Amy McGavin is the pen name of a Scottish wife-and-husband writing team whose real names are . . . Amy and Gavin.

The couple's contemporary romance novels are set in the Highlands. Each story is crafted with humour and heart, with a wee bit of heat thrown in.

The pair live in Glasgow with their daughter and very lively cocker spaniel. When they're not writing, they enjoy exploring Scotland's breathtaking hills, glens, and beaches, then treating themselves to coffee and cake afterwards.

To keep up to date with all their publishing news, and gain access to exclusive bonus content, join their newsletter by visiting amymcgavinbooks.com.

Newsletter

BY THE SAME AUTHORS

The True Scotsman Series

The Highland Kiss

The Highland Fling

The Highland Crush

The Highland Game

For the most up-to-date book list, visit amymcgavinbooks.com.

The
HIGHLAND
CRUSH

The True Scotsman Series

AMY McGAVIN

GRUMPY GROUSE
—— P R E S S ——

ISBN 978-1-916734-05-0

Published by Grumpy Grouse Press

The

HIGHLAND

CRUSH

CHAPTER ONE

IONA

Age eleven

"Go on! If you're so against eating them, set them free." Lewis McIntyre nudges me closer to the pigsty, his dark-brown eyes twinkling with mischief.

I glare at him and push up my glasses. "This is such a stupid dare. I'm not doing it."

"Ha! I knew you wouldn't. You never do *anything* wrong."

My face grows hot. Normally, I'm okay with a bit of playful teasing from Lewis. In fact, I usually join in and am quick with a comeback. But this gibe gets to me. I hear enough comments at school about how I'm the teacher's pet or a goody two-shoes. It hurts hearing it from my best friend.

"Just because I'm a vegetarian doesn't mean I have to free farm animals," I say.

"Aye, but if you don't, one of these piggies might end up in my next bacon roll." Lewis pats his tummy and lets out a contented sigh. "Mmm, bacon."

"That's sick! You can't say that in front of them."

He grins, and even though he's getting on my nerves today, I can't stay annoyed with him when he smiles like that, with his dimples showing. He comes closer, rests his arms on the fence, and sniffs the air. "Wow, they really do stink, don't they?"

"You're being so mean. I think they're adorable."

The six pink pigs snuffling about the pen have pudgy bodies and curly tails. They're far from the only animals on Mr Murray's farm, but they're the ones Lewis zeroed in on for his dare. We shouldn't even be here, but we've been spending the summer holidays exploring the countryside around Bannock, and when we came to the farm and couldn't see anyone about, we decided to have a nosy.

"They are kind of cute," Lewis admits, "but you're lying if you say they don't smell."

"Look them in the eye and tell them you're okay with eating them."

"I'm okay with eating you," Lewis says to the closest pig. "And you, and you . . ." He addresses all six of them.

I bite my lip and hold back a sigh. That is not the response I'd been hoping for. It's been a whole week since I swore off meat, and I've spent the last seven days trying to convert Lewis too, although without success.

"Are you going to do this or not?" Lewis questions. "I'm guessing not, which means . . . forfeit dare! Go up to the chicken coop then flap your arms and cluck as loud as you can. Because you, Ona Pona, are a chicken."

Ugh! Boys can be so stupid sometimes. Lewis normally isn't as silly as the rest of them, but even he has his moments.

"I'm not a chicken, and you know I don't like it when you call me Ona Pona."

"You liked it when we were four."

"Aye, but that was seven years ago."

He smirks and shakes his head. "All right, *Iona*, but you're only making things worse for yourself. Now, as well as clucking, I want you to shout out, 'My name is Ona Pona!'"

"Why am I even friends with you?"

"That's obvious. We live in a small town: options are limited."

"Oh yeah, that's why." I stick out my tongue at him, although in truth there are plenty of other kids we could both play with. But for as long as I can remember, the two of us have been inseparable, and I wouldn't have it any other way. Even if he does wind me up at times, Lewis gets me like no one else does, and I get him.

"The chickens are over there." Lewis points. "Go on!"

I follow the direction of Lewis's finger then glance back at the pigs. Opening the gate to let them out would be irresponsible and the last thing anyone would expect me to do. I don't mind what most people think about me, but Lewis? I care about what he thinks, and it bugs me that he too believes I never do anything unexpected or against the rules.

"I won't cluck like a chicken," I say, "because I'm going to do the original dare." Putting on a brave face, I lift the latch and swing the gate open. My heart races as I wait for the pigs to make a desperate rush for freedom, but . . . nothing happens. With an occasional snort, they continue to sniff around the sty, apparently quite happy where they are.

For a moment Lewis looks shocked that I actually did it, and I take a little satisfaction from that. But he quickly composes himself and shrugs. "All right, now you have to chase them out."

"Nope! I set them free. If they don't take advantage of that, that's on them, but I completed the dare. Anyway, if they're not going to go anywhere, maybe I should just close this gate and—"

"Oi! What in the name of the wee man do you think you're doing?"

We whip around to see Mr Murray striding towards us in blue overalls and welly boots. He slams the gate shut then focuses his attention on me. "Well?" he demands. "It's Iona Stewart, isn't it? What have you got to say for yourself?"

I'd like to bravely tell him I didn't want the pigs to be eaten, but I can't bring myself to utter a single word. I'm not used to getting into trouble and his raised voice scares me.

Lewis steps between me and Mr Murray, acting as a shield. "It's my fault. I dared her to open the gate. You can shout at me, but leave her out of it."

The farmer's bushy eyebrows rise with surprise then he lets out a low chuckle. "Ah, if it isn't one of the McIntyre boys. Which one, I'm never sure."

"Lewis," Lewis says.

"Well, Lewis, don't worry, I'll be telling you off too. Are you aware I supply produce to your parents' hotel, where this one's maw is head chef?" He gestures to me. "I don't think your families would be too happy if they knew you were messing about here. What were you doing anyway?"

Finally I find my voice. "I . . . I'm a vegetarian, so Lewis . . . dared me to . . ."

"Ah." Mr Murray nods seriously. "A wannabe animal rights activist. Believe it or not, I care deeply for my animals. That might be a hard thing for you to get your head around, given what happens to them, but it's true. I'll give the two of you a choice. I can phone your parents right now and demand they drive out here and give you a suitable telling-off. Or you can help me around the farm for the next hour and maybe see that I'm no monster and my animals are treated well. What do you think?"

Lewis glances back at me, the mischievous glint gone from his eyes. Without him having to say anything, I know he feels guilty about getting me into trouble. But doing a few odd tasks around the farm doesn't sound so bad. Actually, it might be fun.

"We'll help out," I say. "And if any poo needs to be scooped up, Lewis is your man."

CHAPTER TWO

IONA

Now

"My laird, you can have my body but not my heart!"

"Nae, lass, I'll take all of ye—mind, body, and soul."

Slowing the car, I pause my audiobook—and just as it was getting to a good bit! Typical, but I've reached my destination: Bannock, a small town nestled in the Scottish Highlands. Its main street has scarcely changed in the nine years since I left, its stone houses and slate roofs simple but charming on this bright August day.

I pull up outside Maw's house and step out, casting a glance across the road at the Bannock Hotel, with its freshly painted woodwork and pretty hanging baskets. I practically grew up in that building—spent almost as much time there as I did in my own home. Unwelcome memories threaten to surface, so I shove them back down and head into Maw's.

"I'm home!" My voice bounces off the walls of Maw's hall.

"Oh, Iona!" She bustles through from the living room and wraps me in a hug. She has the same blue eyes and fair skin as me, and her hair was once blonde like mine but is now grey. "I'm so delighted to have you back. How was the journey up?"

"It was fine—same as ever." Although it's nearly a decade since I last lived here, I have returned for weekend visits and occasional longer stays.

"Och, but it's not the same as ever because this time I get to keep you. With Aidan, Grace, and the bairn just down the road, and you moving in with me, I feel like the luckiest mother alive." She gives me another squeeze and I laugh.

"Why don't you put the kettle on and I'll start taking things in?" I suggest, disentangling myself. "We can catch up properly in a few minutes."

Back outside, I open the boot of my car, which—like the back seat and the passenger seat—is crammed full. Until I had to pack it all up, I hadn't realised how much stuff I'd accumulated over the years. I really should have done a clear-out before moving home.

To minimise trips, I stack a few of the lighter boxes on top of each other. When I lift them, they wobble threateningly, but rather than put them back down—which would be the sensible thing to do—I stubbornly take a few steps towards Maw's door. And . . . the tower begins to keel over.

"Whoa! Let me carry that."

That voice—deep, melodic, and achingly familiar. Before my belongings can spill out for all to see, the boxes are swept from my hands.

"Welcome back, Iona." Tall with carefully tousled chestnut hair and a gym-sculpted body, Lewis McIntyre now sports a smattering of stubble, something I've never seen on him previously. He suits it, but then Lewis could never look bad. He's annoying that way.

"I was getting on just fine," I lie.

His lips curl up, and like the town itself, that smile hasn't changed—even his dimples remain intact. You'd think he was harmless—a friendly giant—but I know better. We may have been best friends once, but it's because of this man I didn't return to Bannock sooner.

He deposits my things inside then strolls back. "Just like old times, eh? Neighbours again." He nods at the hotel.

"Yes, well . . ."

His casual tone annoys me. Why does he always pretend like everything is okay between us? It's not.

He reaches into the boot.

"I've got it from here," I say.

"It's no bother." He lifts another load, his eyes roving over me. "I like your outfit, by the way."

Self-consciously I glance down at my fox-print top and faded jeans. "Er . . . thanks?"

That smile again—then he disappears into Maw's. Truthfully, with his muscles, he'd make light work of unpacking the car, but I'd rather he just left. I hoist up a heavier box, this one filled with books, but when Lewis returns, he plucks it out of my hands.

"You've had a long journey up—let me handle this. If you pop something else on top, I can take that in too."

He's not listening to me when I say I don't need help, and that bugs me. So, in a fit of pique, rather than picking something light, I go for another box of books (yes, I own too many—can't bear to get rid of them). I dump it on the first, hoping to see Lewis flinch, but he doesn't so much as blink.

As he transports just part of my romance novel collection into Maw's, I take a moment to gather myself. I can't let Lewis get to me—I don't want to give him that power over my emotions. Aye, we'll be living opposite each other, but I'll be keeping contact between us to a minimum. I'd hoped he would have understood that without me having to say it.

A car pulls up behind mine then Richard hops out, smiling that goofy grin I fell for a year and a half ago.

"Finally!" I say. "You were right behind me most of the way. What happened?"

"Sorry!" He wraps an arm around me and pecks my cheek. "The scenery was too good not to stop for photos."

He's drawing away from me when Lewis returns, and on instinct I tug Richard back to me and give him an especially fierce hug, like I haven't seen him in weeks. Only after releasing him do I say, "You remember Lewis, don't you? My . . . childhood friend?"

"Of course." Richard shakes Lewis's hand. "Good to see you again, mate."

"And you. I'm just helping Iona take in her things."

"Don't worry about it. I'll get it from here."

Richard is a friendly sort who'll get on with anyone, and most people see Lewis that way too, even if I know there's another side to him. Whenever these two meet, though, there's a chill in the air.

"All right." Lewis nods. "See you around." Shooting one last smile in my direction, he walks across the road to the hotel.

Richard lifts the second-last box from my boot. "Whoa! This is heavy. What's in here? Books?"

"Er, aye," I admit, making a mental note to hide some of the spicier ones somewhere Maw won't find them.

He grins then heads for Maw's. I grab the last box, close the boot, and follow after.

A long-distance runner, Richard has an athletic but lean

figure and his training rarely focuses on upper-body strength. It wouldn't be fair to compare him with Lewis, and yet . . . I notice he lets out a sigh of relief when setting down the box in Maw's hall. I doubt Lewis did that, and he carried two at the same time.

I reprimand myself for this thought. I'm not living in a romance novel. So what if Richard's max load is twenty paperbacks?

"There you are, Richard." Maw emerges from the kitchen and gives him a warm embrace. "Welcome!"

"Thanks for letting us stay, Elspeth. We'll try to be out of your hair before long."

"Och, there's no rush for you to find a place of your own. Truth be told, now that Aidan has moved in with Grace, the house is too big for just me. Anyway, I've made us all tea, and I baked a lemon drizzle cake this morning. You can finish unpacking later. For now, have a seat and recharge your batteries after the drive."

She ushers us through to the living room, and . . . oh wow! The cake is so good—light, fluffy, its delightful tangy flavour bursting on my tongue with each mouthful. Moving back in with Maw is going to be dangerous. My figure is on the curvier side, and while I'm happy with how I look, I'd rather not put on too much more weight.

As we enjoy our sweet treat, Maw asks Richard a few questions about the job he'll be starting as a wind turbine technician. Until a month ago I had no interest in returning to Bannock, but on the same day Richard heard about this new role, Bannock Vets posted a job opening, and it was like it was meant to be.

Rested and refuelled, Richard and I fetch the rest of our things from our cars then haul them upstairs. We stack most of the boxes in what used to be my brother's room but dump the ones containing clothes in my childhood bedroom, which is still adorned with teenage relics. I was eighteen when I moved away—barely an adult. The naive girl I was then seems almost like a different person.

"It's not how I pictured our first place"—Richard lifts a Highland cow cuddly toy and gives it a wee squeeze—"but it'll do for now."

Down in Glasgow we had our own flats, but I'd spend a night or two at his each week, or him at mine, so living together shouldn't be too big a leap.

"Now we're here, it'll be easier to go to viewings and find somewhere to call our own," I point out.

"Yeah. Anyway, how about some music as we unpack?"

My phone is closer, so Richard wakes it and taps the play button without checking what I was last listening to.

"The laird roughly pulled Felicity against him, her voluptuous breasts pressing into his chest. She could feel his throbbing manhood—"

Richard pauses my audiobook, and I giggle, fully expecting a bit of playful teasing for my listening habits.

"*The Laird's Feisty Virgin Bride* was your entertainment for the journey up?" He shakes his head. "Honestly, considering how bright you are, it's a mystery to me why you like such rubbish."

Okay, well, that wasn't so much playful as judgemental. I enjoy what I enjoy—what's wrong with that?

My expression must betray my feelings because he envelops me in a hug. "I'm just joking."

Except it wasn't funny, I think, but I take a breath, let go of my irritation, and snuggle into him. Tracing his chest with one finger, I say, "Maybe those books give me ideas. Did you think of that?"

"Like . . . bedroom ideas?"

He shifts uncomfortably. He can be pretty inhibited when it comes to sex. I mean, we do it, but . . .

"Having your mum in the next room might cause us problems."

"Well, we're not going to go celibate, are we? It could be a few months before we move into our own place. Having to be discreet and do it quietly could be kind of . . . exciting." I kiss his neck.

He pulls away, laughing nervously. "Sorry, it's just . . ." He shrugs. "I don't know. It feels really weird while your mum's in the house. Anyway, let's unpack. While I'm sure you're desperate to hear more about Felicity's voluptuous breasts and the laird's throbbing manhood, I'm going to put on some music."

CHAPTER THREE

LEWIS

The piercing cries of a baby sound over the cheerful Scottish folk music that plays at reception to welcome guests to the Bannock Hotel.

"I'm so sorry about this." Emily's rather frazzled voice reaches me back in the office. "There, there, Ru, you're okay. Now, ladies, I'll just grab your keys and then—"

I put on my best managerial smile and step out to the front desk. "Welcome to Bannock," I say to the two fifty-something women standing on the other side. To Emily, my sister-in-law and colleague, I suggest, "Why don't I take over from here?"

As she bounces and soothes my nephew, Ru, she shoots me a disapproving look. She doesn't like it when I "interfere". Luckily, our guests don't notice her irritation because their focus is on me.

"Well, look at you!"

"A sight for sore eyes—and that accent! It's to die for."

Both women are American—from Texas, possibly, or somewhere in the South anyway.

"Say, did you pose for a calendar of topless men in kilts?"

"Er . . . no."

"Oh. I picked one up in a gift shop yesterday and I swear you're the spitting image of Mr July."

The second woman nods excitedly. "He is! Show him, Barbara. Go on!"

Before I can stop her, Barbara unzips her suitcase and rummages through it. "Wait till you see this. He's just like you!"

Out of the corner of my eye, I catch Emily smirking as she continues to comfort Ru. His sobs have reduced to sad little sniffles.

Barbara slaps a calendar down on the reception desk and flips through it until she reaches July. She then proudly displays it for me and Emily to see.

Under the sun, an axe-wielding Highlander wipes sweat from his brow, a pile of chopped wood on the ground beside him.

"Isn't he your doppelgänger?"

"Er . . . I'm not sure I see the resemblance myself."

I can only assume Barbara's gaze is distracted by the drops of sweat trickling down the man's bare chest. His face is nothing like mine.

Barbara's friend thinks otherwise. "You see it, don't you?" she says, turning to Emily. "The likeness to your husband is uncanny."

"Oh, Lewis isn't my husband. I'm actually married to his older brother, Ally."

Barbara rests her arms on the desk and leans closer to me. "Does that mean you're still on the market? Because I'm recently divorced and wouldn't mind a Scottish boy toy to spice up my vacation."

Her companion bursts into laughter and claps her hands together.

I chuckle, perhaps a little nervously. "That's quite the offer.

Unfortunately, unlike my brother, who started dating Emily here while she was visiting, I adhere to a strict code that forbids relationships with guests, no matter how attractive they are."

"Then you'll just have to quit your job," Barbara shoots back with a wink. "Trust me, I'm worth it."

This sets her friend off again.

I grin. "I can't do that, but what I can do is carry your cases upstairs for you. I'll lead the way."

The two women follow behind me and compliment me regularly on my strength and muscles—plus I overhear an approving whisper about my "ass". I ignore their flattery, although I can't help but wish Iona had shown a bit of appreciation earlier when I was helping her out. Instead, she'd remained indifferent the whole time, even while dumping a second box of books on top of the one I was already carrying.

I decline a last-ditch suggestion from Barbara that I join her in her room (I *think* she's just having a laugh but I'm honestly not sure) then head back down to reception. "Those two are going to be trouble," I mutter to Emily. "We should come up with a safe word in case I need you to rescue me from them."

"If you'd stayed in the office rather than sticking your nose in, you wouldn't need rescuing. I was getting on fine."

"Sorry, you're right."

Emily used to be a wedding planner in London and thrived on creating the perfect day for her wealthy clients. She understands better than anyone the importance of getting every detail just right and so is well aware that a crying baby isn't the first impression we want to give guests of the Bannock Hotel. She knows it, I know it—but I also know I'd get my head bitten off were I to say it out loud.

Ru whimpers again so I reach out and tickle his belly in an

attempt to cheer him up. The way I see it, Emily wants to apply the same perfectionism to the hotel that she did to her wedding-planning business, but she also wants the very best for her son, and at times those demands come into conflict. That's why I'm always happy to step in and help where I can, and yet . . . it irritates Emily when I do. I'm not sure what the solution is.

Ru's cries get worse, so—with a sigh—Emily announces she's going to put him down for a nap. I smile and nod, judging that to be the safest response.

The pair of them have barely left when my younger brother, Jamie, strolls in from the snug—that's what we call the hotel's bar area. He leans against the reception desk, a mischievous glint in his eyes.

"One minute you're tripping over your own feet in your rush to welcome Iona, the next you're chatting up older women. You're coming across a bit desperate, if you ask me."

"I didn't ask you, and anyway, if you overheard that conversation, you must also have heard Ru crying. Didn't it occur to you to maybe step in and help? I was in the middle of something in the office, and I bet the snug isn't busy right now."

"There's not a single customer," Jamie agrees. "I was thinking of coming to help, but I was actually at this really important bit in a game I was playing, so . . ."

I shake my head. Jamie and his bloody video games.

"Anyway, you've missed the boat with Iona," he adds. "She and Richard have moved in together and have new jobs lined up—they're settling down. I wouldn't be surprised if he pops the question soon."

This hits me like a blow to the gut. Are things *that* serious between them? I suppose they have been seeing each other for a while, but surely they're not thinking of marriage?

"They've not *really* moved in together," I protest. "They're just staying with Elspeth for now." But even I can hear what a shallow objection this is.

Shit. Even if marriage isn't on the cards yet, it probably will be at some point, and that terrifies me.

I check the clock. The restaurant doesn't open for dinner for another few hours.

"I'm going to the gym," I say. "Seeing as the snug is quiet, you can keep an eye on it and reception."

I head up to my room to get my things. While throwing a T-shirt and shorts into a bag, I can't resist glancing out my window, and there she is, in the house opposite. She and Richard are unpacking.

Growing up, Iona and I would wave at each other through our windows or fix messages to them. Every year on my birthday, I'd leap out of bed and yank open my curtains to see what poster she'd designed for me—she always worked so hard on it.

As I reminisce, Iona turns and catches me looking. I raise a hand in greeting but she frowns.

Shit. Gone are the days of innocently communicating with each other from our bedrooms. Now she probably just thinks I'm a creep.

I throw my bag over my shoulder, go down to the car, then set off for the Glen Garve Resort, a much larger hotel situated in extensive grounds a short distance from Bannock. Technically a competitor of our own family-run business, it has fantastic leisure facilities, and although they're mainly intended for the resort's guests, there are membership options for locals. I'm a frequent visitor to the gym—it's my sanctuary, a place I can lose myself.

After my warm-up, I head for the squat rack, select a barbell, and load it with plates. I position the bar across my shoulders, take a few deep breaths, then begin my first set of squats.

I never put in earphones while lifting. Instead, I focus on my breathing, which gets heavier as I work up a sweat. Normally, I find peace in the exertion and enter an almost meditative state. Today, though, I can't chase thoughts of Iona from my mind.

When we were younger, we'd spend all day, every day together, never tiring of each other. We'd share everything—there was nothing I didn't know about her, nor she about me. We haven't been like that for so long. Not since—

No, it's too painful to think about that, even after all these years. I was such a fool back then.

After my squats, I move on to lunges, thoughts of Iona still lingering. Now that she's returned to Bannock, I'll constantly be reminded of what I did, and that's going to be torture. To make life bearable, I have to patch things up with her.

There's no chance of anything romantic between us—I've come to terms with that, even though Iona is the only woman I've ever truly wanted. But maybe, just maybe, I can win her back as a friend.

The least I can do is try.

CHAPTER FOUR

IONA

First day on the job and where do I end up? Mr Murray's farm. The same Mr Murray whose pigs I attempted to free when I was eleven.

Still, it's been sixteen years. I doubt he'll even remember.

I step out of my car and breathe in the country air—so much fresher than in the city.

"Look who it is!" Mr Murray strides over, his hair more salt than pepper now, although he remains as strong and sturdy as ever. "Are you here to examine my livestock or to plot another jailbreak?"

Okay, so he does remember. His tone may be playful, but my cheeks heat all the same.

"Hello, Mr Murray. And no, I won't be opening any gates today unless you tell me to." Already I feel like a little girl rather than a confident professional woman.

He lets out a hearty laugh. "Call me Fergus. If you don't mind me saying, isn't a farm vet an odd career choice for a vegetarian?"

"Ah, my vegetarian phase only lasted a few months," I admit

sheepishly. "And actually, I've got you to thank—or to blame—for my career path. Remember how you made me and Lewis help around the farm as a punishment for the Great Pig Escape? We stayed a lot longer than the hour you sentenced us to because we loved it. I reckon that experience sparked an interest in farm life."

"Huh, well I never. All right, let's see how you get on with the cows. I'm hoping a significant number of them are expecting this year."

◆ ◆ ◆

I'm pretty sure I impressed Fergus with my skill at rectal palpation. After all, who wouldn't be impressed by the sight of me with an arm up a cow's backside?

We parted ways on good terms, my act of childhood rebellion water under the bridge. Maybe it's not such a bad thing he remembered anyway. When I was younger, most folk in Bannock saw me as the perpetual goody-goody who never put a foot wrong. In the years I've been away, I doubt their opinion of me has changed much. At least Fergus knows there's more to me than that. I'm a girl who's not afraid to break the rules (or to shove my hand up a cow's arse).

I'm back at the practice now, sorting through a bit of admin work and familiarising myself with my new surroundings. As I'm typing up some case notes, Claire, our receptionist, peeks her head around the door.

"There's someone here to see you."

"Oh? Er, send them in."

I'm not sure who to expect, but I'm caught off-guard when Lewis strolls in, even though I really shouldn't be. In recent years, any time I've visited Bannock to see my maw and brother, Lewis has invariably popped over to say hello. And yesterday, I'd barely got out of my car when he showed up, almost as if he'd been waiting for me. But dropping in at my workplace? That feels like a step too far.

"Lewis, this is a . . . surprise."

I get a hint of spicy aftershave, which makes me worry I might spell of Eau de Cow, but he's not wrinkling his nose up. I think I'm all right.

"Sorry to pounce on you like this." He holds out a cardboard cake box. "But . . . I wanted to give you a wee something to welcome you back—and to extend an olive branch. It's a Victoria sponge."

"Oh."

As a girl, that was my favourite and it still holds a special place in my heart (and stomach). A classic British dessert with layers of light sponge, sweet strawberry jam, and whipped cream, it's basically happiness in cake form. There was a period when Lewis would bake one for me regularly, especially when I needed cheering up. Back then, I'd never have guessed that kind boy was capable of wounding me as deeply as he did—so deeply I'm not sure I've ever fully recovered.

I don't know what to say so I wordlessly take the box and place it on my desk.

Lewis stuffs his hands into his pockets and rocks back on his heels, a gesture he'd do as a lad whenever he felt uncomfortable, and one he apparently hasn't grown out of. It's actually kind of endearing seeing him do it in his filled-out adult body. Yes, he could probably bench-press a Shetland pony now, but some part of the boy I remember is still in there, peeking out from behind the brawny exterior of the man before me.

"Iona, I . . . am sorry. I can't go back in time and change

things. If I could, I would. Now you're back in Bannock, is there any chance we could put the past behind us and be friends again?"

Friends? After what he did?

"I . . . don't know, Lewis," I admit, avoiding eye contact.

"Right." He nods slowly. "Okay." He shifts his weight from foot to foot and puts on a brave smile, those familiar dimples showing. "Well, enjoy the cake. And . . . I'm not going to give up." He bobs his head, faster this time, as if to convince himself. "One day you'll be laughing at my jokes again, just like old times."

He grins with an air of forced confidence. I've known Lewis since we were in nappies—he should know I can see right through him.

"Anyway, I'll let you get on with whatever you're doing." He gestures towards my desk. "Sorry for bothering you. Oh, by the way, your maw has asked me to help prepare a dinner to welcome you back."

Oh joy!

"And to welcome Richard too," Lewis adds. "Tomorrow—at the hotel."

Our families—the McIntyres and the Stewarts—have always been close, and even now, joint meals remain a tradition. They're an opportunity to chitchat with Lewis's siblings while simultaneously squirming every time he glances my way.

"Maw mentioned something about that."

Lewis nods again then, when I offer nothing more, lifts one hand in an awkward wave before turning to leave. There's something oddly charming about his obvious discomfort, and my heart melts, just a bit.

"Guess who my first appointment was with today?"

He stops mid-step and glances back, his eyebrows rising,

apparently surprised but pleased I'm making an effort to keep the conversation going. "Who?"

"Fergus Murray. And he hadn't forgotten about the pigs."

Lewis laughs—a warm, nostalgic sound that evokes memories of long-gone carefree days. "Wow! Who knew something I dared you to do when we were eleven would come back to bite you sixteen years later?"

I give a small smile then tap the side of the cake box. "I really should get on, but thanks for this."

"Anytime, Ona Pona."

Before I can scold him for using that childhood nickname, he's gone.

CHAPTER FIVE

IONA

Age fifteen

Sunlight breaks through the clouds and dances on the surface of Loch Bannock. Lewis sends another stone skipping across the water while I sway gently back and forth on the old tree swing. It's just the two of us—no one else as far as the eye can see—and that's exactly what I need today. I've had it up to here with other people, with their pitying looks and whispered gossip.

"Oh, wow, did you see that?" Lewis grins at me, brimming with pride. "Seven bounces!"

I manage a weak smile. "Nice one."

"All right, the new target is eight." He hunts for another stone, determined to beat his record.

This last week he's been amazing. He hasn't pried or pushed me to chat about things. There's been no judgement in his gaze, only steady support. Any time I've needed him, he's been there for me, even if just to hang out together in friendly silence. His patience has meant the world to me, but . . . maybe it is time we talked.

I kick at the ground, sending a small cloud of dust into the air. "What would you do if you found out your da had another woman?" I say. "And not only that, but another child—a four-year-old half-brother you knew nothing about?"

Lewis pauses mid-throw and considers my question. "Honestly? I'd be a mess. It amazes me you're managing to keep it together." With that, he flings the stone. This one skips six times.

"I don't feel like I'm keeping it together," I admit.

"Aye, well, you're entitled to be upset and confused. The news stunned us all. I'm not going to pretend I know what you're going through—he's *your* da—but . . . I have known him my whole life. Hell, when I was little, I called him Uncle Ewan because your maw and da are practically like an aunt and uncle to me. So maybe I understand the tiniest fraction of what you're experiencing, and . . . it's shit." He shrugs. "It really is just shit."

I swallow and nod. "It is."

He selects another stone, tosses it up in the air, and catches it. "Your turn."

"I've never been able to skip stones."

"I know, and it's time we sorted that. C'mon!"

Reluctantly I slide off the swing and onto the pebbled shore then take the stone from him. With a quick flick of my wrist, I send it flying, but instead of elegantly skimming across the water, it plunges straight in with a splash. I watch the ripples spread, wishing my troubles could sink just as easily. If only life were that simple.

"Er, not a bad attempt, but that was more of a plop than a skip." Lewis chuckles softly. "Want to try again? I can help you with your form if you'd like."

"Nah. I'm not really in the mood."

"Fair enough." He walks over to his backpack and unzips it.

"In that case, how about this?" He pulls out a round biscuit tin and whips off the lid.

Inside is a rich, golden-yellow cake, its top dusted with icing sugar. Jam and cream ooze out from between the layers.

"Victoria sponge!" My chest tightens with a sudden rush of emotion that catches me off-guard. Grateful beyond words for having such a thoughtful friend, I fling my arms around him— only to send the tin tumbling from his hands.

"Crap!"

We both watch as it falls, time seeming to slow down. Lewis instinctively reaches for it, but it's no good: his fingers barely graze the side. A disastrous splat seems a certainty but . . . it lands the right way up. The top layer of sponge slides off slightly, leaving the cake looking a little lopsided, but otherwise—miraculously—it's unscathed.

For a moment, neither of us speaks. We stand frozen in amazement.

Lewis is the first to break the silence with a disbelieving laugh. "Wow, I thought for sure that was going to flip over and splatter everywhere. See? Things don't always go wrong."

"Aye, I suppose you're right." I chuckle, the heavy weight that's been dragging me down all week lifting just a little. "Now, did you bring a knife or do I have to judo-chop myself a piece?"

With a wink, Lewis produces a plastic knife then cuts us each a slice. No sooner has he done so than I grab one, shove it in my mouth, and groan.

"Oh! Fluffy perfection!" I mumble mid-chew. "So . . . good."

"Er, I actually brought forks and paper plates too, but your way does look more fun." Sitting on a root, Lewis copies my method.

"Cake makes everything better," I say, returning to the swing. "By the way, you can squeeze on here with me if you want."

"Nah, it might be a tad tight. I know we both fitted when we were younger, but I think we're a bit big for it now."

"Are you saying I've got fat?"

His eyes widen in horror. "No!" When he realises I'm just messing with him, he breaks into a grin and flexes his muscles. "It's because I'm bulking up so much. Becoming a man, you know?"

He has broadened out—he's no longer the skinny little boy he used to be—and he's finally shot past me in height. His voice has deepened too, and I've got to admit, I like the lower tone.

"I suppose those biceps do need space to breathe," I agree. "The next time we go to the cinema, you'll need to book an extra seat for them."

"Are you kidding? I'll need a whole row for these." Lewis strikes a classic bodybuilder pose and plants a kiss on his arm. "I'm becoming a total beast."

He's no longer as scrawny as he once was, but "beast" is a ridiculous exaggeration, and for some reason this sends me into stitches. It's not even that funny—I think this is just all the bottled-up tension I've been carrying around finally bursting out.

"Aye, laugh it up. I get it—I'm still a bit of a beanpole." Lewis pretends to sulk, sticking out his lower lip, before joining in with the laughter. He isn't offended in the slightest about being the butt of the joke. I think he's just happy to see me in good spirits.

"Okay, enough talk about muscles," I say once I've caught my breath. "I'm far more interested in unhealthy things, like cake." I polish off my slice then hop down from the swing and hold out my hand for him to shake. "You definitely deserve this."

Lewis was inspired to get into baking by *The Great British*

Bake-off, which we watch together religiously. In the show, judge Paul Hollywood rewards bakers who impress him with a coveted "Hollywood handshake". As Lewis's chief taste tester, I've adopted this tradition, and I give him my own version—the "Stewart handshake"—whenever he bakes something that wows me.

Lewis glances at my fingers, observes the cream and crumbs on them, and arches an eyebrow. "Your hand is pretty minging, so I'll pass, but . . . thanks?"

"Hey, you can't turn down a Stewart handshake!" I move closer to him, reach out, and boop his nose, leaving a blob of cream there.

He doesn't immediately wipe it away but instead frowns and tries to look at it, going cross-eyed in the process. I don't know why, but . . . his expression is adorably cute.

"Iona, there's something I need to whisper in your ear," he says. "Come here a moment."

"Nope!" Laughing, I retreat a few steps.

He narrows his eyes then lunges forward. Squealing, I dodge him then try to flee, but he catches me easily and lifts me off the ground. Wow, clearly he is getting stronger. He carries me over to a patch of grass, lays me down, then leans over me and rubs his nose against my cheek.

"Ew, that's gross!" I protest, half cringing, half laughing.

When he pulls back, he's grinning mischievously, but then our gazes lock, our faces only inches apart. A moment passes. Then another. Lewis's playful demeanour shifts, his expression growing more serious. There's an intensity in his deep-brown eyes I've never seen before. Then . . .

He rolls off me and sprawls beside me on the grass, bursting into laughter and shattering the awkward tension.

But my heart is racing. What just happened between us?

Get a grip, Iona. It was just Lewis being silly.

"Really? Rubbing your nose on me?" I say. "How old are you?"

"Aye, well, putting cream on my nose—how old are *you*?"

Our familiar rapport helps restore our usual vibe. I stare up at the sky, cool blades of grass tickling the back of my neck. Overhead, clouds drift lazily, and for a while I allow myself to get lost in their shapes.

"When we finish school, I'm out of here," I announce abruptly, cutting through the tranquil silence. "Bannock is too . . . suffocating."

I hadn't felt that way about my hometown a week ago, but I do now.

"Of course you'll leave," Lewis agrees. "I've always known you would."

The certainty in his voice takes me by surprise, and I prop myself up on one elbow to get a better view of him. "You have?"

"Just look at your grades! Bannock is too small for you. You'll go off to university somewhere fancy then fly high in the world."

"Well, you'll have to come too. I'm not going anywhere without you."

He smirks up at me, the sun highlighting reddish strands in his chestnut hair. "My grades aren't anything to brag about. Besides, I really like the hotel." He shrugs. "Maybe I'll run it someday, when Maw and Da are old and grey. First, though, I've been thinking about helping out in the kitchen. Perhaps your maw could take me under her wing? I already pester her with questions while she cooks."

He's chatting about this like it isn't a big deal, but the thought of being separated from him hits me hard. It's not as if I haven't considered it before, but I've always shoved it to the back of my mind. He's right, though: I am a bit of a geek, and if I want to keep studying after school, I'll have to move away.

"Maw doesn't think you're a bother," I say softly. "She's forever saying how helpful you are, whether you're chopping vegetables or serving dishes. And you're a hit with guests too—especially the ones from abroad."

"Aye, well, who could resist me?"

I give him a playful shove, but there's truth in what he just said. If he'd leaned in to kiss me earlier, I think I'd have let him.

CHAPTER SIX

IONA

Now

When I get back to Maw's, I find her and Richard in the living room, sipping cups of tea and chatting away to one another. Richard looks completely at ease—he's made himself at home in no time at all.

Maw beams up at me. "Well, how was the first day at the new job?"

"Good, thanks, although I could do with a wash." While I love farm visits, I always have a good scrub when I get home, especially after performing intimate bovine examinations. A power shower and some nice-smelling soap are ideal, but I'd take industrial-strength detergent and a pressure washer in the garden if that's all that were available.

"You go upstairs and freshen up, but don't be long. Dinner is in the oven and it'll be ready soon."

Once I'm clean and changed, I head back down, finding Richard already seated at the dinner table. "Did you enjoy your first day as a wind turbine technician?" I rest my hands on his shoulders then lean down and plant a quick kiss on his lips.

"It was really great." Enthusiastically he fills me in on what he got up to. "Oh, and one of my new colleagues says he went to school with you. Joe Campbell?"

"Aye, I remember Joe. He's a nice guy. He'd take the bus in each morning from one of the surrounding villages—Auchenford, I think. How is he?"

We chat for a few minutes and then I call into the kitchen, "Maw, is there anything I can help with?"

"No, you sit down. That's me ready to serve now."

I settle into the chair beside Richard, and moments later Maw enters, expertly balancing three plates—something I'd never dare try, given my uncanny ability to turn the simplest of tasks into a slapstick routine. She sets them down, and as one, Richard and I let out a satisfied sigh. Fresh salmon grilled to perfection, with buttery new potatoes and steamed spinach—yum!

"This looks amazing, Elspeth," Richard says.

"It really does," I agree, the sight and smell of the food awakening my appetite and reminding me how long it's been since lunch. "Oh, I should have said earlier, but I've got cake for after—a Victoria sponge."

A nostalgic smile brightens Maw's face. "Remember when Lewis used to bake that for you?"

"He made this one," I admit.

"Oh, that's lovely. That lad bakes almost as well as Morag at the bakery. Maybe now you're in Bannock again, you and Lewis can go back to how you once were. You used to be inseparable."

Richard raises an eyebrow. "Inseparable, eh?"

"Yes!" Maw's eyes twinkle. "They did everything together, even coordinating Halloween costumes each year. My favourite was when they dressed up as Shrek and Fiona—I'm sure I've got a snap of that in one of the photo albums. We can have a look for it after dinner."

"Actually, Maw, I'd prefer if we didn't go through old photos, thank you very much."

"I don't know," Richard says. "I'd like to see it." He takes a mouthful of food, swallows, then turns to me. "It's funny, when I introduced myself to Joe today, he told me that everyone at your school was *sure* you and Lewis would end up together. I knew your family and the McIntyres have always been close, but I hadn't appreciated you and Lewis used to have such a . . . special bond." He pauses, studying me. "Did you two ever date?"

I chew on a piece of salmon, trying to decide how to respond. Before I can, Maw jumps in.

"Nope! I kept waiting for it to happen, but it never did. I suppose they just saw each other as friends."

That's not entirely accurate, but I'm not about to correct Maw. I will, however, need to have a private conversation with Richard later to set the record straight. I've never told him the full story about me and Lewis because, frankly, I try to think about Lewis as little as possible. I don't see why that man should impact my life any more than he already has. But I also don't want to lie to Richard. He deserves the truth—just not in front of Maw.

The conversation moves on to safer topics, and before long, our plates are cleared.

"That was delicious," Richard enthuses. "Iona and I aren't too skilled in the kitchen, are we? We can do a few basic dishes, but normally we're so knackered after work all we have the energy to do is bung a ready meal in the oven." He pats his stomach. "I could get used to home cooking like this. If you're not careful, you won't be able to get rid of us, Elspeth. Why would we want to move into our own place when we can dine like royalty here?"

Although clearly meant as a joke, this comment pokes at something raw inside me. As much as I love Maw, the idea of staying with her indefinitely is stifling. After nine years away, I'm used to my own space. Richard better not get too comfortable.

Brushing aside these thoughts, I stand and gather up the plates. "That really was brilliant, Maw," I agree. "I'll go cut us all a slice of cake."

CHAPTER SEVEN

LEWIS

Age eighteen

The full moon casts a silvery glow over the calm waters of Loch Bannock. Iona sits on the creaky old swing, the gentle breeze catching her hair, while I lean against the tree, my gaze drawn to her, as it so often is.

"This may be the last time we hang out here like this," I say. The loch has been our go-to spot for years now, a place where we can talk for hours and hours, openly sharing our hopes and fears.

"Jesus, Lewis. I'm moving to Glasgow—it's a three-and-a-half-hour drive away. It's not like I'm never coming back."

"Aye, you're right." I kick a pebble into the water. "But . . . it'll be different."

Iona tucks a lock of blonde hair behind her ear. "You're a bundle of laughs tonight. Is this really how you're going to send me off? And what exactly are you implying—that living in the city will change me?"

I don't say it, but yes, that is what I think. At university she'll be mingling with students almost as bright and clever as she is, sharing experiences with them and forming close bonds, while I . . . stay here in Bannock.

She deserves this—she's worked incredibly hard for it—and I *am* happy for her. But I'm jealous too. Not of her, but of the new friends she'll make—people who'll get to spend time with her while I'm up here missing her.

Iona snaps her fingers and waves at me. "Hello? Are you still there? What's going on in that head of yours?"

"Nothing." I stuff my hands in my pockets. "Well, actually . . . I heard that, at freshers' week, free condoms are handed out by the bucket-load because casual sex among students is a given. Do you think that's true?"

Okay, maybe I'm not just jealous at the thought of Iona gaining some new friends. It's also crossed my mind that she might end up in bed with some sophisticated intellectual types. Lucky bastards—I've had a secret crush on my best mate for years.

"Well, if they're giving out condoms, I'll be grabbing as many as I can to help satisfy my insatiable sex drive. Fingers crossed they've got some glow-in-the-dark ones—I've always wanted to see a guy swing his thing about like a lightsaber."

My jaw drops open, and I freeze mid-breath. Did she really just say that? Has Iona ever even seen a guy's "thing" before, let alone a luminescent one?

She bursts out laughing at my stunned expression. Caught between shock and amusement, I scramble for a comeback. "Oh, so *that's* what girls mean when they say they're looking for a guy who lights up the room."

"Exactly! Who needs a night light when you've got a glowing sword under the covers?"

"Shit, I've been wasting my time with chocolates and flowers.

This is going to revolutionise my dating game. Glad we had this chat."

"Remember, young padawan, it's not enough just to have a lightsaber—you must also know how to wield it. Or as Yoda would say, 'Know how to wield it you must.'" She even attempts the accent.

I grin. "Right, well, as much as I'm enjoying all the penis puns, how about a toast?" I reach into my jacket pocket and pull out a flask.

"What's in there?"

"Whisky. Ladies first?"

She takes it. "What's the toast going to be? Oh, wait, I've got an idea. May my love life be full of light and my partners' sabers forever bright!"

"Great, you've officially ruined *Star Wars* for me—I'll never be able to watch it the same way again. Have you already been drinking?"

"Nope, I'm completely sober."

"Well, that's worrying."

"I think it's the nerves. I'm leaving tomorrow, and I'm feeling a bit jittery. It's making me babble."

"Aye, well, that's eighteen years of memories down the drain. Now all I'll remember about you is that you had an unhealthy obsession with glow-in-the-dark dicks."

"I'll take that. It's a more interesting legacy than being the swotty know-it-all."

"Right, except . . . you've always been so much more than that to me. I was actually going to do a heartfelt toast, but after all your chat about lightsabers, it wouldn't really fit the mood."

"Oh, go on," she encourages. "Tell me how brilliant I am."

"All right. To my best friend and the smartest person I know.

You'll be amazing in Glasgow, but just remember, we'll be waiting for you with open arms in Bannock whenever you want to come back for a visit."

She tilts her head. "Hmm . . . not bad, but I prefer mine."

"Well, I'm not drinking to your partners' sabers being forever bright, so we're going with my toast."

She lets out an exaggerated huff. "Fine!" She takes a sip and immediately coughs, pulling a face. "Jesus! It burns."

"You can't say that! It's unpatriotic." Snatching the flask back, I take a swig and wince. "But fuck, that really does burn."

"Ha! See?"

"Aye, well, they say whisky grows on you. We export it around the world—there must be a reason for it." I take another cautious sip.

"Where did you get that stuff anyway?"

"We're eighteen, Iona—old enough to buy alcohol. But . . . okay, I filled up the flask in the snug when no one else was about. But then Maw walked in and I had to hide it behind my back, although I reckon she knew what I was up to. She asked me where I was going, and when I said I was off to the loch with you, she smiled like she thought . . ."

I slide my hands into my pockets and rock back on my heels. "Well, like she thought you and I were going to get up to something. She does stuff like that every now and again, and it's weird. We've always been friends, so I don't know why lately she's started thinking there's something more between us."

At first Iona doesn't respond, and the gentle lapping of the water fills the silence. Then, almost shyly, she says, "Can I ask you a question?"

"Of course. This might be your last chance, so whatever it is, spit it out."

"Why . . . have you never made a move?"

Shit, I'm not sure what I was expecting her to ask, but it wasn't that. Both of us have dated here and there, but no relationship has ever lasted more than a few weeks. I can't speak for Iona, but for me, that's because there's no lass I want to spend time with more than her.

"Is it because you never wanted to?" she prompts.

I steal a glance at her, admiring the way the moonlight makes her skin glow, the way her blonde waves cascade down her back. My gaze traces the curves of her body, every inch unmistakably woman. Thighs, hips . . . tits. I don't know that I should be looking at those, her being my best mate, but they're impossible to ignore.

I meet her sky-blue eyes, which I've always found the most captivating part of her, framed prettily by her glasses. "It's not that I've never wanted to kiss you, Iona. But . . . how many couples who start dating in their teens actually stay together? Not a lot, right? If we went there, and things didn't work out, I don't know how easy it'd be to fall back into our friendship." *And I can't bear the thought of losing you*, I add in my head. "Plus, with our families being so close, that complicates things, doesn't it? It's not just *our* friendship at stake."

I pause, swallowing hard. "But I've wanted to kiss you. Of course I have."

She falls quiet for a while, considering my words. Then she says, "Well, seeing as I'm leaving tomorrow, this is a bit of a now-or-never moment, don't you think? I see what you're saying, but . . . I think I'd regret living opposite you for eighteen years, hanging out with you pretty much every day, and never once kissing you. Before I go, I'd like to try it, if you would. Would you?"

Butterflies flutter in my stomach. "Just checking, but is this the drink talking?"

She scoffs. "I had one sip, Lewis. It's not the drink."

"Oh. Right. Well . . ."

My heart thumping, I reach out and still the swing, then I lean in to Iona, inhaling the sweet scent of her strawberry shampoo. A shiver ripples through me as our breaths mingle. The kiss begins sweet and slow, but then Iona parts her lips slightly, and I seize the invitation. Our tongues meet, and I'm overwhelmed by her taste, the hint of whisky mingling with something uniquely her.

She runs her fingers through my hair and nibbles on my lower lip, and a new intensity floods through me. Fuck, I'm growing hard. Is that . . . okay? Panic mixes with the pleasure.

At least on the swing she won't notice, but no sooner do I think that than she hops down and pushes me back against the tree. Shit, she *must* be able to feel my erection now—our bodies are flush together. But she doesn't recoil or question it. She keeps kissing me.

Screw it, this is heaven—why should I hold back? I let go of my worries and surrender to the moment, one hand moving to her waist, the other cradling her cheek. She moans softly, which sends a thrill through me. I've been dreaming of this for years, but the reality is better than I ever imagined.

When we finally part, we stare at each other, both panting slightly. Iona's cheeks are flushed.

"Wow," she says. "*That's* what I've been looking for. I've kissed a few boys, but it was never even close to what they describe in books. That, though?" She fans herself. "You took my breath away."

I can barely form words—my mind is still reeling from the feel of her lips on mine.

"What now?" She places her hands on my chest. "Because I'm about to leave for a five-year course, and you're staying in Bannock."

"Shit, we've not timed this very well, have we?"

"No, but I'm glad you kissed me. And . . ." Her gaze drifts downwards, her mouth curving into a mischievous smile. "It seems you enjoyed it."

Heat rushes to my cheeks, and I scratch the back of my head. "Sorry, I—"

"There's no need to be embarrassed. If anything, I should be flattered, shouldn't I? It's like a compliment. Wouldn't it be worse if you hadn't reacted at all?"

"Er, aye, I suppose?"

"Ha, don't take it so seriously—it's just an erection. I'm off to study veterinary medicine, so I'm quite aware of how animals make new animals. I only wish I had one of those special condoms I was talking about on me. Then you could have popped it on, and your boner could have lit our way back home through the dark."

I smirk. "You missed a trick there. I was sure you were going to say something about using my lightsaber to boldly battle against the dark side."

"Damn it!" Iona stamps her foot. "I'm ashamed of myself. I bet another vet student would have made that connection. That's what worries me—I've always done well in Bannock, but it's a small pond. What if in Glasgow I can't compete with other students and their lightning-fast minds?"

"I doubt anyone else on your course is spending their last night at home making up jokes about lightsabers. No one else's mind works the way yours does, Iona. You're one of a kind, and that's your secret weapon."

"Whereas your 'secret weapon' isn't so secret anymore!" she blurts and then pumps her fist into the air. "Ha! That was pretty quick, wasn't it?"

"It was." I wink at her. "Thank you for being you. Other girls might have politely said nothing about my hard-on, but you've made it the subject of a stream of gags. Just what every guy wants."

"I know you're being sarcastic, but I'm amusing myself, and that's the main thing. Anyway, fancy another kiss?"

I don't hesitate. I take a hold of her waist and pull her firmly against me, my self-consciousness forgotten. If she's not bothered by my arousal, why should I be? Our lips meet again, more eagerly this time.

CHAPTER EIGHT

LEWIS

Now

"Hello?" Emily says. "Are you listening to me?"

We're in the hotel office, working on a mood board for the next room refurb. We've been doing them up one by one, giving each a unique makeover and injecting a bit more personality into them.

"Er . . . aye, sorry." I rub a hand over my face. "You were talking about . . . colour schemes?"

"No!" Her brow furrows and she exhales deeply. "We already signed off on the colour scheme. Or did you just say 'yes' earlier without actually paying attention to what I was saying?"

I try not to look too guilty. Normally, I'm fully absorbed by the project of doing up the Bannock Hotel. For the longest time, it was in need of a bit of TLC, and I've been fiercely proud of all that Emily and I have achieved over the last year. Today, though . . . I'm distracted.

"I asked Grace to watch Ru so we could have this meeting

without any baby distractions. I need you present and alert, Lewis!"

"Shit, I really am sorry. It's just . . ." I can't think of a good excuse, but I can hardly admit that Iona's return to Bannock has stirred up old feelings and I've been struggling to concentrate on much at all these last few days.

I'm saved from having to tell a white lie by Elspeth, who sticks her head around the door. "Sorry to interrupt, but I was wondering if I could borrow my sous chef for some help in the kitchen?"

I quite literally jump at the chance. For me, food prep is almost as therapeutic as the gym. "Emily, I like it all—you've got an amazing eye for this stuff. Let's go with your vision."

She raises an eyebrow. "Er . . . okay. Well, that was an easy meeting."

I head off with Elspeth.

"I need to thank you for the lovely slice of Victoria sponge I had last night," she comments as we walk. "Honestly, I don't know how you maintain the physique you do when you can bake sweet treats like that. I still remember the skinny little boy you used to be, and just look at you now—strong as a Highland bull! You'll make light work of chopping all the veg we need."

There's a fair bit: carrots, potatoes, onions, and garlic, for both a beef stew and a vegetable stew, as well as courgettes, tomatoes, and green beans, for the latter only. Including me and Elspeth, there'll be eleven adults tonight at the welcome dinner for Iona and Richard, plus two babies.

Elspeth cuts the meat into chunks and then browns it, its rich smell filling the kitchen. "Beef stew was your father's favourite meal, you know."

I smile. She says that every time we make this dish, but I don't mind. I'm always happy to hear a story about Da or Maw.

"Come to think of it, Ewan and I were eating beef stew with your parents when we hit upon what to call you and Iona."

"Oh?" This is a detail I've never heard before.

"Aye, I mentioned I wasn't sure what to call the wee lassie I was carrying, and your mother said she'd always liked the name Iona. I agreed it was a lovely name—and the island of Iona is such a special place—but I didn't want to steal it in case Mairi ever had a daughter. She insisted that if I liked it, then I should use it."

"Oh, wow, so if you hadn't gone with that name, then Cat would have been called Iona?" My wee sister—Cat, short for Catriona—is currently up in Wick, doing her probationary year as an English teacher.

Elspeth nods. "Funnily enough, your mother, who was pregnant with you, hadn't yet settled on a boy's name. I suggested she could go with a Scottish island name too and threw out a few possibilities: Arran, Harris . . . Lewis. And so you became Lewis."

I blink, give her a sideways look, then grin. "Really? I can't believe I'm twenty-seven and I'm only just now finding out that *you* came up with my name. Well, thanks. I've always liked it."

I go back to chopping, buoyed by this exchange. That's the amazing thing about working with Elspeth: she can still surprise me with new stories. We lost Maw and Da six years ago, and I miss them every day, but whenever Elspeth tells me something like that, it makes me feel closer to them.

"Anyway, talking of you and Iona, whatever happened between the pair of you?"

I'm not prepared for this question. "What do you mean?" I say unconvincingly.

"Oh, come on, you used to be joined at the hip. Your friendship didn't end without explanation, and it was more than just the distance. When Iona first moved to Glasgow, you went down to visit her, a lot. But then that all stopped. It wasn't long after—"

"We just drifted apart," I insist. My grip on the knife tightens, my shoulders tensing. "It didn't happen straight away, but she made new friends and had new experiences in the city . . ."

Of course, that wasn't it at all.

◆ ◆ ◆

As is typical for a McIntyre and Stewart family get-together, the restaurant is far noisier than it is when filled with actual customers. The air buzzes with banter and laughter, punctuated by the occasional squeal from Ru or babble from Callie.

I'm on the far side of the table from Iona and Richard. That's the annoying thing about working in the kitchen—you always get the last choice of seat. I keep on glancing Iona's way, though. She's sporting her usual large-framed glasses and a deer-print dress. Her cheeks flushed from wine, she's laughing at something that David, Grace's brother, has just said. He's here with his partner, Johnny. Our gatherings have grown since Ally and Emily became an item and Aidan and Grace got together, but that adds to the fun: the more, the merrier.

Ally, opposite me, leans forward. "I hear you're planning to extend the time breakfast is served at the weekend. I'm not sure that's a good idea. The restaurant opens for lunch on Saturdays and Sundays. It's important you leave enough turnaround time between meals."

I suppress a groan. Further down the table, Jamie is telling Aidan a joke—a rude one, no doubt. I'd much rather be listening to that.

Until last year, Ally was the manager—or more like, the micromanager—of the Bannock Hotel, but he left that role to set up an outdoor-activities business with Aidan. We've all been happier since—Ally's heart was never in hospitality—but he still lives here with Emily and Ru, and because of that, he just can't resist getting his neb in at times. I do love him, but . . . sometimes I can't help but wish he'd get his own place and move out.

Emily, who has Ru on her lap, pats her husband's back. "Believe it or not, Lewis and I have discussed it in detail—with Elspeth too—and we all agree it'll work. Plus, it's in response to guest feedback. Some people would like a little longer in bed at the weekend, which I can understand."

"Hmm," Ally says. "All right, maybe it's not such a bad idea."

Chuckling, I shake my head. Emily could say anything and Ally would go along with it. My once-stubborn brother is utterly besotted with his wife.

I glance back down the table at Iona. Her blonde hair is half up, half down and frames her face in soft waves. She takes a bite of her dinner then closes her eyes and lets out a satisfied sigh. I'm pleased to see her savouring a dish I helped to prepare. But then she lifts another piece to her mouth, and as her lips close around her fork, an unexpected image flashes into my mind—of those lips around something else altogether.

Shifting in my seat, I realise Richard is watching me, his glare sharp enough to cut glass. Jesus, what's his problem? Okay, sure, I just had a dirty thought about his girlfriend, but it's not as if he can see what's going on in my head.

I turn away to have a few mouthfuls of food then return my gaze to the far end of the table. I'd like to know what they're talking about down there, but it's hard to catch anything over the noise. Emily, Grace, and Elspeth are now deep in chatter, while

Ally, Aidan, and Jamie are cracking up at something. When Ru fusses, I see my chance.

"You finish your food. I'll calm him down." Standing, I scoop my nephew out of Emily's lap and, bouncing him gently, move towards the other side of the room. His cries soften to quiet murmurs, and he nestles his head against my chest.

"With all the work you do with animals," Johnny is saying to Iona, "I bet you'll be wanting your own furry friend soon. Maybe once you and Richard have moved into your own place?"

"Well . . ." Iona begins.

Richard holds his hands up. "The problem is me—I've got terrible allergies. Iona would love a dog or cat to snuggle up with, but a fish or hamster is more realistic. Otherwise, I'd be a runny-eyed, snotty-nosed mess."

I snort. Can't help it. Iona has loved animals for as long as I can remember, starting with Molly, the cocker spaniel I had as a lad. As a girl, Iona always dreamed of having her own dog, but her da never allowed it. Isn't it sad that now, as a grown woman, she can't have one because of her boyfriend?

"Richard, of course, can't help his allergies," Iona says, firing a look my way, and I realise my snort was unkind. "Besides, you can still snuggle up with a hamster . . . kind of."

Jamie, who has apparently noticed me sidling towards the far side of the room, leans over and says, "Richard, did you know that Lewis has always had a thing for Iona?"

I stiffen, a hot flush creeping up my neck. As several pairs of eyes turn my way, I focus on Ru and lightly pat his back. "We were friends growing up," I state plainly.

"Really? Only ever friends?" Jamie teases.

"Yes!" My voice comes out a little sharper than I intended.

I catch Richard rolling his eyes, which makes me wonder . . .

does he know? Iona, of course, has every right to tell him what happened between us—he is her boyfriend—but we've never told our families or anyone else around Bannock. Were Richard to shoot his mouth off, and people found out what I did, I'd . . . well, I don't know how I'd cope. I mean, how could I ever work with Elspeth in the kitchen again? How could I meet her eye if she knew how I'd treated her daughter?

I realise I'm being utterly pathetic, worrying about myself like this. The truth is, I deserve to be shamed and humiliated—just as I shamed and humiliated Iona.

"Don't listen to Jamie," Ally says to Richard. "He's always winding people up. It's what he does."

Jamie smirks. "I'm just saying what we all think. Lewis, can you put a hand on your heart and swear that you and Iona never, you know . . ." He makes a squeaky bed noise.

If I wasn't holding Ru, I'd make Jamie pay for that.

Richard's jaw tightens, his lips pressing into a thin line, but—amazingly—he holds his tongue. He doesn't turn on me or Jamie.

Wow. He's a better man than I am.

CHAPTER NINE

LEWIS

Age eighteen

The University of Glasgow's main building is like something out of a fairy tale—or *Harry Potter*. Its towering spire looms high above countless turrets, a beacon of knowledge stretching into the sky. Were some Gryffindor kids to hurry past on their way to potions class, I wouldn't even bat an eye. But there are no witches or wizards to be seen—just a bunch of students milling around, even though it's evening and lectures must be over for the day. I can't help but feel a bit like a muggle as I stand among them waiting for Iona.

And then I see her. She approaches with two other girls, but I barely notice them because my attention is fixed on my best friend. In just a few short weeks, her entire look has changed. Her hair is thrown up in a messy bun, and she's sporting a retro patchwork jacket, ripped jeans, and combat boots. She looks incredible in the mismatched ensemble, and yet different from the lass I've known my whole life, who left Bannock not so very long ago.

Her face lights up when she spots me, and she sprints the rest of the way before launching herself into my arms. I hold her tight, breathing in the sweet, familiar smell of her strawberry shampoo.

"Lewis! It's so good to see you. Three weeks—it's the longest we've ever been apart."

I pull back a little and smile down at her. "It's good to see you too. You look amazing."

"Aye? Well, you're not so bad yourself. Oh! Let me introduce you." She steps back and gestures to a tall girl with dark hair. "This is Charlotte. And this"—she signals a shorter girl with a beanie hat—"is Erin. They're studying veterinary medicine too."

"Nice to meet you both," I say.

"And you," Charlotte replies. "Iona has told us *so much* about you."

"Er, she has?"

"Yep!" Erin nods eagerly. "She talks about you nonstop. It's been very . . . illuminating."

For some reason the pair of them giggle at this, and Iona rolls her eyes. It must be some sort of in-joke.

"Anyway, thanks for sharing your best mate with us." Charlotte slings an arm around Iona. "She's an absolute riot."

"Yeah, after a few drinks, she's a hero on the dance floor." With zero shame, Erin recreates some of Iona's moves for me. She throws her arms up and shimmies her shoulders, drops into a deep squat, then twirls with exaggerated elegance as though she were in a ballet.

"Stop it!" Iona laughs, hiding her face with her hands.

Wow, I thought I knew everything about Iona, but in just a few weeks, Charlotte and Erin have already seen a side of her that I never have. I nudge her shoulder with my own. "You never did much dancing in Bannock. I've obviously been missing out."

"You have!" Charlotte agrees. "Anyway, we'll leave you two to catch up. Erin and I were just being nosy—we wanted to see you for ourselves."

"Iona kept on going on about how handsome you are, so we had to come check you out," Erin explains. "She wasn't kidding. You are one good-looking guy."

"*So* good-looking," Charlotte echoes.

I scratch behind my ear. "Er . . . thanks?" I'm not used to my appearance being openly assessed like this, like an animal at a livestock show.

"All right, it's definitely past time you two left." Iona shoos them away, and they laugh as they go, promising to have a proper chat with me another day.

I stick my hands in my pockets and grin at Iona. "They seem like fun."

"They are! Quick question: would it be weird if I give you another hug?"

"Nope! Go for it."

Her arms wrap around me, and it feels so nice having her close like this. I've missed her. I don't know where we stand exactly—we've exchanged messages since she left for uni, but neither of us has brought up that night at the loch. Still, I'll never turn down a hug from her.

"So," she says when she finally disentangles herself, "let's grab a bite to eat, then I can show you where my classes are and where I'm staying. Sound good?"

"Aren't your classes in there?" I nod at Hogwarts.

"Nope, that was just an easy landmark for you to find—you can't really miss it. Veterinary medicine is actually on a different campus, a little further out of the city. It's on a huge estate with lots of greenery and woodland areas. I reckon a country boy like you will like it."

"A country boy like me? Are you a city girl now?"

She winks. "Anyway, even though we don't have classes here, Erin, Charlotte, and I are always visiting on account of all the cool pubs, cafés, and shops in this area. Let's go find somewhere that does good grub."

We sit in at an Italian place and feast on some delicious pizza. Iona does most of the talking, filling me in on everything that's happened, both on her course and on her nights out and weekends. I'm happy to listen, not having nearly so much news to share. Bannock is much the same as it's always been, save for the absence of Iona.

Afterwards, we grab a bus to the other campus, which just as Iona said, is set in a vast leafy park. She leads me to her halls of residence then up to her room, which is pretty compact, with a single bed, a desk cluttered with textbooks and stationery, and a wardrobe.

I plop down on the bed. "Well, I take it this is where I'll be sleeping, me being the guest and all. You'll be okay on the floor?"

"Always the gentleman." Sitting next to me, she sticks her tongue out.

I test the bed's bounciness. "I imagine this has seen a *lot* of action since you got here. Am I right?"

"Oh, you know me—I take home a different guy every night. Sometimes two a night, when I'm *really* horny. Usually one after the other, but now and then, both at once. It depends on my mood."

"The poor bed. How do you all fit?"

She grins. "Advanced acrobatics and a lot of imagination."

"I'm impressed. Unless, of course, by 'a lot of imagination', you mean it's all in your head." I nudge her shoulder teasingly.

"Damn it, you saw right through me. Yes, the truth is, I still haven't lost my V-card."

I'm relieved by this news, but I try not to show it.

"I doubt you have either," Iona adds.

"You're right." I sigh. "We're both so utterly tragic. What if we grow old and wrinkly without ever having sex? If only there were a way to prevent that from happening . . ." I glance at her, trying to gauge her reaction.

She meets my gaze, a hint of curiosity in her eyes. "Any suggestions?"

"Hmm . . . well . . ."

We're obviously joking around, but how will she react if I take things a step further? Only one way to find out. I lean forward, moving my mouth tantalisingly close to hers but halting just before our lips touch. The ball is in her court—she can either close the gap or push me away.

She closes the gap, her lips meeting mine, and just like the last time, the kiss quickly becomes passionate, our tongues dancing and exploring. She edges closer, her tits pressing eagerly against my chest, her heartbeat syncing with mine, both pounding fast.

As before, I feel myself getting hard, only this time my cock gets trapped in my jeans as it grows. Wincing, I have to reach down and adjust myself. If there's a subtle way of doing that, I've not learnt it—she notices, of course.

She giggles, breaking apart. "It never takes you long to get in the mood, does it?"

At the loch I was embarrassed, but I'm not today. In fact, when her eyes drift down, far from feeling self-conscious, a thrill shoots through me. I enjoy watching her study the contours of my jeans, like she's trying to decipher a secret code. There's curiosity in her gaze and perhaps a hint of amusement on her lips.

"We agreed it was a compliment, remember?" I remind her. "And anyway, your eyes aren't complaining." I can't quite keep the smug tone out of my voice. She's still not torn them away, and I'm revelling in her attention, experiencing a surge of masculine pride. Throughout most of my teens, erections have come at inopportune moments and have been things to conceal. There's an exhilarating freedom in finally showing off my bulge without shame.

"Staring isn't nearly as fun as touching," I add cheekily.

It's this that causes her to look up and meet my eye. I stare right back at her, holding her gaze, not backing down. I can't quite believe I had the guts to say that, but my cock is straining against my jeans, aching for her touch.

Iona bites her lip, glances away for a moment, then makes eye contact again. "Lewis," she says hesitantly, "did you know that in the animal kingdom it's usually the male birds that are bright colours?" She pauses, as if second-guessing herself, then continues, "They're also the ones who perform fancy dances to impress females."

"Er . . . okay?" Given a million chances, I'd never have guessed she'd reply with that. Am I not thinking straight because all the blood in my body has gone south? What am I missing?

"If there's going to be any touching involved, there's something you need to do first." She opens a drawer and takes a small packet out.

"A condom? Aye, no problem, I can put that on. Protection is a good idea."

"It's not just any condom. It's . . . a glow-in-the-dark one."

I raise an eyebrow and sit up a little straighter. "Aye? Why have you got that?"

"It was a present. From Erin. As a sort of . . . joke."

"All right, you're going to have to explain."

"Well, Charlotte and Erin were sharing stories about things they've been getting up to since they got here—encounters with boys, I mean. Then they turned to me, and . . . being a virgin, I didn't have a lot to discuss. But I felt I had to offer *something*, so I told them about how you kissed me at the loch. I mentioned that you got an erection and that we had a bit of a laugh about lightsabers."

Ah, earlier Erin said something about how meeting me was quite "illuminating". So that was another lightsaber pun.

"You told them about our night at the loch?"

She grins sheepishly. "Sorry! But honestly, compared to some of Charlotte's and Erin's anecdotes, mine was so tame. You got a hard-on—so what? It's perfectly natural. Anyway, a couple of days after I told that story, Erin handed me this. She dared me to try to get you to put it on the next time I saw you. So I was think-ing . . . " She tosses me the condom, and instinctively I catch it. "How about it?"

"Wow, this is a bit . . . left-field. I've had a lot of sexual fantasies—many of them involving you, actually—though none has ever gone like this. But . . . okay, let's say I put it on. Can we then get down to it?" I shoot her a mischievous smirk. That seems a fair deal to me.

"Not quite. Going back to my chat about male birds . . . the condom will give you the bright colour you need, but you'll still have to perform a courtship display."

I frown in confusion, so she adds, "A dance, Lewis. With the lights off. Just your . . . thing waving about in the dark."

I throw my head back and laugh hard. "This is a wind-up, right? It's a good one. Very funny."

"It's not a wind-up. But if you don't want to do it, that's fine. We can both remain sexually frustrated virgins. Your choice."

I narrow my eyes, thinking through this incredibly strange offer. "All right, just hypothetically, let's say I do this. Do we then get to . . . 'mate'?"

"Well, maybe not *mate*—at least, not today. I'd rather work my way up to full-on sex. But I could definitely have some fun with . . . you know . . ." She nods at the bulge in my jeans.

Heat surges through me. I lick my lips, imagining her soft, warm hand wrapped around me, stroking and teasing me. *Fuck!*

"That sounds . . . good," I say, struggling to keep my voice steady. "But it's not enough. If I dance for you, your clothes will be coming off afterwards. I will strip you naked and inspect every inch of you. *Every . . . inch.*" To drive my point home, I lower my gaze to her tits and drink them in, picturing how beautiful they'll look when I unclasp her bra. Never before have I stared at them so brazenly, but given she openly studied my hard-on, it seems only fair.

"Deal."

I glance back up to find a playful smile dancing on Iona's lips. I blink, scarcely able to believe my luck. "Really?"

"Yes, but you have to go all out with the dance. I want to see some real creativity."

Wow. If I'm going to get to see her naked, then making a fool of myself is a small price to pay. To hell with my dignity. Iona took a courageous step when she left her old life to come to Glasgow. Now it's my turn to show I can be daring too—and also spontaneous, fun, and a little bit silly.

"All right, how does this thing work?" I lift the condom wrapper and inspect it.

Iona's face lights up with a mixture of excitement and anticipation. "You're really going to do it? This is going to be the best thing ever. So, you have to hold it up to a light for thirty seconds. Once you've done that, we get this room as dark as possible, and then . . . you can begin. Unless you chicken out, of course."

"Not going to happen. But are you sure you want me to do this?"

I study her. Yes, there's an eager, playful glint in her eyes, but this act—daft though it may be—will represent a major shift in the dynamic between us. If we go ahead with this, our relationship—one we've had our whole lives—will never be the same again.

"I'm sure," Iona confirms.

"Okay, then let's do it."

I turn on Iona's desk lamp then tear open the wrapper and hold the contents to the bulb. Iona, meanwhile, draws the curtains and shoves her dressing gown at the bottom of the door to block out any slivers of light. Once we're ready, we flick a few switches, plunging the room into darkness . . . save for a green glow that shines from the wrapper in my hand.

"Wow, it's really bright," I say.

"Time to stick it on. And don't just drop your jeans down to your knees or whatever. I want you to take *everything* off."

I squint at her. I can just about make out her outline—she's sitting on the bed—but nothing more.

"It's not like we can see each other," I say. "What difference does it make?"

"I want to *know* you're naked, Lewis. And I'm the one setting the rules. You're just the guy who has to follow them."

I chuckle. "All right, fine." I put the condom wrapper on the desk then kick off my trainers, yank off my socks, and pull my T-shirt over my head. I drop my jeans too then hesitate. *What are you waiting for?* I ask myself. *Just do it!* And so, taking a deep breath, I tug my boxer briefs down and discard them. Now I'm standing naked, just a few feet from Iona, with a throbbing erection.

"I can't really see you," Iona whispers, "but . . . I can tell you're not wearing anything." She giggles.

"If this is a practical joke, this is your last chance to say so. Otherwise, the condom is going on."

"It's not a joke, so stop stalling. Get it on your dick already."

Her words send a thrill through me. Hearing her say "dick" instead of some euphemism is a total turn-on, and the fact she just commanded me to do something with it is scorching hot.

"All right. Here goes nothing." I remove the condom from the wrapper, position it at the tip of my erection, then carefully roll it down my length.

There's a sharp intake of breath followed by stunned silence.

"Bloody hell," I murmur. "My cock looks radioactive."

At this, Iona erupts into laughter—rolling waves of it that fill the room. "It does!" She gasps for breath. "You know, in the opening of *The Simpsons*, how Homer leaves the nuclear reactor with a glowing rod stuck in his clothes? It looks just like that!" She's laughing so hard it almost sounds like she's crying.

I don't quite know how to react. Do I join in with her laughter? This whole situation is utterly ridiculous, but I know Iona well enough to be confident she's not mocking me. She's just having a good giggle, and that's okay, I suppose.

"No need to put on a hazmat suit before touching it," I offer.

"Oh, good one!" Iona's silhouette inches closer. Is she coming in for a better look? "It's kind of . . . big," she observes.

"Aye?" In the dark, my chest puffs out.

"I mean, I've nothing to compare it against, but . . . it's bigger than I imagined it would be. Crap, I shouldn't have said that. I can't see your face, but I can already sense the smugness radiating from you."

"I feel like a footballer who's just scored a hat-trick," I confess. Her approval causes some primal part of me to surge with pride—an instinctual, almost caveman-like satisfaction in knowing that she's impressed by my size. "Now you strip."

"What? No way! My clothes aren't coming off until you strut your stuff."

Shit, I forgot about that bit.

"All right, but . . ." Maybe it's too late to redefine the terms of our deal, but I decide to try. "I don't just want to see you naked," I confess. "If I do this, I want to touch you too." In the safety of darkness, it's a lot easier to admit this desire than if I were looking my best friend in the eye.

"You won't be seeing or doing *anything* unless you start dancing," she points out. "And I'm growing impatient."

"Fine," I mutter, steeling my nerves. "But you better brace yourself because this performance is going to blow your mind."

And so, squaring my shoulders, I begin my courtship display.

CHAPTER TEN

IONA

Now

It's late—long past time I should have left the surgery and headed home—but I'm still here. I've been analysing blood samples from a few ewes who were displaying signs of lethargy and poor appetite. The results from the haematology analyser indicate an infection, so I ring the farmer to let him know and discuss next steps.

I'm just finishing up the call when Donald, the senior vet, peeks his head around the door. He waits till I hang up then asks, "We're not working you too hard, are we? That's me off now, and I hope you're not staying much longer. A good work-life balance is important, Iona."

I smile. "I'll only be a few more minutes. And don't worry—I love this job."

"All right, well, I'll leave you to lock up. Have a good night."

After he leaves, my smile fades slightly. I do love the job—it's the "life" part where I'm having some issues. I'm not exactly in a rush to head back to Maw's.

What I'd really like to do is vent about a few things—get them off my chest—but I can't chat with Maw or Richard about them because . . . they're at the heart of the problem. Donald is nice, but I'm not about to off-load my personal problems on a colleague, so . . . who can I talk to?

For my last few years in Glasgow, I shared a flat with Cat McIntyre. We told each other everything—well, except for what happened between me and her brother Lewis. I kept *that* to myself. Otherwise, though, if something was bothering me, talking it over with her always helped. I decide to give her a ring.

"Hello, stranger!" Her voice is lively and cheerful, as usual.

"Hey, you. How are things going in Wick?"

Like me, Cat has returned to the Highlands, in her case to do her probationary year as a high school English teacher. She was hoping to be posted to Bannock or at least somewhere nearby, but instead ended up a two-and-a-half-hour drive north of here, almost at the very tip of the British mainland.

"It's a nice enough place, and the kids are all right, but man, I used to think Bannock was remote. I was so naive! You can get from Bannock to Inverness in forty minutes, but up here there's nothing but quiet hamlets, tiny villages, and very occasionally a small town. Mostly, though, it's just miles and miles and miles of rugged landscape."

I can see the problem there. I know Cat, and that doesn't sound like her scene at all. She liked to hit the clubs when she was in Glasgow.

"Next year you'll have a bit more control over where you work," I offer. "Hopefully, you can come back to Bannock. I miss having you around."

"I miss you too—and my stupid brothers. Anyway, how are you getting on?"

"Well . . ." I hesitate, unsure how to begin.

"Shit, that doesn't sound good. Tell me everything—I need some news to help me feel connected to the world."

"The job is going well," I say, "but . . . living at Maw's isn't easy."

"Oh? Is she making you too much food? I love Elspeth, but if I moved in with her, my waistline would never forgive me."

"That *is* a bit of an issue, but . . . it's not Maw who's the main problem."

"Oh crap, it's Richard? What's up?"

"Well . . ."

Richard and I actually had a disagreement within days of arriving, when I admitted to him that Lewis and I were at one point more than friends. He wasn't too keen on the idea of living opposite Lewis after learning that, nor was he best pleased when I asked him to keep the details to himself. He felt that amounted to defending Lewis, something he doesn't think Lewis deserves.

With hindsight, of course, I should have made my admission about Lewis *before* Richard and I moved to Bannock. I messed up, but to be fair to Richard, he came around, and I have to give him credit for that. And yet . . . since we got over that initial wobble, other issues have cropped up.

"You know how, when we were in Glasgow, I'd spent a few nights at Richard's each week, or he'd spend a few nights at our flat? That worked really well. It turns out living with him seven days a week is a little more . . . challenging."

"Ah."

"Sometimes, after work, all I want to do is curl up with a romance book and lose myself in the story. But Richard . . . I don't know, it's almost like he isn't capable of entertaining himself. He always wants to do things together, and maybe that's sweet—maybe I shouldn't be complaining—but I find it a bit . . . draining. It's like he's used to weekend me and is expecting me to be the same person on a weeknight, but I'm just not. After a day at work, I don't always have a lot left in the tank. Plus, while I'm glad he's enjoying his new job, I've already heard more than enough about wind turbines for a lifetime."

Cat laughs at this. "So you're saying you'd rather spend time with your latest book boyfriend than listen to Richard prattle on about renewable energy? I'm not sure that's a big issue, Iona."

Isn't it? I'm literally admitting I prefer the company of fictional men to that of my actual boyfriend. Then again, I suppose a lot of women in happy relationships enjoy romance books, so maybe Cat *is* right and it isn't something to worry about. But if that's the case, why do I have this nagging feeling in my gut?

"Here's what I think," Cat says. "Even though your issue isn't with your maw, living with her will be putting a strain on your and Richard's relationship. That's not a dig at Elspeth—you know I love her—but Richard probably feels he has to be on his best behaviour all the time. Maybe all he wants to do is lounge around in his underwear, watching football and drinking beer, but he can't because your maw is in the living room. So he's hanging out with you instead."

That is a good point. Life will be different once we have our own place—I have to remember that. Then again, Wednesday through to Sunday, Maw works at the restaurant, so it's not as if Richard and I haven't been getting any time to ourselves. But today is Monday, so Maw will be there when I get back, and maybe that is contributing to my sense of dread.

"Perhaps you and Richard just need an evening away from each other," Cat adds. "Yes, you want to read your romance stories, but perhaps what you *really* need is a girls' night out. Why don't you organise something and have a bit of fun?"

"Er, this is awkward, but . . . why do you think I'm on the phone to you, Cat? I've been away for nine years. I don't have any girlfriends in Bannock."

"Bollocks! What about Emily and Grace? They may not have grown up in Bannock, but they're Bannock girls now."

"They're both great," I concede, "but . . . they have their babies, plus their relationships seem so perfect. I'm not sure a night out with them would make me feel any better about myself."

"Good point. It is a little sickening how head over heels they are about their men. We grew up with Ally and Aidan—we remember how daft they once were. Okay, let me have a think. Hmm, right, this is why you shouldn't have spent your entire childhood hanging out with Lewis. If you'd thrown your net a bit wider back then, you'd have more options now. Oh, wait! How about Maisie in the Pheasant? She's a laugh, plus she's single so there's no risk of her banging on and on about how wonderful her man is."

Maisie was in the year below me at school and now works at the local pub, the Pheasant. She's really friendly.

"I do like Maisie. I actually bumped into her a few days ago—we chatted for a few minutes and then went on our way again. How do I . . . sorry, I realise how pathetic this question sounds, but . . . how do I go from that to having a night out with her?"

"Er, you ask her if she wants to grab a drink and have a chat?"

"You make it sound so easy."

"Because it is?"

"Isn't there something a little tragic about begging her to

hang out with me because I don't have any other single friends in Bannock?"

"Hmm . . . oh, crap, something has just come up. Is it all right if I call you back?"

"Sure, no prob—" The call cuts off before I can finish.

Weird. I wonder what could have "just come up" in Wick that demanded Cat's immediate attention. But then my phone pings, and a notification informs me that Cat has created a group called "Bannock Babes". To it, she's added herself, me, and Maisie.

Ah. She's always been impulsive—never one to hum and haw. Instead of wasting time trying to convince me to get in touch with Maisie, she's taking matters into her own hands. That's why she ended the call.

The first message comes in.

CAT

Hey, Maisie! 👋 I was just chatting with Iona. She's been pretty lonely since she moved back to Bannock and needs some girl time. Fancy meeting up with her for a drink or two?

Oh dear. I realise Cat is being nice, but it does come across as a bit tragic. "Pretty lonely"? I only wanted to vent to someone— that's all.

I'm wondering whether to call Cat and ask her to delete the group when I see the words *Maisie is typing* . . .

Too late. She's already seen it.

MAISIE

Hey, Cat and Iona! Sure. Tonight isn't great for me, but things should be quieter in the Pheasant tomorrow evening, if that suits?

If you come along, I can take a break from the bar for a while to sit down for a chat. Sound good?

IONA

That'd be brilliant, but please don't feel you have to adopt me as a friend!!! I'm sorry about pouncing on you like this. 😬

MAISIE

LOL, don't be silly, it'll be fun. Shall we say eight?

IONA

👍

MAISIE

Great. Now, Cat: can you really call yourself a "Bannock Babe" when you live in Wick?

CAT

Excuse me? I'll always be a Bannock Babe at heart. But if you're going to be pedantic . . .

A message pops up informing me that the group's name is now "Scottish Sirens".

CAT

Sorted! All right, Iona, you've got something to look forward to tomorrow, but what about tonight? I think you could do with some me-time. How about a swim and sauna at the Glen Garve Resort?

MAISIE

Good idea, or you could pump some iron at the gym. 🏋️

CAT

> Ha, having lived with Iona for a few years, I'm pretty sure my suggestion is more up her street.

Cat is right, of course, but it's not like I *never* go to the gym. I just don't go very often. And because of that, I normally end up cancelling my membership, which means . . .

Okay, fine, I never go to the gym. But maybe now I'm back in Bannock, it's time to turn over a new leaf. Perhaps it's what I'm missing in my life. Exercise *is* important—for the mind and the body. It'd be healthy to work off a few frustrations.

IONA

> Cat, you don't know me as well as you think you do. Thanks for the suggestion, Maisie. I'm going to go get my sweat on.

CHAPTER ELEVEN

LEWIS

My back flat on the bench, I press the barbell up, my arms shaking as they straighten, my muscles screaming under the heavy load. With a sharp exhale, I lower it, feeling the burn. Just two more reps. Almost there . . .

I lift again, my chest tightening. And then . . . down. All right, last one now.

Grunting, I raise the bar for my final rep, the strain in my chest and arms almost unbearable. Then, with a satisfying clang, I drop the bar back onto the rack. My muscles protest with a fiery ache, but it's a good pain, the kind that tells me I've pushed myself hard. Still, I'm not done yet—two more sets to go.

For a few moments I just stare up at the ceiling, sweat trickling down my temples, then I sit up and roll my shoulders to ease the tension. Grabbing my gym towel, I wipe my face and neck then stand and walk a few paces, psyching myself up for the next round. I'm about to settle back down on the bench when something—no, someone—catches my eye.

The gym has been quiet this evening, just me and two other men I don't recognise, who must be guests at the Glen Garve

Resort keen to squeeze in a workout during their stay. Now, though, who do I spot but Iona, in a plain white T-shirt and black leggings—a simple outfit, much more conventional than some of her animal-themed ones, but it looks good on her. Then again, what doesn't?

"Iona!" I raise a hand in greeting.

She glances my way, and while she doesn't quite roll her eyes, she's clearly not thrilled to see me. Ouch. Oh well, that's her standard reaction to me nowadays, and I've learnt I can't let it hold me back. So, undeterred and beaming widely, I go over to say hi.

"Lewis." She offers a stiff smile. "As I was driving over, it occurred to me that I might bump into you here. I know how much you like to work out."

"And here I am! Lucky you." I adopt a fake stern expression. "Have you been avoiding me? I've barely seen you since the welcome dinner."

"Ha!" There's no amusement in her tone. "Well, I'm going to go make a start. On . . . something." She adjusts her glasses and glances around the gym a little uncertainly.

"If you like, I can show you—"

"I'll be fine." Her voice is sharp, but after a moment, her features soften slightly. "Sorry, but I came here for some time to myself—I'm sure you understand. Anyway, seeing as you're a sweaty mess, you're obviously mid-session, so I'll leave you to it."

I maintain my smile even though it stings to be so quickly dismissed, given how close we once were. "Aye, of course. Have a good workout."

She's absolutely right—the need for time away from others is one I fully understand. I come here to escape everything, including thoughts about Iona. God knows how I'm going to manage that when she's just a few metres from me.

Back at the bench press, I lie down and grab the barbell, searching for the mental calm the gym usually provides me. I lift, striving to focus on the motion, but invariably my mind drifts to Iona. I don't want to be staring up at the ceiling—I want to be glancing over at her.

By the time I finish the set, my chest feels like it's on fire, but it's a satisfying burn. Standing, I have a stretch and can't resist checking to see what Iona's up to. She's on the lat pulldown machine, yanking the weight down with sharp jerks, arching her back while doing so. Her grip is too wide, and she's using her momentum more than her muscles. Yikes, that's a sure-fire way to end up with an injury. I know she wanted space, but . . .

I walk over. "Er, Iona? You really need to keep your back straight and—"

"God!" She drops the weight and glares at me. "Can't a woman come to the gym without some know-it-all man bothering her? What year is this?"

The other two guys halt their workouts and look over.

"We're friends," I assure them, raising my hands in a gesture of peace.

"More like acquaintances," Iona corrects. "But aye, I do know him—unfortunately—and he's not troubling me. But thanks."

With nods, the men leave us to it.

"Sorry," Iona mutters, rubbing her arm sheepishly. "That was a bit dramatic of me, but I was releasing some pent-up frustration during that exercise, and I could have done without the interruption."

"No need to apologise. I don't want to be 'some know-it-all man', but if you continue like that, you're going to hurt yourself."

She sighs. "All right, fine. What am I doing wrong?"

"First, let's reduce the weight. Once you've got the motion right, we can increase that, but for now, the main thing is to concentrate on your form. Next, bring your hands a wee bit closer together on the bar."

She adjusts them.

"That's better. Now, keep your back straight, and when you pull the bar down, do it in a nice, controlled way, keeping your elbows close to your body. Let your muscles do the work. Like this." I put my hands on either side of hers, taking extra care not to accidentally brush her fingers, especially after her earlier comment. In fact, I'm so focused on this that I'm completely unprepared for the whiff of strawberry shampoo I inhale as I lean close to her.

Damn, that smell is a time machine, and suddenly I'm drowning in memories of . . .

No, pull yourself together, Lewis. This isn't the place for such thoughts.

Gathering myself, I demonstrate the motion for Iona, showing off the smooth, controlled rhythm. "All right?" I say, fighting to maintain an even tone, despite the rush of intimate recollections. "You try it now."

She does, and this time her movement is fluid, her back straight.

"Perfect!" I flash a grin, hoping my exterior is composed and masks the emotions I'm wrestling with inside. "Now finish the set. Normally, I'd say ten to fifteen reps, but as it's a low weight, I'm confident you'll make fifteen no bother. Go for it! You can do it."

As she works through the set, I try not to be too mesmerised by the way her muscles flex and relax under her T-shirt, or by how the movement accentuates the curve of her hips. I swallow hard, willing my traitorous eyes to behave and focus on her form and nothing else.

"That's it," I say, figuring that speaking might distract my brain. "Feel it in your back, not your arms. There you go, thirteen, fourteen, fifteen—done!"

"Phew!" She catches her breath. "All right, what next? Another set of this or should I move on to another machine?"

I half thought she might have dismissed me now I've shown her what to do, but it seems she's okay with me hanging around a little longer. Obviously, that's great, but . . . a part of me wonders whether it'd be better if I hurried to the men's changing room for a cold shower.

Nah, screw that. If she's happy for me to stick around, I'm sticking around.

I get her to do another set of lat pulldowns, this time with a bit more weight, to see if she can maintain her form when it's more of a challenge. She smashes it, so I suggest we move on to the chest press machine. Normally, once I start a workout, nothing can distract me from it, but today I couldn't care less that there's one last set of reps waiting for me over at the bench press.

After selecting a weight I reckon Iona should manage, I go first, doing a couple of presses to demonstrate the movement, even though this one is harder to get wrong than the lat pulldown. We switch over, and I stand in front of her to observe and guide.

"Keep your elbows in line. Good."

If anything, this machine is more distracting than the last one. As she pushes through each rep, the white cotton of her T-shirt stretches across her chest, revealing the dark shape of her sports bra beneath. I can't stop my gaze from flicking down, but I mentally slap myself and refocus on her technique.

Once more, I try to keep my mind busy by chatting. "You mentioned something about pent-up frustration. A bad day at work?"

Exhaling forcefully, she presses the handles away from her. "What is this, a therapy session?"

"Aye, I suppose it is." I grin. "I'm kind of a unique personal trainer—I offer the full holistic experience, training your body and mind at the same time. So, talk to me about what's bothering you. Is being a farm vet in Bannock harder than in Glasgow?"

"It's nothing to do with my job," she says, completing the set. "And you're not my personal trainer, Lewis." Unprompted, she increases the weight then goes at it again.

"All right, well . . . I know!" I click my fingers together. "You've been missing me. You regret not having spent enough time with me since you moved back, and that's been getting you down."

She scoffs. "It's definitely not that, and I never asked for a therapy session, so—"

"Problems with Richard?"

Her jaw clenches, and I realise I've hit the nail on the head. Pausing for a moment between reps, she says, "No." Then she continues.

"Hmm, really? I'm not sure you're being honest with me. Bottling up your feelings isn't healthy. I'm a modern man—I get that. It's good to get things off your chest."

Oi, Lewis, what are you doing? Just because you said "chest" doesn't mean you should check hers out again. Eyes back up. I said, EYES BACK UP!

I rub my forehead, attempting to disguise the fact I've just sneaked another glance at her breasts. Not the smoothest move—I doubt she's fooled.

Clearing my throat, I say, "If something isn't right between you and Richard, you can tell me. When we were younger, we didn't keep secrets from each other. No topic was off the table. Remember?"

She finishes her second set. "Aye, but that was back when I could trust you."

I wince. "Ouch! Low blow, Iona. Careful, you should be nice to your PT. Otherwise, I might make you do extra reps."

She goes straight into a third set, completing each chest press with new force, her annoyance fuelling her movements. "As I've already said, Lewis, you're not my personal trainer, and I'm not talking to you about my problems with Richard."

"Ah, so your problems *are* to do with Richard. Interesting." I rub my chin thoughtfully, mimicking the therapists I've seen in films, although I doubt actual therapists do this.

"If you don't . . . shut up . . . maybe I'll give you . . . a literal low blow." She's struggling now, and her words come out in strained bursts.

I glance down, taking in our relative positions and the ease with which she could, if she wished, kick me in a rather sensitive spot. Laughing nervously, I take a step back and playfully wag my finger at her. "No threatening your PT. It's against the rules."

Finishing the set, she rests, her breath coming in quick gasps. "You're really beginning to get on my nerves."

"Hmm, well, I reckon you've got one more set in you. So, keep going, and let's talk through why you're getting worked up." It turns out I can do a pretty good calm-and-collected therapist voice. "Of what sort of nature is your problem with Richard? One relating to the bedroom, perhaps?"

"Lewis!" she warns.

But I'm having fun. I like seeing the spark back in her eyes, even if she is glaring at me. The last few years, whenever she's come to Bannock for a visit, things have been so awkward between us. I've been terrified of doing or saying anything to hurt her even more, and because of that, I've been way too polite and careful around her. That's only widened the rift. If ever I'm going to win her back as a friend, we need to reignite some of our old banter.

"When was the last time you and Richard expressed your love physically?" I probe.

"*Lewis!*" She's just begun her next set, and this catches her off-guard. She pauses between reps. "Have you forgotten my threat about the low blow? Your crotch is right there." She nods at it.

I doubt she'd act on her threat, but I can't be sure so I clasp my hands in front of me, just in case.

"Anyway," she goes on, continuing the chest presses, her voice strained from effort or irritation or both, "not that it concerns you, but it hasn't been long at all."

"Oh. In that case, is the sex unsatisfying?"

Her eyes narrow into dangerous slits. "You're insufferable."

"Aye, but you know what? Whenever you get annoyed with me, you start to really go for it with the exercises. It's clearly an effective motivational technique. I'll have to make teasing an integral part of all our sessions."

"Tonight is definitely a one-off."

"You say that now, but we both know you're having fun, really. Before you leave here, we'll be comparing calendars on our phones to see when we can do this again. Tomorrow, maybe?"

"Nope, I'm catching up with Maisie tomorrow." She catches herself then clarifies, "Not that that matters—like I've said, there won't be a next time."

"We'll see," I say cockily.

Her lips press into a thin, hard line. I notice her cheeks are getting rosier with every push and release, and her skin glistens with a sheen of sweat. In the past, when I saw her getting hot and bothered like this, it was because . . .

Glancing down, I observe how she straddles the seat, and a memory comes to me of her straddling me like that, riding me with wild abandon.

My cock twitches. Damn it, I *cannot* get a hard-on right now. These gym shorts wouldn't hide anything, and anyway, she's sitting in front of me, her line of vision not a whole lot higher than crotch level. I shift my stance and casually adjust my waistband.

To clear my thoughts, I look away for a moment, but when I turn back, an idea hits me—a cheeky one—and I can't resist leaning a little closer. "So, going back to your sex life . . . do you still read smutty historical romances?"

She lets the weights drop with a resounding clang. Red-faced and panting, she hisses, "You can't ask me that!"

I nod, the therapist persona returning, one hand on my hip, the other rubbing my chin. "If the answer had been no, you'd have said no. So that's a yes. Interesting."

Her foot shoots up, and I instinctively flinch, but she doesn't make contact.

"That was your last warning, Lewis. Maybe you should be a little less worried about me suffering an injury and a little more worried about yourself—specifically, your balls. No more sex talk. Understood?"

Grinning, I give her a mischievous wink.

CHAPTER TWELVE

IONA

Age nineteen

It's a dreich spring day and the rain is relentless. By the time Charlotte, Erin, and I make it back to the halls of residence, our shoes are squelching. We head up to our rooms to change into something dry. Entering mine, I find Lewis lounging on my bed in a grey T-shirt and blue boxer briefs, a book in his hand. He sets it aside and flashes me that cheeky grin of his. God, he's gorgeous. His chestnut hair is just how I like it—neatly trimmed on the sides and deliciously tousled on top—and those dimples? Irresistible.

He got here yesterday. It's been nearly half a year since the "courtship display", and since then he's visited me at least once a month.

"Make yourself at home, why don't you?" Hanging up my coat, I nod at his underwear, which is somewhat distracting—it's a snug fit, if you know what I mean.

"Aye, well, my jeans got wet. Besides, I hate lying down in denim: it's too stiff and annoying. These boxers, though?" He places his hands on his thighs and lets out a contented sigh. "They're *so* comfortable. Here, come feel how soft they are."

I laugh and shake my head. "Wow, so subtle, Lewis. I'm literally just back, and already you want me to put my hand near your penis? You're not wasting any time."

He winks then stretches his arms up behind his head, flexing.

The night of his first visit, I had a lot of fun with his glow-in-the-dark dick. We giggled and whispered jokes to one another, and in time Lewis's laughter gave way to low moans until . . . well, you know. Afterwards, we stuck a light on and I explored his body properly and let him explore me. Since then, whenever he's come down, we've ended up naked together.

We've not admitted to people back home what we've been getting up to, nor have we put a label on this thing between us. It's complicated, especially as we live so far apart and don't get to catch up often, but it's exclusive—neither of us is seeing anyone else.

"All right, you caught me out, but these boxers *are* really comfortable." He studies me, his playful expression turning more serious. "Crap, you're soaked through, Iona. We can't have you catching a cold. I swear I've no ulterior motives here, but for health reasons, I think you should strip. I can help you out of your clothes, if you like?"

"God, Lewis! You're so randy. Have you been lying here all day having dirty thoughts while I've been out at classes?"

"Pretty much." He runs a hand through his hair, messing it up even more. "But I've got you to blame for that."

"Oh? Am I so attractive that, even when you're not in my presence, you can't stop thinking about me?"

He considers this then nods. "Aye, you're fucking gorgeous, but that's not what I meant. I was out exploring Glasgow earlier but got completely drenched, so I came back. I got a bit bored, so I had a wee rummage around, and . . . I found your secret stash of naughty books."

My cheeks warm. "Wait, what?"

He lifts the book he's been reading: *Rival Clans, Secret Riches* from Aurora McKenna's *Highland Hearts and Hidden Treasures* series.

Oh my God. Lewis and I have always told each other more or less everything, but my love of spicy historical romances is something I've kept to myself. Mortified, I wait for him to give me stick for enjoying "trash", but instead he says, "It's so good! I'm almost done. I really hope they find the treasure in the end. After all they've been through, they deserve it—Eilidh, especially. I'm rooting for her."

"Wait, you're properly reading it? Not just skimming through for the naughty bits?"

"Aye, although I am paying extra attention to those scenes." He shrugs shamelessly.

I perch on the bed, my embarrassment giving way to interest. "Did they . . . turn you on?" I trace patterns on his bare leg, his soft hairs tickling my fingers.

"Of course. I mean, that scene in the great hall, where it was just Douglas and Eilidh, and Douglas said he wanted a feast? Except he wasn't talking about food but . . ." Lewis's gaze drifts downwards and settles on my lap. "Let's just say I made a few mental notes. There are some things I'm keen to try out."

A wave of heat floods my body. Since he explored me that first night, Lewis's tentative touches have grown in confidence. He approaches my pleasure with curiosity and fascination, eager to experiment. He's not at all embarrassed about asking questions or seeking feedback—all that matters to him is finding out what I like. Just knowing he's been reading one of my books and drawing inspiration from it is incredibly hot.

"But," Lewis goes on, "some of the words the author uses—ha! His *staff*? Her *hidden garden*? Once it was *claymore* and *scabbard*—I chuckled at that. Another time, he pushed his dick into her *feminine folds*."

That's the one thing Lewis hasn't done yet. We've tried pretty much everything, save for actual sex.

"I doubt he pushed his 'dick' in," I say. "More likely it was his love lance or something."

Lewis throws his head back and laughs. "Ha! I've not come across love lance—I'd have remembered that. Anyway . . ." He cocks his head to the side. "Are you going to stay in those wet clothes, or . . . ?"

"Hmm. Well, I suppose this top *is* pretty damp." I pull it off and throw it aside. "That's better."

His gaze, predictably, drops to my cleavage. You'd think it was his first time seeing me in just a bra, but no. He's seen every inch of me, and yet whenever I take off a piece of clothing, this daft look crosses his face and he completely forgets where my eyes are. He's such a boy, but I'd be lying if I said I wasn't flattered by the attention.

"So . . ." I bite my lip, unsure how he'll react to what I'm about to suggest. "What would you think about . . . acting out one of the scenes from the book?"

He sits up straighter. "I'd be up for that."

"Really?"

He nods. "I'm pretty sure I can channel my inner Highland warrior. How about the scene where she's tending to his wounds by the campfire and then . . . well . . ."

"Isn't that the one where they have sex for the first time?" I'd been thinking more along the lines of the great hall scene.

A mischievous smile tugs at Lewis's lips. He's suggested we go all the way a few times now, but I've wanted to take thing slow. It seems this is his latest attempt to test the waters.

"Well . . ." I consider his suggestion. "Okay."

"What?" Surprise flickers across his face. "You're kidding, right?"

"Nope."

"Let's be clear here. Are you saying I can put my cock inside your . . . feminine folds?"

"Not if you use that term. Aurora McKenna can get away with it because her stories are set centuries ago. It sounds bloody weird coming out of your mouth."

He grins. "All right, fine. Your pussy."

"That's better. And yes, we can have sex. I'm ready."

There's a stirring in Lewis's underwear—the idea obviously excites him—but he asks, "Is this a trick?"

"Nope. And you don't even have to wear a glow-in-the-dark condom. A regular one will do."

He chuckles and rubs the back of his neck, glancing away for a moment before meeting my gaze again. "Are you sure about this?"

"Are you honestly trying to talk me out of it?"

"No, I'm desperate to have sex with you, but I'm also your friend, and I want what's best for you. You only get to lose your virginity once, Iona, and you pick today? It's pissing down outside. I'm hanging around your room in my boxers. It's a single bed. If we're going to do it, shouldn't we at least, you know, dress up first? Go out for dinner? I might be able to cobble together

82

some cash for a hotel room so we can have a double bed. I mean—"

I hold up a hand, cutting him off mid-sentence.

"Sometimes, Lewis, you're just a horny young man with sex on the brain."

His expression falls. "Oh."

"But other times you can be so . . . sweet."

He pulls a face. "Nah, I prefer the first description. Being sweet is lame."

I give him a playful shove. "I'm being serious. A lot of people spend their lives looking for someone who really gets them, but I literally grew up opposite you. How lucky is that? You're my best friend, and I can't imagine having sex with anyone else. I want to do it with you. Going out for a fancy dinner isn't very us—we don't have the money for it—but doing it here, in this wee room, on a single bed after you've been reading one of my smutty books? That feels right somehow. So . . ."

Impersonating Eilidh, the feisty daughter of the neighbouring clan's chieftain, I say, "You're hurt, Douglas. Let me tend to your wounds." I take a hold of Lewis's T-shirt and gently tug it over his head.

He clears his throat then lowers his voice. "These injuries torment me, lass. Your gentle touch is the only thing that can ease my suffering."

I scoot closer to him and trail my fingers over his chest. Lewis must mistake this for an invitation because he reaches for my bra and I have to swat his hand away.

"Oi! Did Douglas do that at this point in the scene?"

"Shit, no, you're right. Sorry. I . . . got carried away. That comes later."

"It does. Now, where were we?" I find Eilidh's voice again. "Ah, yes. Your wounds, Douglas . . ."

CHAPTER THIRTEEN

IONA

Now

Richard is in a good mood as he pulls on his work things. "That was fun last night, wasn't it?"

"Aye, it was." I have to force a smile as I get myself dressed and ready for another day of farm visits.

Until last night, Richard had only been up for sex at times when Maw was out of the house. He'd always said no if she was in, even when I was certain she was fast asleep. But after my gym session, I finally convinced him, arguing it'd be exciting and a wee bit naughty to do it while she was downstairs watching TV. I'd hoped it might liven things up, but . . . it ended up being much the same as always.

Sex with Richard is never *bad*—in fact, it's pretty good—but . . . well, as much as I enjoy Christmas dinner, I'd get bored if I ate it every day. Variety is the spice of life, but Richard obviously missed that memo when it comes to his sexual technique. I've tried chatting with him about exploring new things, but there's a disconnect somewhere.

"Right, that's me off." He gives me a quick kiss. "After work, Joe and I are going to grab some pub grub in Auchenford, so I won't be back till later. Enjoy your girls' night."

"I will. Say hi to Joe for me."

He heads downstairs, calling goodbye to my maw, then the front door thuds shut behind him. I'll be following him before long, but now that I've got a moment to myself, I sit on the bed and attempt to untangle a few troubling thoughts I've been having. I'd never admit this to Richard, but there have been times where, to make things a little more interesting for myself, I've imagined scenes from my favourite books as we've been doing it. I probably shouldn't let my mind wander when we're supposed to be sharing an intimate experience, but I honestly never considered it to be a major problem.

But then yesterday, *while Richard was inside me*, an image flashed into my mind of Lewis, in his form-fitting T-shirt and shorts, his muscular arms and legs on show, his skin glistening with sweat from his exertions at the gym. Of course, I immediately banished the vision—I'd never cheat on Richard, even in my head—and yet guilt gnaws at me that it happened at all.

What makes the guilt worse is that, well, sex was *never* boring with Lewis. Yes, it's hardly fair to compare my current boyfriend's sexual proficiency with that of a former partner, but it's the truth. I don't recall Lewis ever saying no to anything I suggested, whether it was something really hot or else something a bit silly and out there. He had a playfulness about him and a complete lack of inhibition around me.

Like one time, when I was still at university and hanging out with Lewis in my room, I was bored and looking for something to do. So . . . I asked Lewis if I could use his dick for a game of hoopla. It was such a stupid request—like, unbelievably ridiculous—but he didn't even hesitate or question it. He just shrugged, got his thing out, then let me toss bangles at it like I was at the fair. And you know what? It was fun. We both cheered whenever I got one of the makeshift rings on target.

Richard would never agree to something like that—he'd find the idea humiliating. That's okay—they're different men—but what I miss even more is the way Lewis's playfulness could ignite into searing passion in a heartbeat. When the mood *really* took a hold of him, he'd become like an animal, wild with lust. He'd throw me onto my back, bury his face between my thighs, and eat me out, his tongue and lips making every nerve in my body sizzle to life. Or he'd push himself into me, maintaining eye contact as he teased me with slow, shallow thrusts before quickly working up to a fervour that'd leave me gasping as he drove us both towards ecstasy. When he was like that, the intensity of our sex was off the charts.

Of course, I shouldn't be thinking about this stuff, but last night in the gym was the longest one-on-one interaction I've had with Lewis in years. He was my first, and my childhood best friend, so it's hardly surprising that the workout stirred up certain memories. But they're obviously problematic, for a whole variety of reasons.

After Lewis tore all my self-esteem away, I worked hard to restore it. I moved on and built a life for myself—finished my studies, established myself in my career, eventually found Richard. I can't let my history with Lewis spoil all that I've accomplished. Aye, Richard may not be as exciting as Lewis in some ways, but he's kind, steadfast, and reliable, and that counts for a lot.

Lewis, on the other hand? He *knew* how my da's secret tore me apart—he comforted me when it happened and saw what it did to me. He knew better than *anyone* how important trust is to me, and yet he did what he did anyway.

Well, you know what? I'm perfectly entitled to come back here, to this town where I spent my first eighteen years, and I'm perfectly entitled to find happiness in my relationship with my new boyfriend. I won't let these old memories ruin things for me. And there's no way in hell I'm letting Lewis McIntyre, with his unwanted "therapy sessions" and nosy questions about my sex life, fuck everything up.

I clench and unclench my fists, trying to release some of the nervous tension that's building inside me. When I leave here, I need to be focused and professional, so these thoughts and emotions have to go—for now, at least.

Standing, I head downstairs, give Maw a quick kiss on the cheek, then set off for work.

CHAPTER FOURTEEN

IONA

Age twenty

It's eleven thirty and the restaurant, a burger place, is quiet, although I'm sure it'll soon be bustling with the lunch crowd. Lewis and I are sipping on Irn-Bru and killing time until my da arrives. The only other table that's taken is in the far corner, where a young couple, about our age, sit nestled close to each other. The guy has one arm casually draped around the girl's shoulders, and with his other, he picks up fries and pops them in his mouth as they chat away.

Lewis shifts in his seat, his leg briefly brushing against mine. The contact may have been accidental, but I liked it. It makes me wish he and I could be more open with our affections when I'm up north. I can understand the secrecy when we're in Bannock, but right now we're in Inverness, the "Capital of the Highlands". We're sitting side by side, so I wouldn't mind snuggling up to him and having his arm wrapped around me, especially as it's a cold February morning and I'm still shaking off the chill from outside.

Drumming my fingers on the table, I decide to voice my

thoughts. "Is it weird that we've not told anyone back home about us? We *have* been hooking up for a year and a half now."

Lewis snatches up the menu and holds it in front of his face then peeks out from behind it and puts a finger to his lips. "Shh! You never know who might be listening. Bannock folk are always popping through to Inverness at the weekend." He ducks back under cover like a really bad secret agent.

I groan. "Stop messing around. I'm being serious."

He tosses the menu down and winks. "Sorry. I don't know. Weren't you the one keen to keep things casual?"

He's right. University is hard work, and although my inner party animal has emerged since leaving home, I haven't lost my nerdy instincts. I just wouldn't have the time for a proper boyfriend. Meeting up with Lewis once a month, or occasionally twice, but being able to focus on my studies the rest of the time? That's perfect.

"We do need to keep it casual for the moment," I concede, "but do we have to keep it a secret?"

"What do you suggest I say to my maw and da?" Lewis shoots back. "*Nah, we're not boyfriend and girlfriend—we basically just meet up every few weeks to shag each other senseless. Any questions?* Maybe some people can talk candidly about that stuff with their parents, but not me, and I don't think you have that sort of relationship with your maw either. Besides, can you imagine what my siblings would say? Jamie would have a field day. *You'd* be able to escape his jokes down in Glasgow, but I wouldn't. I'd be stuck with him in the hotel, and it'd be nonstop. I'd never hear the end of it."

I smile at this. Lewis is right: Jamie would tease him mercilessly. "Fair enough. Anyway, I suppose what we've got is pretty good, isn't it? Like, take Charlotte and Erin. I've never known either of them to see the same guy more than a couple of times. Generally, they meet someone at a club, go home with him afterwards, have a bit of fun, and then never meet up again. That just isn't my scene—I much prefer what we have."

"Right. Your brother does the same thing, and every time I spot him with yet another random lassie, I think to myself, *Poor Aidan. Sleeping with all these beautiful young women—that can't be an easy life.* Me, though? I get to go celibate for, like, twenty-nine days a month. I'm living the dream."

I slap Lewis's thigh with just enough force to sting. He chuckles.

"There is so much wrong with what you just said," I accuse. "First, I don't want to hear any details about my brother's sex life, thank you very much. And second, you know you'd never find another woman as fun in the bedroom as me. I'm worth waiting for."

"That is true." Lewis takes a sip of his drink then leans close to me. "So . . . read anything hot lately? Any new things for us to try? If so, count me in."

"Shouldn't you hear the ideas first before saying you're game?"

He shrugs. "Nah, I'm up for anything."

"That's perfect because I've been reading about some of the things that dominatrices get up to, and I was thinking it'd be fun to kick you in the nuts. Repeatedly."

Lewis barks out a laugh. "Piss off."

"Oi, watch your tongue when speaking to your mistress. I'm being completely serious." I place a hand on his shoulder and fix him with an earnest stare. "It's a fantasy I've never admitted to you before, but finally I've found the courage to open up. You've already told me you'd be up for anything, so there's no backing out now. The next time you come to Glasgow, it's happening. We'll buy a bag of ice for afterwards—you'll want to nurse your poor balls."

Lewis shudders. "All right, so maybe I'm not up for *anything*. What I meant is anything you're *actually* into because I don't believe for a second you're into that. I've a good idea of the sorts of things that turn you on, Iona." He nudges my shoulder. "We're pretty sexually compatible, you and me."

"Iona!"

Our conversation comes to an abrupt end because my half-brother, Archie, runs over, sporting a bright smile that's missing a few teeth. He's nine years old and utterly adorable.

They say every cloud has a silver lining. Well, as devastating as the revelation of Da's secret second life was, Archie is the one good thing to have come out of it, even if I don't see too much of him. He lives here in Inverness with my da, who left Bannock after the truth came out, and Kirsty, my da's new woman. I get on *okay* with her, but I wasn't exactly disappointed when Da said she couldn't make it today.

"Hi, you." I wrap my arms around Archie and give him a squeeze.

My da strolls over. "Good to see you, Iona." He places a hand on my shoulder then bends over and kisses my cheek. "And Lewis! It's been much too long. You're a man now."

Grinning, Lewis stands and shakes Da's hand. "You're looking well, Ewan. And Archie, hi! My name is Lewis. Can we shake hands too?"

They do, then Da and Archie sit opposite us at the table. We catch up and order burgers. I ask Archie the usual questions about how school is going and how he's getting on at his sports clubs, while he asks me what I've learnt about snakes and lizards on my course. He really wants to get one, but Da is less keen.

Soon Archie's interest turns to Lewis. "Are you Iona's boyfriend?"

"No, we're just—"

"Yes!" I interrupt, taking Lewis by surprise—and myself too. I bite my lip then offer Lewis a shy smile.

Archie scrunches his face up, puzzled by this contradiction.

"Well, he's sort of my boyfriend," I clarify, wondering how to explain this. "He lives in Bannock and I live in Glasgow, so we don't see each other very often. But when he visits me, it's like we're boyfriend and girlfriend."

"Oh." Archie shrugs.

Da chuckles, his eyes twinkling. "I always knew you two would end up together. You were inseparable growing up."

"Aye, well, we've not told anyone in Bannock," I say. "We're not planning to either—it's hush-hush. I trust you can keep quiet about it. After all, you're no stranger to a secret relationship."

Da raises his brows, unsure if this is an attack, but I smile to let him know I'm just teasing. At some point, you have to be able to joke about these things.

I glance at Lewis. "You don't mind that I said, do you?"

He grins. "Not at all. It means I get to do this." He slings an arm around me and pulls me close, giving me a quick peck on the lips.

"Ew!" Archie protests. "I don't want to see you kissing!"

A rush of warmth spreads across my face, and I can't help but giggle. It's both thrilling and mortifying to be kissed in front of Da and Archie.

Our food arrives and we chat some more as we enjoy it, then afterwards we say our goodbyes. Archie, who's already bored of grown-up talk, is excited about going swimming with Da, while I'm happy to have Lewis to myself for a while. We'll drive through to Bannock later, so I can catch up with Maw and Aidan, but once there we'll have to revert to just being friends. For now, we'll hang out together in Inverness. It isn't nearly as exciting as hanging out in my bed in Glasgow, but it's something.

We go for a chilly walk by the River Ness, and despite the risk of bumping into someone from Bannock, Lewis holds my hand. His is warm, as it always is, even on a day like this, and that sends a pleasant tingle through me. We can chat endlessly, he and I, but we're just as comfortable in silence, and today we're quiet as we stroll, simply enjoying the scenery and each other's company.

After a while, I sing under my breath:

> Gin a body meet a body
> Comin' thro' the rye,
> Gin a body kiss a body
> Need a body cry?

"Oh, I know that one," Lewis says. "'Comin' thro' the Rye' by Robert Burns, right?"

I shoot him a sideways glance and arch an eyebrow. I've known him my whole life, and he's never expressed any interest in old songs and poems.

"Charlotte, Erin, and I went to a Burns supper at the end of January, and that one stuck in my head. How do you know it?"

"Er, because it's practically our theme song, Iona."

I blink. "It is?"

I think through the lyrics. In old Scots, *gin* is another word for *if*, so the lines basically mean: if two people meet in a field of rye (and so away from prying eyes), need anybody get upset if

94

they kiss? It was written in the eighteenth century, at a time when society frowned upon casual romantic encounters, but the song suggests a kiss between two people isn't something to get worked up about.

"Okay, now I think about it, I can see the connection. You and I do kiss in secret, after all."

Lewis scoffs. "We do a lot more than that. The version you sang is the innocent one, but Burns wrote another for . . . less sensitive sorts. In it, instead of *kiss*, the lyric is *fuck*."

"Bollocks. You're having me on."

"Nope." Lewis shakes his head. "I promise you he did. That's the only reason I know that song. When things have swear words in them, I always pay more attention."

"But . . . people didn't speak like that back then!" I protest.

Lewis throws his head back and laughs hard. "Ha! Characters may speak politely in the historical romances you read, with all those funny euphemisms for penises and vaginas, but the truth is, in the past, Scots were just as dirty-mouthed as we are today. The meaning of the song is: what does it matter if two people fuck in secret? Burns didn't see any harm in casual sex. As I say, it's our theme song."

"Oh, wow." I give Lewis's hand a squeeze. "My estimation of our national bard has just gone up. It's nice to know he'd approve of what we get up to."

"Aye, well, I could really do with a field of rye about now, if you know what I mean." Lewis's dark-brown eyes meet mine, and I spy that all-too-familiar flicker of desire in his gaze.

"In February? Good luck with that."

"You're right. Oh well, in that case I'll just have to find a nice secluded spot on the drive to Bannock. We'll pull over, and you and I can have a bit of fun on the back seat."

A thrill of excitement ripples through me. Sex in a car is something we've never done before. I'd quite like to tick it off the list.

"Deal. As lovely as this walk is, how about we make a move now?"

"Aye, let's do it."

Hand in hand, and laughing as we go, we dash for Lewis's car, both eager to get to it as fast as we can.

CHAPTER FIFTEEN

IONA

Now

"Do you think that was *really* Ronan Dunbar's dick?" Maisie asks. "And not, like, a prosthetic or something?"

"Oh, it was his dick," I assure her. "As soon as the credits rolled on that episode, I googled that very question."

"Ha! Great minds think alike." Maisie grins and winks. "But wow! It was some size, wasn't it? Good on him for getting it out on camera. Makes me wonder what it looks like when it's hard."

We both giggle at this. We're in the Pheasant, which is something of a Bannock institution, a charming country pub owned by Maisie's father and where she works as a bartender. She's off duty right now, and we're seated near the fire, which crackles and pops as the flames dance. There's a decent crowd of locals in, and cheerful chatter and laughter fills the air, although I've seen the place busier. Maisie did say she expected tonight to be a slower evening when she suggested it for our meet-up.

"It's a good thing male nudity is *finally* becoming more

common in TV and films," Maisie says. "It makes things more fun for us ladies, eh?"

"I'll drink to that," I say, and I do, having another big gulp of white wine.

Maisie, who's moved on to soft stuff after having one with me, chuckles and has a sip of cola.

We are, of course, talking about *that* scene from *Highland Legacy*, the big-budget TV drama that's a mashup of *Game of Thrones* and *Outlander*, and which features a significant number of sex scenes and, yes, willies. But it wasn't until the fourth episode of season three that the main actor, Ronan Dunbar, finally joined in on the naked fun, stirring up quite the reaction online, with screenshots and video clips being widely shared. Ronan's penis has even been credited with causing a spike in the show's viewing figures. Apparently, a lot of people who'd previously passed on *Highland Legacy* binge-watched it after seeing, or at least hearing about, Ronan's appendage.

"So, how many times did you rewatch that scene?" Maisie asks coyly.

I chuckle. "A few. And you?"

"Aye, a few at the time, but by now it's popped up so many times in chats and on message boards that I've honestly lost count. Anyway, I've always loved fantasy and dragons and all that stuff. It's great that shows like *Highland Legacy*, with the help of Ronan's willy, can make the genre more mainstream and less geeky. Have you played the video game it's based on?"

"Nope, I'm not much of a gamer. Is it good?"

"So, so good!" She nods enthusiastically, her cherry-red bob catching the light. She's always changing hair colour—a few months ago, it was teal. "It's this massively multiplayer online role-playing game where . . ."

She tells me all about it, enthusing about avatars and battle strategy, and even though video games aren't my cup of tea, I am interested to hear how it relates to the TV show. Besides, Maisie talks with such enthusiasm that she could make any subject captivating. Working in the pub all day, serving locals and tourists alike, has clearly given her the gift of the gab. She's the kind of person who could get along with anyone. I reckon she figures out what makes people tick, finds some common interest, and then chats away, be that about sport, current affairs, or . . . Ronan Dunbar's willy. I don't know how, based on what little she knows about me, she guessed that would be a good topic for conversation, but she was absolutely right.

But while I do enjoy the odd sword fight and mythical creature, it's the romantic aspects of the TV show that hook me most, and apparently these feature less prominently in the video game. As such, my interest dips a little, but Maisie immediately picks up on this and takes action.

"Anyway, enough about video games. Want to hear a funny story about something that happened this week?"

"Sure," I say, my attention rekindled.

"All right, well, you know how there are places across the UK with rude-sounding names?"

"Like Cock Bridge in Aberdeenshire?" I giggle. "Oh, or Dick Place in Edinburgh!"

It's true, the wine is getting to me—and I'm working tomorrow!—but when was the last time I had a girls' night? I'm taking full advantage of this rare opportunity and letting my hair down. Quite frankly, if I can't make penis jokes tonight, when can I?

"Ha! Exactly," Maisie says. "Or Twatt in Orkney, or Shitterton in Dorset. And then there's my personal favourite: Sandy Balls in Hampshire." She lets out a loud laugh. "That can't be comfortable for the poor lads in the area—I bet the name alone makes them itch.

"Anyway, I was chatting with some American tourists the other day, and they were really amused by all this stuff. They'd already taken photos of themselves standing in front of a few funny signs. They asked me what places I knew about, so I told them all the ones I could think of. But then, since they seemed like the sort of folk who'd appreciate a joke, I kept on going, adding ones I was making up on the spot: Arsebrook, Nipplewick, Wankers Way."

"Wankers Way!" I repeat, snorting.

"They eventually cottoned on, of course, but we had a good laugh about it. Anyway, Iona, I have a question for you. If *you* had to make up a rude place name, what would it be?"

"Hmm . . ." I stroke my chin, giving this erudite question the lengthy consideration it undoubtedly deserves. "I'd have to go with . . . Boobington. Or maybe Ticklewilly Forest."

A roguish smile tugs at Maisie's lips. "Nice. I'd quite like to visit Ticklewilly Forest—it sounds like a fun place." She takes another sip of her drink. "You know, I'm really enjoying myself, Iona. You're great company."

"You mean I'm not the bookish swot everyone remembers me as?"

Her eyes widen. "I didn't mean that!"

I laugh. "It's fine, I know that's how a lot of people around here still see me, but I was away for nine years. I grew and changed a good deal in that time."

"Right. If I'm honest, I suppose my perception of you is that you're a very studious and polite person—not that those are bad things. But, aye, I'd never have guessed you're a big fan of a dick joke. That's the nice thing about getting to know someone better:

you discover the hidden quirks of their personality. I'm getting the impression that, beneath your well-educated and professional exterior, there's quite the wild streak in you, Iona Stewart."

I grin. "There is. And . . ." My smile falters, as if a cloud has passed over my sunny mood. "I think that's part of the problem."

"Oh. Problem? Does this relate to Richard?"

My expression must convey my surprise because she gives me an apologetic look.

"Sorry, Cat mentioned you were having some relationship issues—I hope you don't mind. She didn't go into details, though. If you want to talk about it, I'm all ears, but equally if you'd rather keep the mood light, that's fine too. It's totally up to you."

It would be good to get a few things off my chest, but I don't even know how to begin. I take a few moments to gather my thoughts then say, "Richard is . . . such a nice guy. He really is. And handsome too, and eager to do well in his career. I bet a lot of people around Bannock see us together and think, aye, they're a good fit. But . . ."

"He doesn't have that secret wild streak that you have?" Maisie guesses.

I sigh. "Right. When it comes to Richard, what you see is what you get. And that's not a bad thing, but . . ." I tilt my head to the side. "I just . . . don't know if it's enough. But this isn't the time to be having doubts! We've literally just moved up north together. Why couldn't I have questioned things a month or two ago? If we'd tried living together in Glasgow before coming here, maybe I'd have realised there were problems, but now . . . well, there's no way I can break up with him having just moved to Bannock with him. I'd feel too guilty. And like I say, he's a nice guy, so . . ."

"So the only thing to do now is wait for him to propose, marry him, then spend the rest of your life in an unhappy marriage," Maisie finishes flippantly.

"When you put it like that, it sounds ridiculous, but—"

"It *is* ridiculous. You're allowed to be happy, Iona. And if Richard doesn't make you happy, that's okay. It doesn't mean there's anything wrong with him, just that he's not the right match for you. It's notoriously difficult to find a life partner. A lot of people spend years searching for 'the one', and along the way, they go through plenty of relationships that don't quite fit the bill. *But* . . . we're getting ahead of ourselves. I'll be the first to point out that I'm no expert in this stuff, but can I ask if you've had a frank and honest discussion with Richard about how you're feeling?"

I bite my lip. "Er . . . no. I mean, I've talked with him about trying to . . . spice things up a bit. But I've probably not been clear with him about how important that is to me."

"Well, maybe that's a good place to start. Don't get me wrong, all options are on the table. If ultimately you decide he's not the one for you, that's fine, but chat with him first. Give him a chance to fix this."

Wow, Maisie is so practical and sensible. That is exactly what I needed to hear. When it comes to my job, I know what's what, but sometimes navigating relationships can feel like trying to read a map in the dark.

"You're right. I'll sit down with him and have a proper heart-to-heart. Thanks, Maisie."

I finish off my wine. Without a word, she takes my glass, walks up to the bar, fills it up, then returns to her seat, setting it in front of me.

"Cheers, but this will definitely have to be my last one. I've got farm visits tomorrow."

"Very sensible, but I wouldn't mind loosening you up a wee bit more because, if I'm honest, I'm curious to hear more about this wild side of yours. I bet dating in a city like Glasgow is pretty different to how it is here. Feel free to tell me to shut up at any point, but . . . did you have a few fun flings before getting together with Richard?"

"Hmm. Actually, the most fun I ever had was a little closer to home."

"You mean Lewis McIntyre?"

A flush creeps up my neck. "Shit. How did you guess that?"

She looks at me like I've just asked the stupidest question she's ever heard. "Iona, everyone in Bannock assumed you two would end up together. Also, please don't look so worried. What happens on girls' night stays on girls' night—that's the rule. The things we discuss here won't go any further than this table."

"Because if Cat finds out—"

"She won't. She and I get on really well, but it's not my place to tell her you've slept with her brother."

I relax a little. "Thanks."

"So . . ." Maisie leans closer and lowers her voice, not that anyone else in the room would be able to hear us over all the laughter and merriment. "Again, you don't have to tell me anything you don't want to, but . . . what do you mean, Lewis is the person you've had the most fun with?"

My flush spreads to my cheeks, but I answer honestly. "Well, he was my first and I was his, and maybe it's because we were exploring everything together for the very first time, but . . . the sex was always fun and hot. *Always.* Any fantasy I wanted to act out, he was up for it, no hesitation. And . . ." I hesitate, my inner voice warning me to reconsider what I'm about to say, but I say it anyway. "If ever Ronan Dunbar needed a body double for another nude scene, Lewis could step into the role quite easily. Trust me, the public would not be disappointed."

Oh my God. What is this wine doing to me?

"Really?" Maisie arches an eyebrow with interest.

"Yes, not that men deserve any credit for the size of their things, of course. It's all genetics and luck—nothing they have any control over. But still, it's a pretty impressive sight."

"I bet. So, good sex, a huge dick, and I think everyone in Bannock would agree Lewis is a nice guy. Like, of the three brothers, Jamie is the joker, Ally was the grumpy one—until Emily sorted that out—and Lewis is just . . . nice. Everyone loves him, and even your maw is forever singing his praises, saying how talented he is in the kitchen, how well the hotel is doing under his management, and that he's such a lovely lad. Which brings us to the big question: what went wrong?"

Just thinking about it makes my chest tighten painfully—I can't say it out loud. I'll need some time to mentally prepare myself before sharing that story.

"We've already had one major revelation for this girls' night," I say. "Let's leave that tale for the next one."

Maisie smiles. "Aye, I'd like this to be a more regular thing—we'll have to get another catch-up arranged. I wish this one could go on, but I did say to my da I'd be taking an hour off, and it's already been more than that. Time has flown. I really should get back behind the bar and help him out."

"Of course. Well, thanks for this, Maisie. It's been exactly what I needed, especially the detailed analysis of *that* scene from *Highland Legacy*."

Chuckling, she stands and is about to give me a hug when her gaze flicks to the door. "Oh shit, it's Mr Big Dick himself."

Clearly, I've had too much wine because my first thought is, *Heart-throb Ronan Dunbar has come to our small town to grace us with his presence?* I turn to the door with a burst of exhilaration, but . . . it's only Lewis.

Oof, talk about disappointment.

Spotting me, he grins and heads over.

"Shall I send him away?" Maisie whispers.

"Nah, I can fight my own battles."

"All right, if you're sure. If you change your mind, give me a wave and I'll be right over."

I nod and Maisie leaves. Lewis, dressed in a well-fitted burgundy shirt that accentuates his broad shoulders, reaches the table a few seconds later.

"Hey, gym buddy," he says cheerfully. "Fancy seeing you here."

I frown with suspicion. "Wait a minute. I told you yesterday I couldn't go to the gym tonight because I'd be here. Is that why you've shown up? Are you stalking me, Lewis?"

His eyebrows shoot up and he rubs the back of his neck. "Er, wow, that's a strong word. No, I just thought I'd pop by to see if you fancied a chat."

"It's a girls' night, Lewis. I'm sure I mentioned that."

"You did, but it looks like Maisie has gone back to work and you're at this table on your own. Surely you'd rather have company than drink by yourself, even if that company is me?"

"There are other faces here I recognise. I'd be welcome to jump into any number of conversations."

"I'm sure you would," Lewis agrees. "But c'mon, we both know I've got better chat than anyone else here."

As he says this, he leans closer to me, and maybe it's because of his proximity, or because of what Maisie and I were just discussing, but my gaze flicks down to the crotch of his jeans. It takes me a moment to realise what I'm doing and tear my eyes away again. *Get it together, Iona!*

Because I'm a little flustered by having just peered at Lewis's bits, I don't say anything for a second or two, and he apparently interprets my lack of objection as an invitation to sit. He takes the seat Maisie vacated and beams at me.

This annoys me, naturally, but then again, the table does block my view of his lower half, so at least I won't be tempted to have another sneak peek at his package. If only he could also put a bag over his face to hide his irritatingly good looks.

Oh God, where did that thought come from? Am I just tipsy or am I drunk? I'm not entirely sure.

Don't make a fool of yourself, Iona. Finish your drink then get out of here as soon as you can.

"Well," I say drily, adjusting my glasses, "seeing as you've already sat down, what would you like to talk about? You've got five minutes then I'm off. And please do try your best to amuse me because I've had an absolute riot with Maisie and I'd rather not end the night on a dull note."

Lewis's lips curl into a playful grin that shows off his dimples, and he leans back in his chair. "Challenge accepted."

CHAPTER SIXTEEN

LEWIS

Iona hasn't left yet, and it's been twelve minutes since I sat down with her—that's more than double the five she originally offered me. That's a win in my book, albeit a small one. I don't want her to go anywhere anytime soon, though, so I have to keep this conversation rolling.

What I'd really like to do is talk about something meaningful—maybe reminisce about times from our childhood and teens. We've so many shared memories, but we never relive them together because . . . well, she doesn't much like chatting with me about anything. If I steer the conversation towards our personal history too soon, I'm worried she'll get up and leave, so I'm keeping my chat general for now. I'm easing her into this, taking things slowly. The bridge between us collapsed a long time ago, and rebuilding it won't happen overnight.

Unfortunately, my current topic—funny things guests have left behind in their rooms—isn't going down as well as some of my earlier banter.

Lewis, you cannot afford to mess this up. You've got to bring your A game.

As I mentally scramble for a new topic, old Hamish walks past our table, heading for the door, his brown-and-white springer spaniel in tow. The dog, Ruby, pads over to Iona for a sniff, and Iona melts, as she always does around animals. She bends down and pats Ruby's head, scratches her chin, and ruffles her ears.

"Oh, look at you. You're adorable!"

Ruby's tail wags furiously and she pants happily, her tongue lolling. She's clearly delighted by the attention. She reminds me a lot of my childhood dog, Molly, who was a cocker.

Apparently, I'm not the only one to notice the similarity. After Ruby follows Hamish outside, Iona turns to me, her blue eyes sparkling.

"Did you notice it was *me* Ruby came to say hello to? Who does that remind you of?"

"Oi!" I say, a smile tugging at my lips. "Don't even try to pretend Molly preferred you to me."

"Oh, she absolutely did. We settled this debate on multiple occasions, or have you forgotten?"

And just like that, without me having to engineer it, the reminiscing has begun. Thank you, Ruby.

"Those tests were rigged!" I accuse. "We're twenty-seven now—it's time for you to fess up. How did you do it? Did you always have a treat in your pocket? I never was able to figure it out."

As kids, Iona and I would stand at opposite sides of a room or field and both call Molly's name. She *always* went to Iona, the little traitor.

"There was nothing *to* figure out, Lewis. She liked me best. That's all."

I cover my heart with my hands. "You're killing me here. She was *my* dog, Iona."

"Aye, I know, and you were her second-favourite person. That's not bad. I'll concede she preferred you to Ally or Jamie or Cat. That's something. She just didn't like you quite as much as she liked me."

"She slept in *my* bed at night. It was *my* job to fill up her dog bowl. And yet all you had to do was call 'Molly!', and her allegiance to me was forgotten." I shake my head and let out a theatrical sigh. "The betrayal still stings to this day."

"What can I say? She probably just thought I was more fun. And kind. And better in every way, really. Oh, and I know she slept in your bed normally, but do you remember what would happen if I stayed over at yours?"

When we were young, if Iona's maw and da ever went away for a night, to see a show in Inverness or whatever, Aidan would kip in Ally's room and Iona in mine. That practice stopped come puberty, after which Iona bunked with Cat instead.

"Crap, Molly would snuggle up with you, wouldn't she? I'd forgotten about that."

"She would, and I think that tells you everything you need to know. I was definitely the favourite. Don't beat yourself up about it, though. I mean, who wouldn't fall in love with this?" She gestures to herself.

And she's absolutely right—who wouldn't? She's got the personality, the looks, everything. Tonight she's in a quirky grey dress covered in white hares and yellow flowers, and her hair is in its usual messy bun, with stray waves falling down to frame her bonny face. Her cheeks are rosy, probably more from the wine than the fire, and it only makes her all the more beautiful.

Who in their right mind would let this incredible woman slip through their fingers? Oh, aye. Me.

"Do you remember the time Molly ran into the haunted cottage?" I ask.

"Oh my God! I'd forgotten we used to think that place was haunted."

The cottage in question has since been demolished, and a nice new property now stands in its place, but when we were young, it had lain empty for many years and fallen into disrepair. It was situated on the very outskirts of Bannock, far enough from other houses to give you the sense that, even if you screamed, no one would hear you. Ally and Aidan used to spook me and Iona with stories of strange goings-on and dreadful, terrible things that happened to any child who entered the place. Big brothers can be such dicks sometimes.

"You and I were walking Molly one day," I say, remembering. "We were, what, ten, eleven? Suddenly she bolted—I think maybe she chased a squirrel?"

"Aye, that was it. We ran after her, calling her name, but she kept on going. Then she came to the cottage and went straight in, and you stopped dead. Soon Molly was barking like mad, and you were sure she was being tormented by ghosts. You paced and paced, psyching yourself up to go in and rescue her, but you took so long that I got fed up waiting. Without a word to you, I went in and got her."

"To this day, still the bravest thing I've ever witnessed."

Iona laughs. "Well, even as a kid, I don't think I ever *really* believed in ghosts. And what do you know, it turned out the only reason Molly was barking was because she'd cornered the squirrel and didn't know what to do next. But you, Lewis? You believed *all* the stories about that place. In general, you had more guts than me, but when it came to ghosts and spirits, you were such a coward."

"I didn't like horror films back then and still don't." I pat my left bicep. "These guns are no use against the supernatural."

"God, it's clear why Molly liked me best. She obviously realised that, between you and me, I'm the alpha."

I bite my tongue, even though I'm desperate to add a caveat or two to that statement. When we were hooking up, that wasn't our dynamic—at least, not always. Sure, I let her boss me around a lot of the time: *Stick on this glow-in-the-dark condom, Get your dick out so I can use it for a game of hoopla*, and all that stuff. She always did get a kick out of treating my cock as her personal plaything, and I was happy to go along with that and let her do whatever she wanted. But when it came down to it, when we were actually doing the dirty, our roles were clear—and hers was surrendering to my every thrust, her body arching, as I commanded her breathless moans. *I* was the alpha then.

"You know," Iona says, "I was talking with Maisie earlier about how I reckon people in Bannock see me in a way that doesn't match how I see myself. That story reminds me that, even as a kid, I could be pretty gutsy."

"You absolutely could—I've always known that. And if that's not how people see you, then you obviously have to reinvent yourself."

She drains her wine, and I worry this may be her cue to leave, but she says, "And how would you suggest I do that?"

The local band are setting up: Neil on the accordion, Eileen on the fiddle, Scott on drums. They often play a bit of live music of an evening.

"You just have to do something no one would expect you to

do. Like, nobody would expect you to get up right now and sing a song in front of everybody."

"Hmm, aye, that might do it. But I'd need company, of course."

"Er . . ." I drum my fingers on the table. I'd expected her to immediately veto the suggestion. "Are we joking about this? I can't tell."

"I'm not joking. Are you? It was your idea. I've done karaoke before—it's not a big deal. The question is, are *you* up for it, Lewis McIntyre?"

Shit, *I've* never done karaoke—it's not a thing here in Bannock. Also, I'm a terrible singer—and stone-cold sober. I was too worried that, if I went to the bar to get a drink, Iona would use that as an opportunity to leave. Mind you, if I refuse now, *that* might encourage her to leave, so . . .

"Sure," I say, feigning far more confidence than I feel.

"Great!" She bounces up to her feet. "Let's go have a chat with the band."

So, reluctantly, I go up with her. The band aren't immediately opposed to the idea but they do wonder what song we have in mind. They play traditional Scottish music, not popular stuff, and there's no karaoke machine to display the lyrics.

"Hmm, what trad songs do Lewis and I both know the words to?" Iona ponders. "Oh! We both know 'Comin' thro' the Rye'. Do you know that?"

The band do, but . . . really? That tune? Our theme song from a time in our lives when we engaged in casual sex? I suppose it's not like anyone in the pub is aware we have a personal connection to the lyrics, but still. Is Iona too tipsy to realise that might not be the best choice, all things considered, or does she just not care?

Before I can process that we're actually going to do this, Neil suggests we address the crowd to introduce the song, and Iona elbows me to indicate this duty should fall to me.

Awkwardly I clear my throat. "Hello! If I could have your attention for a moment, please."

Conversations trail off as people turn to me with interest. Damn, I so wish I'd had some alcohol to give me courage for this.

"Er, as I'm sure you all know by now, we're lucky to have Iona back in Bannock, and she's making a great addition at Bannock Vets."

There are a few cheers, and glasses are raised in Iona's direction.

"No doubt we all remember her brother, Aidan, was pretty adventurous growing up. Hell, he now runs Bannock Adventures with my brother, Ally, so there you go. Iona, though, always had a reputation for being a bit of a bookworm, but she's so much more than that—she can be daring too. It's time we all saw there's another side to her, which is why we're going to start off tonight's entertainment with a song. If you know the words, please join in. It'll help drown out my terrible vocals."

There's a ripple of chuckles.

I turn to Neil. "All right. Ready?"

He nods then the band plays a short musical intro.

Iona leans close to me and says, "We're singing the clean version, by the way."

"Er, aye. Of course."

And then it's time for us to sing, so we do.

Gin a body meet a body
Comin' thro' the rye,
Gin a body kiss a body

Need a body cry?

I'm nervous and stiff, but Iona goes for it with abandon, her voice strong and clear. She first sways as she sings then does a jig on the spot. Her energy is infectious, and soon the whole pub is clapping and singing along. As their enthusiasm builds, my self-consciousness fades, and when Iona loops her arm through mine, we spin together ceilidh-style, the room whirling around us in a blur of laughter and music. Grinning, I belt out the rest of the song with a new-found surge of confidence.

> Gin a body meet a body
> Comin thro' the glen,
> Gin a body kiss a body
> Need the warl' ken?

It's a good question: need the world know if two people kiss (or fuck, depending on which lyrics you prefer)? Well, they never did know about me and Iona.

When we get to the end, there's applause, and Iona, beaming, grabs my hand, lifts it into the air, and bows, like we're a rock band lapping up the appreciation of a loving crowd. It's a tad over the top, but hey, if she wants to hold my hand, I'm not going to stop her. From the bar, Maisie whoops.

Iona lets go of me then leads the way to our table, receiving a number of pats on the back and encouraging words from those she passes.

"That felt good!" she says, sitting again. "Great idea, Lewis. I have officially reinvented my image."

"Er, right. Well done."

"I'll have to go soon—I'm working tomorrow—but I'm buzzing after that."

The bands starts up the next song, and Iona taps the table along to the music. I'm also working tomorrow, like every day, and I'll have to get up early to prepare breakfast for the guests. But I'm not going to be the one to suggest we wrap things up.

Maisie walks over and sets down a lager in front of me. "This one's on the house—your payment for the entertainment. And for you, Iona . . ." She places down a glass of water. "I thought you could do with this. You did say you weren't going to be having any more wine."

"I did," Iona agrees, eyeing the glass glumly.

As soon as Maisie leaves, I take a greedy sip of lager. Mmm, the smooth, malty richness and slightly bitter undertone hits just right. Man, I've definitely earned this after that song.

"Anyway, where were we?" Iona says. "Oh, ages ago, you were telling me about things guests have left behind in their rooms. Have there been any other funny things you've not mentioned yet?"

"Er . . ." That topic had been dying a death, but then again, I deliberately missed out some of the racier things I've found. Is talking about them a bad idea, given our history? Hmm, she seems pretty relaxed, and besides, I know her well enough to know the kinds of things that pique her interest.

"Well, one time, under the bed, I found a pair of fluffy hand-cuffs. Kinky, eh? And let's just say the guests who'd been staying in that room weren't on the young side."

I'm testing the water, making sure she's amused rather than offended, but she lets out a chuckle, so I take that as permission to go on.

"On another occasion, a collar and lead were left, and that

couple did *not* bring a dog with them. Then there's the time I found a set of Kama Sutra cards. Wow, those images were detailed!"

"Oh, you looked through them, did you?"

I shrug. "Nothing wrong with being curious. And let's just say I learnt a thing or two. I'd never even thought of some of those positions before."

I wonder if this is too close to the bone, but Iona raises an eyebrow, intrigued. Maybe she's thinking what I'm thinking, which is that when we were together, there weren't many positions we didn't try.

She takes a sip of her water.

"Oh, and then there was the set of nipple clamps attached to a twelve-inch strap-on."

Iona's eyes bulge and she chokes and splutters, spraying water everywhere, but mainly over her dress.

"Shit." I jump to my feet. "I was only joking about that one. Are you okay? I'll run to the bar and grab something."

She waves me back to my seat and clears her throat. "No, I've got tissues here." She pulls a few out and dabs at her dress . . . specifically, her breasts.

Crap, she's dabbing her wet breasts in front of me. *Whatever you do, Lewis, don't stare. Oi, I said don't stare!*

"Er . . ." To distract myself from what she's doing, I should really keep the conversation going, but unfortunately my mind has gone blank. I cannot think of a single thing to say.

"So . . ." I stare at the fire. *C'mon, Lewis, you can think of something. Anything!* "Do you think your niece and my nephew will grow up being as close as we were?"

There's only a week between Callie and Ru. What's more, Ally and Aidan are best mates, as are Emily and Grace.

I redirect my attention to Iona, maintaining eye contact, refusing to let my gaze dip.

"Quite possibly," she says. "But I'll politely encourage Callie to spend more time than I did fostering relationships with female friends. Those bonds are important—for when your male best friend inevitably screws you over."

Ouch.

The conversation is veering away from the light-heartened mood I've tried hard to cultivate, but I can't stop myself from asking, "Do you ever wonder if it was a mistake to make our relationship sexual? Because we were such good mates, you and I, but . . . we've lost that."

Her eyes narrow. "*That* wasn't the mistake, Lewis. The mistake came later—and was entirely on you."

I wince. "Aye, you're right. And I realise this isn't good enough, but . . . I am sorry. I'm still beating myself up for it now, six years on."

I'm expecting her to say something like, *And so you should be.* But instead she sighs.

"Look, I should hardly be the one to comfort you—it doesn't make any sense for that job to fall to me. But for what it's worth, I'm aware you haven't had much luck in relationships over the last few years."

Understatement of the century. I've tried, I really have, but nothing ever lasts because, quite frankly, no one can compare to Iona. Every other woman on the planet falls short. I had it all, and I messed everything up.

"Again, it shouldn't be me who says this, but sort yourself out. Move on. I mean, I've found Richard, and he's . . ." She hesitates, searching for the right word. ". . . nice. You should try to find someone too."

Wow. She's being kinder to me than I have any right to expect her to be, but there's a problem—a rather significant one.

I take a gulp of lager. "I don't know that I can move on," I admit. "I doubt I'll ever find anyone even half as good as you." As soon as I make this admission, I realise it's probably a step too far.

Iona watches me quietly for the longest time before rising to her feet. "I think this is where we should leave things."

"Fuck, sorry, I shouldn't have—"

"It's fine, but like I said, I have work tomorrow. I've already stayed longer than I should have. Good night, Lewis." And with that, she leaves.

Bollocks. Tonight was the closest I've felt to her in years. Why did I have to blurt out something stupid and drive her away?

CHAPTER SEVENTEEN

LEWIS

I stick my head back into the office. "Oi, Jamie, I asked you ten minutes ago to set up the restaurant for dinner, and you've still not started. Move your arse!"

He doesn't even look up from his laptop. "I'm going to do it. Just give me one more minute." He continues to tap away.

The joys of working with family. Aye, he's my wee brother, but when a manager tells an employee to do something, shouldn't they get straight onto it without fuss?

I walk in and glance at his screen. As I expected, he's playing that *Highland Legacy* game he's obsessed with. I close over the laptop lid.

"Bloody hell, Lewis!" Jamie scowls at me and flings his arms out in frustration. "I was in the middle of chatting with someone."

"Oh, were you typing messages to a wee gamer friend? I'm so sorry, I hadn't realised. My mistake—take all the time you need." I open the laptop back up—then immediately shut it again. "On second thoughts, I couldn't give a fuck. Get your arse in the restaurant. Now!"

He leans back in his chair and folds his arms, smirking. "Wow, someone's tetchy. This is what happens when you stay up late drinking—oh, and singing duets with the lass you've had the hots for your whole life."

I flick his ear with my finger and am rewarded with a satisfying yelp. "With my *friend*," I correct.

"Aye, right." He rubs his ear. "Remember the time Ally and Emily danced together in the Pheasant? Remind me, how long was it after that before they started going at it like rabbits on speed?"

A loud groan escapes my lips. "You really are the absolute worst. Iona has a boyfriend."

"*I* know that"—he gestures to himself—"but do you?" He points to my face, then lowers his finger. "And what about your dick?"

With that, I've had enough. I wrestle him out of his chair, and we tumble to the floor, grappling with each other as he laughs and tries to fend me off.

"You wee shite," I growl, planting my forearm firmly across his chest and pinning him down. "Do you ever shut up?"

"Not when winding you up is this easy. I know it's Iona you really want to be rolling around with, but I'm flattered I'm your second choice."

God, he never gets any better, and he always has a wisecrack ready. In a moment of clarity, I realise the absurdity of this situation. We're both well into our twenties, and guests will soon be arriving for dinner, yet here we are, in a tangle of arms and legs, like we're still teenagers. Normally, I'm more professional than this, but Iona's return has stirred up some old emotions, and I seem to be reverting to immature ways of coping with them.

I stand and straighten my shirt then hold out a hand to Jamie and hoist him back to his feet.

"Sorry, but could you *please* just set the tables and stuff? I need to help Elspeth in the kitchen."

"Fine." Grinning, he dusts himself down.

We head out of the office, go around the reception desk, and manage a couple of steps towards the restaurant when the front door opens and Richard enters. Oh, shit. Why is he here?

I nod at him and even offer a small smile, acting more relaxed than I feel. "Hi, Richard. How are you doing?"

He doesn't return the smile. "Can we talk?"

Jamie rubs his hands together. "Are you two going to fight? This is going to be so good! Lewis has just had a warm-up—he was practising WWE moves on me in the office."

Abandoning my earlier resolve to remain professional, I give Jamie a shove. "Sure, we can talk," I say to Richard. "Let's head out to the garden—we should get a bit of peace there. Jamie, you get the restaurant set up."

I lead Richard into the function room, out through the French windows, and into the garden. On the far side of the grass are a couple of benches. I approach them and gesture to one, indicating for Richard to sit. He makes no attempt to do so but does inspect the plaque on the bench. It reads IN MEMORY OF ANGUS AND MAIRI MCINTYRE, SORELY MISSED BUT FONDLY REMEMBERED.

"Your parents?"

"Aye."

He nods. "I'm sorry you lost them. I'm going to stand, though."

Shrugging, I sit. I've no wish to fight this guy, and standing feels more confrontational.

"So, how can I help?" I'm pretty sure this is about last night, but I act like I've got no idea why he's here.

Richard doesn't answer straight away, as if he's considering his words. Eventually he says, "Yesterday Iona went to the pub for a girls' night, but I hear she spent a fair chunk of it with you. To be honest, it would have been hard for me *not* to have heard, the way word gets around this town. The duet you and Iona did is all anyone is talking about today. It's pretty humiliating to hear people chatter about the two of you when she's *my* girlfriend."

I hold up my hands in a gesture of peace. "Mate, it was only a song. You've got this all wrong. Iona and I are just friends."

"Yeah, but you've not always just been friends, have you?"

And there it is. So he *does* know about my history with Iona.

"Ah." I can't think what else to say.

Arms crossed over his chest, he stares at me like he's searching for something in my expression. "I don't know how she still talks to you—no, how she still *looks* at you—after what you did to her."

His words cut deep because I've had the same thought myself.

"I don't get the dynamic between you," Richard adds, "but it makes me uncomfortable. Can you just tell me what the fuck is going on? Do you have feelings for her?"

I rap my fingers on my thigh. "Nothing is going on between us. We sang a song—that's it. But . . . I do have feelings for her."

He bristles, the corners of his lips pulling down as though he's trying hard to steady his emotions. "I'm not just talking about friendship feelings here. I'm talking about the other kind."

"So am I."

For the longest time, he says nothing. Then, "Well, this is shit. I've come to this town with Iona. We literally live opposite you.

And . . . what, you're going to try to win her off me? How can you even think you deserve her? The way you treated her . . ."

In a quiet but assured voice, I say, "She's not a prize to be won. And all I said was I've got feelings for her—I've no idea how she feels about me. As you may know, our history is . . . complicated."

He stares at me a while longer then blows out. "Fuck!" He opens his mouth as if to say something more then thinks better of it and shakes his head. Without another word, he turns and walks off.

Alone in the garden, I contemplate this new development. If Iona were my lass and I found out another guy was sniffing around her, how would I have reacted? Despite all my weight training, I've never been one to pick fights, and yet I don't know that I could have kept my cool as well as Richard did.

He's clearly not a bad guy, and he has every right to be pissed off. In truth, though, I don't think I've overstepped any boundaries. Hanging out together at the gym? Having a chat in the pub and singing a quick song? Those are the kinds of things friends do, aren't they?

Then again, I did ask her if she still reads smutty books, and when she spilled that water over her chest, I was pretty distracted. So . . . aye, maybe my interest hasn't been entirely innocent.

But fuck, I know a lot of people don't believe in "the one", but I do, and for me it's Iona—it always has been. She's not just some lass, she's the only lass I've ever wanted to be with, the only one I can imagine ever wanting to be with. So if there's even a chance I can win her back, then I'm going to take that chance. And if that means I have to go through Richard, then I don't care how nice he is—I'll go through him.

CHAPTER EIGHTEEN

IONA

"I'm back!" I close the front door behind me. "Sorry I'm late."

For several seconds there's no response, then Richard says, "Through here." He sounds weary.

I plonk down my gym bag then head through to the dining room. He's by himself at the table, an empty plate in front of him, a few crumbs the only remainder of his dinner. At my usual spot is a plate of food that has long since gone cold.

"Oh, I didn't realise you were going to serve dinner. Sorry. My quick after-work gym session turned into a much longer session—I thought it might undo some of the damage the wine did last night." It's a joke, and to be fair, the corners of Richard's mouth twitch, only the smile doesn't quite reach his eyes.

"It's fine." The despondency in his tone suggests it isn't.

Attempting to stay upbeat, I walk over to my seat and inspect the grub: chicken breasts stuffed with haggis and served with whisky sauce, mashed potatoes, and veg. "Oh, wow, Balmoral chicken—nice. Did Maw make this earlier?"

"Nah, I did. She gave me the recipe, though."

Shit. He went to the effort of preparing something special, and I didn't even show up on time to eat it. Guilt gnaws at me.

"You should have called." No sooner do I say it than I remember I put my phone in my bag before my workout then stuffed my bag in my locker. I haven't taken it out to check it since. "Ah, you did, didn't you? But I didn't have my phone on me." I give him a sheepish grin. "What am I like?"

He gives a wee smile, and this time there's a little more warmth behind it. "Really, it's fine. Anyway, I'm sorry I didn't wait for you, but I wasn't sure when you'd be back, and I got hungry. I'll heat up your plate for you. I don't know if it'll taste as good, but hopefully it'll be okay." He stands.

"I can—"

"I've got this. You sit."

I do and he picks up my plate and starts towards the kitchen, but then—turning back—he leans in and plants a quick kiss on my cheek.

"It's good to see you. I feel I've barely spent any time with you the last few days."

That's been by deliberate design, of course, but now I just feel even more guilty. I *am* touched by his gesture of preparing dinner, and with his face so close to mine, my gaze lowers to his mouth and I wonder . . .

Gently I cup his jaw and guide him closer, our lips meeting in a soft kiss. I wait for the spark, the flutter of excitement, but nothing comes. Nothing at all.

I pull back and force a smile. "It's good to see you too."

He flashes me a grin then straightens. "You must be hungry. I'll be right back." He disappears into the kitchen, and the beep of buttons is soon followed by the soft hum of the microwave. A few minutes later, it pings and Richard returns, laying the plate in front of me once more.

"Bon appétit. I hope it tastes all right reheated."

He joins me at the table, watching me, and so I duly lift my knife and fork and tuck in. The chicken is still flavourful, but it's dry in places and slightly tough to chew, while the haggis isn't as rich as it should be. The mash isn't bad—it retains some of its creaminess—but the vegetables are a write-off. They're soggy and bland.

"It's delicious," I say. A white lie, but I'm sure the dish would have been delicious had I eaten it when I was supposed to.

He's pleased by the compliment.

"So . . ." I promised Maisie I'd have an honest and open discussion with Richard about how I've been feeling. With Maw away, this is a good time to do it, but how to begin?

Richard broaches the subject before I can. "You were at the gym on Monday evening, out for drinks yesterday, and then at the gym again today. Should I be worried you're trying to avoid me?"

I take my time chewing on a piece of chicken before swallowing. "I've . . . maybe been finding it a little much, living here with you and Maw seven days a week," I admit eventually.

"Right. Except your mum is at the restaurant tonight, so is it really just me you're having a hard time living with?"

It'd be so easy to deflect this question. I could argue that a lot of boyfriends would approve of their women going to the gym and keeping healthy, or else that couples don't have to spend every minute of their evenings and weekends together. But I'm not trying to win an argument. No, the aim is to be honest with Richard about some of the doubts that have been going through my head.

"Well, it *has* been a bit of an . . . adjustment, going from

126

spending a few nights with you when we were in Glasgow to living with you full time like this."

He nods diplomatically. "Fair enough." Then he adds, "Did Lewis make an appearance at the gym tonight?"

The question takes me by surprise. "No. He helps Maw in the restaurant on Wednesdays."

"Okay. It's just by all accounts you and him got on well at the Pheasant yesterday, at your girls' night."

I chew my bottom lip. So he's heard about that. I should have realised he would: word travels fast around Bannock, always has. With hindsight, getting up with Lewis and singing "Comin' thro' the Rye" wasn't my greatest idea. I blame the wine.

"It really was a girls' night," I assure him. "I wasn't expecting Lewis to show up, and we didn't chat for long. But . . ." If I'm going to be honest with Richard, there's something I should confess. "Lewis *was* at the gym on Monday. Trust me, that was a complete coincidence, and I wasn't happy to see him when I spotted him."

"Wow." Richard drums his fingers on the table. "So you've barely seen me the last few days, but you've seen your ex twice? I actually went to the hotel earlier to have a chat with him. I wanted to get his take on what the deal is between the pair of you. And do you know what he told me? He said he still has feelings for you, Iona. The last thing I want is to be some awful over-bearing boyfriend, but can you understand why it's pretty difficult for me to hear you've been spending time with someone you have a sexual history with and who still has feelings for you?"

A lump forms in my throat. "Aye, I get that can't be easy." I could argue that I didn't plan to meet Lewis at the gym or the Pheasant, and that would be true. Then again, I could—*should*— have done more to shoo him away.

"And bloody hell, the guy literally couldn't live any closer. We can see into his bedroom from your window."

I put down my knife and fork. I can't eat any more, not because the food is dry but because of the knot that's forming in my stomach. "The whole situation is a mess. I'm so sorry. I really do feel terrible about it."

He studies me for a while, then his gaze softens. "The past is in the past. What concerns me more is the future. I can cope with Lewis still having feelings for you—that's not something you or I have any control over. What I want to know is if you still have feelings for him."

I don't reply to this straight away but take a bit of time to formulate my thoughts. "What you have to understand, Richard," I say eventually, "is he's not just some ex I can forget about. Long before we hooked up, he was a huge part of my life, a constant throughout my childhood and teens. When I think of a happy memory from my younger days, chances are Lewis is in it because he was always there. We went to school together, and in our free time we hung out together. To this day our families still have meals together, and Ally, Jamie, and Cat are like cousins to me. Hell, I'm probably closer to them than a lot of people are to their actual cousins. It would be hard for me to feel *nothing* for Lewis, but . . . well, you know how things ended between us."

Richard gives a curt nod. "I do. But I don't want you to be with me because you'd *really* like to be with Lewis, but you can't forgive him for what he did, so I'm an okay second choice. I want you to be with me because you actually want to be with me."

These words hit me harder than they probably should. "Of course. I get that. And . . ." I take a deep breath. "I want to lay all my cards on the table—I want to be as open with you as I can. So let's put Lewis aside and focus on you and me. You're a great guy,

Richard, but . . . I have been having some doubts lately about whether we're a good fit."

Pain flickers in his eyes, and I can't help but wince. This is tough—I've no wish to hurt him.

"That's not to say I want to end things," I add. "I just . . . well, we've been together for almost eighteen months now, so it's natural to be looking at the relationship and thinking, *Am I happy with everything? Is this the person I want to spend the rest of my life with?* I'm sure you've been having similar thoughts?"

He doesn't say anything. Okay, so maybe he hasn't been having similar thoughts.

"We have a lot in common," I continue. "We share a lot of the same values, and our life goals are pretty compatible. But there are also differences between us, as there should be—no two people are identical, and it'd be boring if they were. But I've been asking myself how significant those differences are, and . . ." I shrug. "For me, the big thing is I'd like a bit more excitement in my life. I'm worried we're already getting a little too settled, a little too stuck in a routine, and I'm not ready for that. I want to be surprised, to be swept off my feet. And honestly, that includes in our sex life. It's becoming pretty predictable, and I'm someone who needs to keep things fresh, exciting, and spontaneous. I've just not been feeling the passion recently—not in the bedroom, and not in other parts of our relationship either."

Am I being *too* honest with him now? But no, we have to be able to talk about these things, don't we? I no longer have that urge to tear Richard's clothes off and jump into bed with him, probably because our sex life has become so monotonous that it's hard to get excited about it. And he doesn't seem to have that burning desire to touch me and make passionate love either. But . . . I want to be with someone who struggles to control themselves around me! Last night, in the Pheasant, when I spilled that water over myself and was trying my best to dry off my chest with tissues, I spotted something in Lewis's gaze, a look I once knew well. He had to tear his eyes away and stare at the fire because he was getting turned on.

When we were seeing each other, I'd pride myself on how easily I could get Lewis going. He could be chilling, watching TV or scrolling on his phone, completely relaxed. But with a single sultry glance, or a few teasing words, I could have him shifting uncomfortably and tugging at the front of his jeans, his dick snapping to attention like a soldier ready for duty. You know the way they talk about cars: zero to sixty in four point three seconds? I should really have grabbed a stopwatch and timed how quickly I could make Lewis hard—because it was blink-and-you-miss-it fast.

Of course, we were younger then, but based on how he reacted to me dabbing my top, I reckon I could still get him in the mood any time I wanted to—*if* I wanted to, which I don't. But in any case, I don't seem to have that same power over Richard, and he doesn't have it over me.

Richard scratches his arm. "Well, obviously that isn't an easy thing to hear," he says eventually, "but I appreciate you being honest with me. We're clearly on rocky ground at the moment, but I'm glad you're talking openly with me about things rather than making any hasty decisions. How about, this weekend, I organise something fun and exciting for us? Let's see if we can't move past this. All right?"

"Aye." I offer a tentative smile. "I'm looking forward to seeing what you come up with."

CHAPTER NINETEEN

LEWIS

Age twenty-one

There's a knock on my bedroom door. "Lewis? Are you ready to go?"

I open it slowly, rubbing my temple with one hand. "Hi, Maw," I mumble.

She's in a beautiful black velvet dress, her hair styled in a chic twist. Behind her stand Jamie and Da, both looking sharp and ready for the evening ahead.

With horror, Maw takes in my white T-shirt and grey joggies. "Lewis! What are you wearing? You can't go like that!"

The four of us are supposed to be heading to Inverness for a casino-night fundraiser at Jamie's rugby club. Neither Ally nor I ever took a shine to the sport the way Da hoped we would, but Jamie is a mean winger. I don't particularly like complimenting him, given how annoying he is as a wee brother, but I'll concede that when he gets the ball, it's an impressive sight. He's fast and can really tear down the pitch with it. He's hoping to go pro, and

Da—who's ridiculously proud of him—reckons he's got it in him.

Leaning against the doorframe, I cough and clear my throat. "I don't think I'll make it tonight," I say softly, as though even speaking causes me pain. "I've got this terrible headache."

"Oh, my baby!" Maw draws me into a hug.

Jamie, meanwhile, laughs. "Bollocks! Developing a mysterious illness on a night Iona is home from Glasgow? C'mon, Lewis, you're not even trying to be subtle anymore. Just admit it already: the two of you are shagging."

"Oi! Da, are you going to let him speak like that?"

"Your brother's right," Da says to Jamie in that low, rumbling voice of his. "Don't say that kind of thing when we're in a corridor. A guest might hear you."

"*That* wasn't my objection," I say. "My objection was Jamie saying it at all. Iona and I are just friends—and I really am ill."

"Pfft. Aye, right." Jamie folds his arms.

"You two go downstairs and get in the car," Maw says to Da and Jamie. "I want to have a quick chat with my baby to see if he's okay. He *is* looking a little peaky."

"Why do you always call Lewis your baby?" Jamie questions. "He's not the youngest—Cat is. He's not even the youngest boy—that's me."

"Aye, but just look at him." Maw cups my face in her hands and gives it a squeeze. "Butter wouldn't melt. When you were children, unlike the rest of you, Lewis *never* wriggled out of a hug or protested about being kissed. Even now . . ." She gives my cheek a peck. "See? He lets me do it. Would you, Jamie, without some cheeky comment? Or Ally without a grumble? Or Cat without a moody teenage tantrum? No. But Lewis? Always. He may be the second oldest, but he's the only one who still lets me fuss over him."

Jamie tuts and shakes his head. "Mate," he says to me, "your relationship with Maw is *so* unhealthy. And Maw, are you forgetting he's supposed to be ill? Actually, don't worry about that—I don't think you can catch being super horny for Iona."

I thump Jamie's arm for that, and he grins, rubbing it.

"Shoo! Off you go, both of you!" Maw waves Da and Jamie away then comes into my room with me and closes the door behind her. She feels my forehead. "Hmm . . . no temperature. Maybe Jamie is right about your mysterious illness."

"Maw!"

"Sorry, I know it's nothing to do with me. I'm sure all those trips down to Glasgow are perfectly innocent. No doubt you and Iona just meet up for coffee and cake." The sparkle in her eyes suggests she doesn't believe that for a second. "For what it's worth, though, the idea of you and Iona being an item warms my heart." She places a hand on her chest. "I've waited and waited and *waited* for you to tell me, 'Maw, I've got something to admit: Iona and I have been seeing each other for a few years.' But the confession never comes! How much longer before you finally spill the beans?"

"Jesus, Maw, you're as bad as Jamie tonight. There's no confession to be made, so—"

"She's my best friend's daughter, and you've known each other since you were babies. It's perfect!" She's not listening to me.

"Well, Da and Jamie are waiting for you, so it's time for you to go." I guide her towards my door.

"Okay, I'll leave you alone, but promise me one thing. You do use protection, don't you?"

"Aye, of c—" I catch myself, but it's too late. Shit. I was in such a hurry to get her out, I said that without thinking.

Maw giggles delightedly. "I knew it! *I knew it!*" She does a little dance. "This is the best news ever. You know, when you were *very* wee, Ally and Aidan often shared a bath, but so did you and Iona. You'd splash about, giggling away, naked and utterly shameless. And now you've graduated from bath-time buddies to bedroom buddies!"

"Oh my God, Maw, just stop talking! Why would you even say that? That's so weird! Here's my door, so if you could just—"

"Wait till Elspeth and I have a chat about this. Oh! She's going to be as excited as I am."

"So I can't trust you to hold your tongue, then? Keep the secret? No?"

"Well, I need to talk about it with *someone*. Would you rather I natter about it with your da and Jamie on the drive to Inverness?"

"No! Under no circumstances may you tell Jamie. I'd never hear the end of it."

"In which case, Elspeth and I will have a wee chat tomorrow." Maw rubs her hands together. "I can't wait! She's going to be over the moon. My darling boy and her gorgeous girl!"

I scratch behind my ear. This is a disaster. "Aye, well, Iona wanted to keep things casual, okay? She's focusing on her studies. You know what Elspeth is like—she'll be as thrilled about this as you are. Then she'll start chatting about it with Iona, and then *I'll* get it in the neck for letting it slip."

Maw considers this. "Hmm. I can certainly *ask* Elspeth to keep it to herself, but . . . you're right. She probably won't."

I sigh. "Great. Well, I suppose I'll have to warn Iona. At least we managed to keep it a secret for a few years, eh?"

"So secret that Jamie was making a joke about it just five minutes ago." Maw grabs my face again and kisses my cheek. "Anyway, you've made me so happy. My baby—all grown up!"

"Jamie's right: maybe the baby stuff *is* a bit weird."

"Och, wheesht! You'll always be my baby, Lewis." She plants a kiss on my other cheek. "Right, well, I'll leave you to your night of . . . lying about in your room feeling under the weather." She winks. "I'll have a quick word with Ally and Cat before I go and tell them you're not well and should, under no circumstances, be disturbed." A thought comes to her. "Is it hard sneaking Iona up here, or—"

"I'm not discussing any details with you, Maw. Please just go."

"All right, my wonderful, handsome son. I'll see you in the morning. Remember to get some sleep in between all the . . . you know . . ."

My cheeks blaze, and she laughs, a warm, melodious sound that fills the room. She's getting a kick out of how embarrassed I'm getting. I couldn't ask for a better mother—she really is incredible in every way—but she seems to think her motherly duty includes making her kids squirm.

Finally I get rid of her, and I wait five minutes before padding down to reception and peeking into the restaurant. There are a good number of customers for a February evening. Cat is serving, and even though I can't see Aidan, I know he's helping Elspeth in the kitchen, stepping into my usual role. Next, I glance into the snug and spot Ally behind the bar, pulling a pint for a customer while chatting away to the man. I quickly retreat before he spots me.

Lately Ally and Aidan have been taking on odd jobs wherever they can—they're planning to go travelling soon and see the world, so they're keen for any extra cash. As for Cat, she *was* invited along to the casino night, but at seventeen she wouldn't have been able to drink or gamble, so it wouldn't have been much fun for her. Understandably, she chose to stay behind.

When I agreed to go with Maw, Da, and Jamie, I didn't know Iona was going to be home this weekend. After learning she was, I couldn't think of any good reason to pull out, other than faking a last-minute illness. Anyway, I'm hardly going to go through to Inverness to hang out with some rugby guys when Iona is right here in Bannock.

With the coast clear around the front door, I shoot off a message to Iona, telling her to come over now. A minute later, she's here—and soaking wet.

"It's awful out there!" She gives me a quick kiss on the lips—dangerous, considering the others could stroll into reception at any moment. "Even just running across the road, I got drenched. Is your da really okay driving to Inverness in this?"

"Shh! We'll chat in a minute." I take her hand and tug her towards the stairs—in a rush because I don't want to get caught but also because I last saw Iona a month ago and I'm desperate to be alone with her. There was a joint McIntyre and Stewart family lunch earlier, and, as always, it was torture spending time with Iona without being able to touch her.

I don't speak again until we're up one floor and I'm leading Iona along the corridor to my room. "Da will be fine. He's forever saying to guests that, in Scotland, if you cancelled your plans on account of the weather, you'd never do anything."

At my door, I release Iona's hand to get my key.

"I love you in joggers," she whispers as I open up. "They're so soft, and I can feel everything through them." She gives my arse a playful squeeze.

I grin at her then we head in. She removes her waterproof jacket, revealing a light-blue sweater dress that clings to her every curve. Fuck, she looks good. Maybe I should have made more of an effort and put on jeans and a shirt. Then again, she doesn't seem to be objecting to my joggies. In fact, her gaze is fixed on them right now.

"Lewis, are you *already* getting hard?"

I glance down. "Aw, shit. Aye."

Her eyes gleam with mischief. "Another reason I like you in joggers: they don't hide anything. At all." She points. "Is that just from the arse squeeze?"

"Well, *that*, and the fact I've been frustrated all day. It isn't easy having lunch with you without being able to touch you, you know." I shift my weight from foot to foot. "I reckon my body knows what's coming, so it's getting ready for action."

She throws her head back and laughs. "But what if your body has it wrong and all that's coming is a hug and a long chat? Maybe that's all I'm in the mood for tonight?"

I scratch my neck. "Aye, well . . . in that case, we can just hug, I suppose." I'm sure she's teasing me—she loves to torment me when she knows how worked up and desperate I am—but I play along. "So long as you're okay with my cock jabbing you while we hug, of course. There's nothing I can do about that—the thing has a mind of its own."

Giggling, she draws me into her arms, holding me tight, her tits pressing against my chest. Her hands slowly slide down my back to my arse, which she squeezes again, both cheeks this time, then she pulls me closer to her, pinning my cock snugly between us. She rests her head on my shoulder and lets out a long exhale, her breath hot on my neck. Then she moves her hips against me, creating a friction that sets my blood on fire.

"So . . . what do you want to talk about?" she asks.

"Talk?" I croak, struggling to latch onto a coherent thought amid the torrent of sensations. "Er . . . oh, shit, there is something we need to talk about. Something serious."

It's the last thing I want to do, but with a monumental effort, I peel myself away from Iona's deliciously warm embrace.

"Er . . ." I gently slap my cheeks with both hands. "Crap, we probably shouldn't be chatting about this while I've got a boner. Could you be a bit less irresistible for a few minutes?

"Sorry, this is just how I am." She gestures to herself. "I'm hot as hell and I can't hide it."

I chuckle. "Aye, and I wouldn't have it any other way. All right, we'll just have to ignore the bulge in my joggies. Here's what's up: I was chatting to Maw earlier, and she was pestering me with all these questions about you and me. As usual, I denied everything, but then she tripped me up and . . . well, long story short, she now knows what's going on between us—and she's going to talk with your maw tomorrow." I wince. "I'm sorry. Are you pissed off with me?"

"Oh, Lewis." Solemnly she shakes her head, her eyes locked on mine. "Oh dear, oh dear, oh dear. What have you done?" A smile creeps onto her lips. "God, you actually look worried. I'm teasing you, Lewis—it's fine. To be honest, it's probably long past time we told our families. This isn't the best moment to say this, what with your whole tenting situation, but this *is* about more than just sex for me. Don't go getting cocky, but . . . I do *kind of* like you. What I mean to say is, you're not bad—as boys go."

I puff out my chest. "Just as well you warned me not to get cocky—I'm feeling pretty smug right now, but I'll try my best to rein it in. You 'kind of' like me—nice. For my part, you've been my best friend my whole life, and these last few years, you've been something more—much more. I'm sure there's a word out there that describes how I feel, but I can't think what it is at the moment."

She tilts her head slightly and bites her lip. "Well, you obviously need to mull it over. Maybe another hug will get those gears whirring again." She steps towards me, but instead of wrapping her arms around me, she lays her hands on my chest, guides me to my bed, then shoves me down onto it.

"Perhaps a little more skin contact could help too." She tugs her dress over her head and slides down her leggings.

I take in her pale-blue lace bra with matching underwear—the same colour as the dress she just discarded—and my breath catches in my throat. Her nipples press against the delicate fabric, entrancing me, while her underwear clings to her hips perfectly.

"Fuck." I lick my lips. "I've never seen these before. When did you get them?"

"Yesterday, as a wee treat for you. Don't go getting used to this kind of thing—my student loan isn't meant for lingerie. But as a one-off, I thought, *Why not?*"

"Any time you want to shop for this stuff, let me know and I'll transfer you money. I can't think of any way I'd rather spend it."

My mind is a whirlwind of desires. I want to reach out and cup her tits, to feel that lace beneath my fingers and tease those hard nipples. But another part of me is desperate to press my hand to her pussy—to feel her warmth then trace the outline of her folds with my fingertips, checking to see how wet she is for me. Then again, the sight of her in these scanty pieces is almost more than I can handle. As much as I love how she looks, I've this overwhelming urge to strip her completely bare.

As it turns out, I don't get to do any of these things because

Iona takes control of the situation. She climbs onto the bed and straddles me. "Where were we? Oh, aye, I was going to give you a hug." She places her hands on my chest then rubs her pussy along my length, from base to tip and then back again. She lets out a soft moan.

I shiver. Fuck, I love it when she uses my cock like this, for her own pleasure.

"Is this okay?" she asks, continuing to move against me. "As hugs go, I mean."

"Er . . . mmm . . . a-aye," I manage to mumble, sounding like a caveman discovering fire for the first time.

There's something incredibly hot about lying back, doing nothing, and letting her do all the work. The problem is it turns me on *so* much that I always get this primitive desire to grab her hips and grind against her—or when I'm inside her, to thrust. *In theory*, I'm happy for her to take the lead, but my body just won't allow it—it never does. As the mood takes over me, instincts kick in, and I have to be in charge. Luckily, that's exactly how Iona likes it.

Already my hands are gripping her curves, pressing her more firmly to me, dictating her movement and her speed—although I'm sensitive not only to my needs but hers too. I want to make her moan again, and when she does, it nearly has me losing control of myself. Despite the layers of clothing between us, I can feel the heat radiating from her, and a dampness too.

"Bloody hell. If we keep this up much longer, I'm going to make a mess in my boxers. Can I put a condom on, push this expensive underwear to the side, and fuck you?"

She lets out a soft chuckle then bends over and kisses me. "Of course."

◆ ◆ ◆

Later, we lie cuddled up under the covers, both naked, Iona's lingerie finally discarded. We've had sex twice. The first time was fast and frantic—neither of us could hold back after a month apart. Our second session, though, was slower and more deliberate. We savoured every touch and sensation.

I reckon we've got one more round in us, maybe two, but for now I'm resting my head against Iona's warm breasts, using them as a pillow while she runs her fingers through my hair. I don't think there's anything more relaxing than snuggling up like this after we've both come.

By the sounds of it, outside the weather has got even worse—rain batters my window—but in here I'm snug and content with Iona. It's as though we're in our own private world.

Until, that is, a flicker of light catches my eye. At first it's faint through the curtains, barely noticeable. But soon enough it becomes persistent and intrusive, flashes of blue breaking through our sanctuary. I lift my head and squint against the brightness.

"What is that?" I say, as much to myself as to Iona.

"I'm not sure," she murmurs. "Maybe you should check?"

"Aye." Reluctantly I pry myself from her warmth and climb out of bed, the cool air nipping at my bare skin. As Iona props herself up on one elbow, I pad over to the curtains and open them a crack, just enough to peek through.

Down on the street, a police car is parked outside the hotel, its blue lights pulsing rhythmically, illuminating the pelting rain.

The shiver that courses through me has nothing to do with the cold. Something is wrong. There's no other reason the police would show up on a night like this.

What's happened?

CHAPTER TWENTY

LEWIS

Now

I woke early after a restless night and couldn't get back to sleep, so I'm already down in the kitchen preparing for breakfast, cutting fruit for the continental selection and chopping mushrooms and tomatoes for the hot options. Elspeth may be the head chef for dinners and lunches, but I'm the breakfast chef and have been for years—it's a role I started long before becoming hotel manager. Getting up early has never bothered me. For some reason, I enjoy setting things up while everyone else in the building is still asleep.

It's been two days since Richard dropped by to ask me what the deal is between me and Iona. I haven't seen her since the Pheasant, when I stupidly admitted I'd never get over her. That's not what kept me awake last night, though.

Jamie traipses into the kitchen, yawning, also up earlier than usual.

"You couldn't sleep either?" I say.

"Nah. But don't worry, when the guests come down, I'll plaster on a smile and pretend everything is sunshine and roses."

He rubs his eyes then pours himself a cup of the coffee I prepared earlier. "She'd have been fifty-nine today."

I let out a small sigh. "I know."

The last time I saw Maw, I was literally shoving her out of my room. She'd been so looking forward to gabbing with Elspeth about me and Iona, but . . . she never got the chance. The car she, Da, and Jamie were travelling in came off the road and crashed into a tree. Maw died. Da too. Jamie, in the back, survived, although his injuries dashed any hopes of him ever playing rugby professionally. He doesn't even watch the sport now. I reckon he finds it too painful—maybe because it was how he and Da bonded.

Me, though? I was fine. Because I faked an illness that night.

Jamie takes a sip of coffee then places his cup on the work surface. By looking at him, you wouldn't know what he's been through. It's pretty amazing how he's recovered. On a whim, I cross the kitchen and pull him into a hug. Normally, he'd shove me away for attempting such a thing, but today he doesn't protest. Neither of us says anything, but there's comfort in our shared silence. I clap his back then withdraw again, in time to see Ally enter the kitchen.

"Jesus," I say. "Can't remember when I last saw *you* up this early."

Since setting up Bannock Adventures with Aidan, Ally has passed his former breakfast duties—of serving as front of house—to Emily. That means he usually gets to stay in bed longer than the rest of us.

"Aye, well, the one night Ru sleeps through without stirring, and I'm lying awake the whole time because I can't sleep." Ally stretches his arms above his head then lets them drop back to his sides. "I figured I might as well get up and be useful. Is there coffee going?"

He pours himself some. As he sips on it, he taps out something on his phone. Moments later, both Jamie's screen and mine light up. There's one new message in the McIntyre Clan Group Chat.

ALLY

How you doing, Cat?

"Wow," Jamie says. "Inspiring stuff."

"Aye, well, it can't be easy for her being up in Wick today, away from family and friends."

Jamie chuckles. "I'm not disagreeing with that, Ally. My point is you sent her four words—not even a kiss. Bloody hell, I thought Emily had thawed that frozen lump you call a heart."

"Jesus Christ! All right, fine." Ally taps his phone a couple more times.

ALLY

X

Jamie howls. "That's even worse! A single kiss as a message on its own. You're the eldest—the leader. Can't you come up with anything more moving to unite our family today?"

Ally leans against the counter. "All right, if you're so good at this stuff, why don't you send her something? You normally communicate solely in GIFs. Is there one for *I'm sorry you're in Wick by yourself on what would have been Maw's birthday*?"

"Hmm . . ." Jamie furrows his brow and scratches his chin. "I bet there's something from the US version of *The Office*. There always is."

As though suddenly struck by inspiration, he taps away on his phone, and soon an animated image appears on my screen. It shows the character Meredith speaking to camera and holding an alcoholic drink. As her mouth moves, a caption flashes up: *You're not alone, sister. Let's get a beer sometime.*

"Not bad," Ally begrudgingly admits. "That one actually works pretty well."

Jamie gives a smug smile. "There isn't a single emotion or sentiment in the entirety of the human experience that can't be communicated with a four-second clip from *The Office.*"

Shaking my head, I compose a message of my own.

LEWIS

> Cat, it's a shit day, but I hope you're all right. When can you come back to Bannock for a visit? We miss you. x

After maybe thirty seconds, all three of our phones light up with a new notification.

CAT

> Wow, so none of you could sleep either? Love the predictability of your messages—Ally with the bare minimum, Lewis with the genuine feeling, and Jamie with the inappropriate GIF.

JAMIE

> Excuse me? That was VERY appropriate. Ally thought so too.

CAT

> To be fair, of the three messages, I did like yours best.

Jamie posts another *Office* GIF, this one of Michael and Dwight doing the Raise the Roof dance.

CAT

But you do realise THAT GIF is inappropriate. Right?

JAMIE

CAT

Anyway, I'll try to pop home soon. BTW, I may live far away, but even I've heard about the duet in the Pheasant. What's going on, Lewis? I thought you and Iona barely talked anymore.

JAMIE

Aye, it's been a REALLY long lovers' tiff.

LEWIS

🖐 We were never "lovers". I'm so tired of saying that.

Jamie posts yet another *Office* GIF, this time of Ryan holding up a sign. It says, *Kelly, I know you are with someone but I love you. I will wait forever.*

JAMIE

That's you, Lewis. Just replace "Kelly" with "Iona".

I put down my phone, grab a wooden spoon, and chase Jamie around the kitchen, intent on smacking his arse with it. Grinning, he dodges and evades me, proving that, even though rugby matches may now be behind him, he can still move quickly when he wants to.

Ally sighs and grumbles that it's too early in the morning for such shenanigans, but we both ignore him.

"Like I said," Jamie calls over his shoulder, racing around the kitchen island with me hot on his heels, "that show covers the entirety of the human experience—even your bloody weird relationship with Iona!"

CHAPTER TWENTY-ONE

IONA

Richard's fingers drum on the steering wheel as we drive through lush green hills blanketed with swathes of purple heather. He's taking me to the activity he's organised for us, whatever it is—apparently, secrecy is part of the fun. Soon a series of wind turbines come into view, looming large against the blue sky, and I begin to suspect it may be to them that we're headed.

"I don't mean to sound rude, but . . . are we going to where you work? Is that your big surprise?"

He glances my way and winks. "I want you to trust me. Okay?"

"Aye. I can do that." That's the least I owe him.

We park near another car, and I recognise the man standing outside it waiting for us: Joe Campbell, Richard's colleague and a former schoolmate of mine. Stocky and broad-shouldered, he has a shock of sandy hair and an easy-going smile.

"Hello, Joe! Long time no see." As I get out, I take in the harness he's already wearing—and the other two that sit atop his car, alongside three helmets. "Er, so . . . what is it we're doing here?"

Joe chuckles and turns to Richard, leaving it to him to explain.

"We're going to go up one of these marvels." Richard nods towards the nearest turbine, whose blades—unlike those of the others—aren't moving.

I crane my neck back and take in its full height. Wow! From a distance these things look big, but up close they're bloody colossal. We're really going to go all the way up there? At least I can't accuse Richard of coming up with something boring. Remembering his request that I trust him, I don't immediately veto the idea, tempting though that is.

"How tall is it?" I *try* to sound calm, but my tone betrays the fluttering in my stomach.

"Including the blades, a hundred and forty metres," Joe says. "But the tower itself is only ninety metres."

"*Only?*" I gulp.

Richard pats my back. "We'll keep you safe. It'll be fun—something a little different. I mean, you've never climbed a wind turbine before, right?"

"Er, no. This is definitely going to be a first for me."

We get geared up, Joe and Richard talk me through some safety procedures, then we head into the base of the turbine.

"There are two rest platforms on the way up where you can take a wee break," Joe explains. "Just to warn you, it is quite a climb—it keeps me and Richard fit."

At the bottom of the first ladder, he shows me how to connect to the fall arrest system, which will catch me should I slip. Peering up at the ladder's intimidating height, I'm relieved there's a safeguard.

Joe heads up first. I'll be going in the middle, with Richard following behind. As I watch Joe ascend, I'm glad we picked this order. He's a nice guy, but if anyone is going to be staring up at my arse while I climb, I'd rather it were Richard.

Once I'm clipped in and it's my turn to go, my knees tremble and my palms become clammy. *Thanks, body. That won't make this any easier.*

"I'm really nervous," I admit.

"You'll be fine," Richard assures me. "You've got this."

I nod then make a start, a rung at a time, each step echoing in the confined space. Soon I understand why Joe said scaling turbines keeps him fit—it's like a session at the gym. When I eventually reach the top of the first ladder, my heart is thumping fast and I'm breathing heavily.

After a rest, we continue, the hum of machinery and the occasional whoosh of wind echoing through the tower. The entire structure sways gently in the breeze, which the men assure me it's supposed to do, although their words don't stop my stomach from doing little flips.

Finally we reach the "nacelle" at the top, where the generator lives. There's limited space here, but we all fit.

"Oh my God," I say, catching my breath. "We made it! I can't believe I did that."

Richard and Joe exchange an amused glance.

"You've done really well," Richard says. "But . . . we still have to go through there." He points to a hatch in the ceiling.

"We're going *outside*? You're kidding? We're ninety metres in the air—off the top of a hill!"

Richard lays a hand on my shoulder. "You don't have to do anything you don't want to, but . . . I did ask you to trust me, and you've already come this far. We might as well take in the view, right?"

I swallow hard. "Fuck it. Let's do this."

The lads cheer. Again, Joe goes first, attaching a safety lanyard to himself then pushing open the hatch and climbing through it. I clip myself in next, take a very deep breath, then hoist myself up and out. Immediately the wind batters me. My legs turn to jelly, and I don't dare take in the view at first—not until, under Joe's watchful eye, I securely attach myself to an anchor point on the platform. Only then do I raise my gaze.

My God. It's unlike anything I've ever experienced before. It's not like observing the urban sprawl from a high-rise, nor like admiring the scenery from the summit of a mountain. We're atop a tower that juts straight into the air and offers a three-hundred-and-sixty-degree view of the surrounding countryside. It's surreal.

Rolling hills stretch as far as the eye can see, a patchwork of green and purple from the heather, while lochs glisten like jewels in the sunlight, their surfaces rippling in the wind. It's incredible.

Richard, who's also now up on the platform, gently nudges my shoulder. "Worth the climb, right?"

I nod, unable to tear my eyes away from the stunning landscape. "Definitely. I've never seen the Highlands like this."

Despite the height and being buffeted by strong winds, a strange sense of calm washes over me. My nerves recede and all that matters is soaking in every detail around me. My fear is replaced by amazement—and then by a sudden surge of excitement.

"Can I . . . scream?"

Richard chuckles. "Course you can. Let it all out."

So I throw my arms back and yell into the wind, and it feels so good. Jack may have felt he was the king of the world on the *Titanic*, but he never experienced this.

As I let loose, something shifts inside me, and with a flash of clarity, I realise I need to be brave and do what's right. Life is too short to do anything else—you never know what's around the corner.

I make a silent decision then and there, but I keep it to myself until we're back on solid ground. After collecting our harnesses and helmets, Joe drives off, leaving me and Richard to it.

"Well?" he says. "What did you think of my surprise?"

"It was incredible," I reply honestly. "But . . . it made me realise something."

In the romance books I read, there always comes a time when the heroine just *knows* she's meant to be with her hero for the rest of her life. I've never had that certainty with Richard, and I know I never will. It's not fair on me or him to drag out this relationship any longer.

I break it to him as gently as I can.

He accepts my words stoically, although when I'm finished, he asks, "Is this because of Lewis?"

I shake my head. "I'm well aware how Lewis feels about me, but I don't know if I could ever enter into another relationship with him. As for us, though, I'm sure we're not meant to be. I like you, Richard, I really do, but . . . I don't love you. I'm sorry about that, but I have to be honest with myself and with you. I feel terrible that we travelled to the Highlands together, and I know this puts you in an awkward position, what with the fact you're working here now and will need to find a place to stay. We'll . . . sort something out."

Richard glances away, staring at the distant hills for some moments before meeting my eyes again. "Thanks, but there's no 'we' anymore. *I'll* sort something out. But it's okay—I get it."

"You do?"

"Don't get me wrong, it sucks, but yeah. You're not sure about me, and I don't want to be with someone who's having doubts, so . . . this is for the best, I suppose. I am experiencing stronger emotions inside than I'm maybe letting on, but I get this is how things go. And for what it's worth, I like this job. It's interesting, and it feels important to be helping Scotland towards a greener future. Plus, hey, climbing up the turbines is just fun.

"I don't regret coming here, and I don't plan on leaving the role, although I will be looking to stay in a town or village other than Bannock. Who knows, maybe I'll find another Highland girl, one who's a better fit for me. Don't they say everything happens for a reason?"

I flash him a grateful smile, impressed by his composure, then give him a quick hug.

Pulling apart, I say, "Right, well, awkward car share back to Bannock?"

Richard gives a small wistful smile and nods. "Yeah, awkward car share back to Bannock."

CHAPTER TWENTY-TWO

LEWIS

"So, it looks like Richard is moving out," Jamie says.

"*What?*" I snap my head up, the paperwork I was immersed in immediately forgotten.

"Come see for yourself!"

Suspecting this may be one of Jamie's wind-ups, I come out from behind the reception desk and join him at the window. Across the road, Richard is piling things into the boot of his car. It does very much look as if he's packing up to leave. When he glances up and spots us gawking at him, we jump back like we've been caught red-handed.

Jamie is the first to peek again. "Oh shit!" He laughs gleefully and bounces from foot to foot. "He's coming over! You know how to throw a decent swing, right? A few jabs?" He punches the air, demonstrating some moves.

This time I'm convinced Jamie is winding me up—but no. When I check, I see Richard really is headed this way.

"Oh shit!" I parrot. "What does he want?"

If he's moving out because things have ended between him

and Iona, maybe he blames me and is intent on payback? I desperately run through some potential scenarios and responses in my head, not that I've a lot of time to prepare. I'm not worried about getting hurt, but this is my place of work and I'd rather stay professional. Besides, I honestly don't wish the guy any harm.

The door opens and in he comes.

"Er, Richard," I say. "Hi. How are things going?" I try to sound casual while remaining on guard, ready for whatever may happen.

He takes in my rigid stance and chuckles drily. "I just thought I'd pop in to say I'm leaving."

I nod. "Right."

"Iona and I have . . . split up," he elaborates.

"Oh." What am I supposed to say to that? "I'm, er, sorry to hear that."

He smirks. "Sure you are." He casts a glance at Jamie then turns his attention back to me. "Fancy stepping outside?"

I tense at this, so he clarifies, "Just for a chat."

"Ah. Of course."

We head out to the street, which is quiet on this late afternoon. Richard watches as a solitary car passes. His eyes follow it until it disappears from sight. Only then does he speak.

"Iona said the break-up had nothing to do with you."

"Aye, well, I haven't even spoken to her since the Pheasant."

His jaw tightens, and he crosses his arms over his chest. "Are you going to try and get back together with her?"

How to answer that? *Should* I even answer that? Is it his business if they're no longer boyfriend and girlfriend?

"I . . . don't know if that could ever happen," I say eventually. "But I do want to be her friend again, if she'd allow that."

Richard studies me in silence for some moments. "And you honestly think you deserve that?"

I shrug. "Probably not, no. But that's for her to decide."

He blows out. "Yeah, you're right. That is for her to decide. But if you do reconnect with her, don't fuck it up again. She's special, and she deserves to be happy. That's all I wanted to say."

He turns to go.

"Wait!"

He hesitates then glances back.

As tense and uncomfortable as this is, I respect him for looking out for Iona. He's a decent guy—even if he hates my guts.

"I wish you all the best," I say.

With a curt nod, he returns to packing up his things.

Back inside, Jamie wants to know if things are over between Richard and Iona, and I confirm they are.

"Why was that so boring, then? I was watching through the window, and no blows were exchanged. I wanted to see you going at each other! How come you'll chase *me* around the kitchen with a wooden spoon, but you're all civil to that guy?"

"Because he's a decent human being and you're an annoying wee brother."

"Oh, you should *not* have said that." Jamie pulls a pose that looks like something out of *Karate Kid*. "Hi-ya!" He kicks the air dramatically. "Prepare to pay for your insolence!"

Just then some guests come down the stairs, and Jamie immediately drops his arms and smiles at them. "Heading out? Okay, see you later."

After the door clicks shut behind them, he waits a few moments for good measure then springs back into action. "Ready to face my wrath?"

"Nope." I don't have time for this nonsense right now. I'm busy pondering what, if anything, this break-up might mean for me and Iona.

From the kitchen, Elspeth calls, "Lewis! It's not long till the restaurant opens. Could I have your help with some prep, please?"

Jamie grins from ear to ear. "Elspeth doesn't know yet! I'm going to go tell her *you* broke Richard and Iona up."

"But I didn't! And don't you d—"

Already he's rushing towards the kitchen. I race after him, but bloody hell, even though his rugby days are long behind him, he's still fast.

He gets there before I can intercept him and proudly announces, "Richard is moving out!"

"*What?*" Elspeth, who was in the process of tasting the mushroom and barley soup, drops her spoon in surprise.

"And Lewis is the one who split them up." Jamie points at me.

"That isn't true!" I protest. "I had nothing to do with it."

"Oh, aye? And yet this comes just days after you sang with Iona at the Pheasant, an incident that was the subject of a lot of town gossip. Before the day is through, everyone in Bannock will be buzzing about how *you* broke up a happy couple."

"But—"

"That's how gossip works, Lewis," Jamie says. "The truth is less important than what people *think* the truth is."

My mouth opens and closes like a fish out of water. "I . . . but . . ."

"Boys! Will one of you *please* fill me in on what's going on?"

I find my voice. "Aye, I will. Jamie, you can keep an eye on the snug and reception. If you stay here, you'll only confuse things with your inevitable meddling additions."

"Aw, but this is going to be so good!"

"*Jamie!*" I use my no-nonsense tone so he knows I'm not messing around.

"Pfft, fine." Dragging his feet, he shoots me a mischievous grin before leaving.

Alone with Elspeth, I explain about Richard packing up his belongings, and I assure her once again that it was nothing to do with me.

"Hmm." She taps her foot. "Are you sure? Because I wouldn't mind at all if you've finally come to your senses."

"Come to my senses?" I repeat.

"Oh, Lewis." She smiles kindly. "Why don't we be frank for once? I have eyes—I'm pretty sure you've been in love with Iona since you were both fifteen."

My breath catches in my throat. A lot of people have teased me about my feelings for Iona over the years—not least, Jamie— but Elspeth has never before referred to the subject so bluntly.

"Your mother saw it too," she goes on. "Back when you'd visit Iona in Glasgow, we both suspected there was more to your relationship than simply friends catching up. We gossiped about it, naturally. We were so pleased."

My chest tightens. It's impossible not to replay my final conversation with Maw—her excitement about my accidental revelation. Without warning, my eyes sting, and I have to look away for a moment. Jesus, am I about to cry? What the fuck is wrong with me?

"Oh, Lewis. Come here." Elspeth wraps me in her arms. She's always given good hugs. Not as good as Maw's, but not bad.

"I . . . broke Iona's heart." I can't quite believe I'm admitting this. I take a breath and try to go on. "It was years ago now, but . . ."

Suddenly shame washes over me, and a mental gate slams shut. I can't continue. Elspeth wouldn't be holding me like this if she knew the details.

Drawing back, but keeping her hands on my arms, she looks me in the eye. "Whatever you did, maybe this is a chance for you to fix things. I remember, as a lad, you got up to just as much mischief as your siblings, and yet, of the four of you, your kind and caring nature shone the brightest. Your maw loved you all equally, but she had a soft spot for you because she understood you could be a wee bit more . . . sensitive at times."

Instinctively I cringe. I doubt many guys would appreciate *that* word being used to describe them.

"Not that anyone would know it to look at you, of course." Elspeth pats my biceps. "Anyway, the specifics of what happened are between you and Iona, but my point is, maybe you've already beaten yourself up enough about it? As your maw's best friend, I'm confident if she were here, she'd tell you to be kinder to yourself."

"Aye. I can imagine her saying that."

That smile again, her eyes crinkling at the corners. "Now, I don't want to run away, but if Iona and Richard have split up, I really should go see how my daughter is doing."

"Oh shit, of course."

"Will you be okay here for a while preparing things by yourself? I know you're confident about the menu—I mean, okay emotionally."

"Jesus, of course I'll be fine. I'm not *that* sensitive."

"Good. There's a lot that needs to be done, so I'll be back as soon as I can, but I need to see how Iona is getting on. Anyway, food prep has always been a calming distraction for you."

I nod. "It has."

"All right, bye for now."

Alone, I make a start on preparing the garnishes, so they're ready for when it's time to plate up. *Be kind to yourself*, I repeat in my head as I work. But can I really forgive myself for what I did?

CHAPTER TWENTY-THREE

IONA

Age twenty-one

After driving three and a half hours without a break, my stomach churning the whole way, I finally reach Bannock. I dropped everything and skipped classes to be here. I had to, after the message Lewis sent me earlier.

> **LEWIS**
> Iona, this isn't working. It's over between us.

Abrupt, cold, devastating, and completely out of the blue. Well, maybe not *completely*. He's been keeping me at arm's length for weeks now, shutting down every time I reach out to him, whether in person or over the phone. It's as though he's been determined to handle his grief alone. I thought that was part of the process and would pass—I never expected him to do this.

When I saw his message, I called him, but he wouldn't pick up. After trying him maybe ten times, I got in the car, and here I am.

I pull up outside the hotel, step out, and take a few breaths to steady myself. I'm upset—of course I am—but I need to handle this situation delicately. Lewis is hurting, and I have to make him understand that I can help him, that we can face this together. But . . . I don't know how to get through to him.

We're all devastated. His parents were like an aunt and uncle to me, and it's unbearable thinking I'll never again hear Angus's friendly, booming voice or see Mairi's warm, infectious smile. Lewis was especially close to his mother, and maybe that's why he's acting the way he is, but he should be leaning on me for support—or if not me, at least his siblings or my maw. But he isn't.

He has, however, started going to the gym. A lot. On the surface that's healthy, but Maw says he goes every day—sometimes twice a day. He also now meticulously tracks everything he eats. I'm sure he's trying to regain some sense of control after what happened, but there's a fine line between dedication and obsession.

As ready as I'll ever be, I head inside. The hotel has always felt like a second home to me, the backdrop for countless joint family dinners filled with laughter, storytelling, and friendship. Now, though, the building feels different. Not visibly—the decoration hasn't changed—but the life and energy Angus and Mairi brought to the place is gone.

Ally is behind the reception desk, on the phone. He's frowning, although when he looks up and sees me, he forces a smile. I can't begin to imagine what it's been like for him. The eldest sibling, he's had to take on the running of the hotel. I don't know how he's managing, given he—like the rest of us—is still reeling from it all. But the building is not only the family home, it's their source of income—and Maw's, as head chef. I suppose he hasn't had a choice.

"Sure, I can bring Jamie in on Friday. What time?" Ally scribbles something down. "All right, thanks. Bye." He hangs up.

"One of Jamie's medical appointments?" I guess.

Jamie had a lengthy hospital stay immediately after the crash but is recovering at home now, although he's going in regularly for follow-up care.

"Aye, that was the physio, and then he's seeing the orthopaedic consultant next week. He's getting on okay, though. You know what he's like—still cracking jokes, despite everything."

Somehow I can believe that. We all have our own ways of coping, I suppose.

"Is Lewis about?"

Ally shrugs. "In his room, maybe? Or at the gym—he's always there nowadays."

"Thanks. I'll try upstairs."

He nods, lifts a mug, and takes a long sip of something—coffee, probably. I imagine he needs a lot of caffeine to help him get through the day. He doesn't ask why I'm here mid-week. With everything that's on his plate, it likely hasn't even struck him as odd.

Ascending the stairs, I make a mental note to check in on Cat at some point. Unlike Lewis, she's been replying to the messages I've sent her, but it's coming up for exam season at school and this is an important year for her. I've no idea how she's managing to focus on studying after what happened. For now, though, I have to give Lewis all my attention. He clearly needs it.

I knock on his door. Noises come from within—an exasperated grumble, followed by the creaking of floorboards.

"Aye? What is it?" His voice is somehow both familiar and strange.

"It's Iona."

There's a pause, then the door opens, revealing Lewis in only a pair of joggers. They sit low on his hips, the waistband of his boxers peeking out above them. Even though I'm here for a serious conversation, I can't help but notice the transformation in his physique. His shoulders have broadened, and his chest has taken on a firmer, more defined shape. The change may be impressive, but it's startling that it's happened in such a short time.

He crosses his arms. They too are stronger, each muscle now clearly pronounced. "What do you want?"

I smart like I've been slapped. *This* is how he greets me? After the message he sent me earlier? Isn't it obvious why I'm here?

Despite his frosty demeanour, I force myself to stand tall and look him in the eye. It's grief that's making him behave like this— I have to remember that.

"I know you're in pain, but . . ."

My words trail off because something catches my attention— a flicker of movement further inside the room.

A woman, half-hidden under the covers of Lewis's bed, stares at me with wide eyes.

Suddenly it's a struggle to breathe. My insides twisting, my knees weakening, I place a hand against the wall to support myself. "Lewis . . . what the fuck is going on?"

He glances over his shoulder then meets my gaze again. "Isn't it obvious?"

My vision blurs. "But . . ."

"What's the problem?" His voice is chillingly emotionless. "I broke things off with you. Besides, it's not as if we were ever properly going out. It was casual. I only messaged you out of courtesy."

I can't believe this is happening. My legs feel like they're about to give way beneath me. "So these last few years . . . I've just been your fuck buddy?"

"Isn't that how you wanted it? So I didn't interfere with your studies?"

His words cut through me like a knife. My maw thought she knew my da, only to discover he had a secret life. I, though, was *sure* I knew Lewis. I didn't think him capable of a betrayal like this.

Tears spill down my cheeks. I don't want him to see how much he's humiliating me, but I can't hold back my emotions. "How could you?"

He just shrugs—doesn't even bother to answer my question with words. After twenty-one years of friendship, an indifferent shrug is all he offers as an explanation for why he's tearing apart my heart.

I open my mouth to say more, but nothing comes. I can't think what else to say. Unable to process this, I take a step back from him. Then, turning on my heel, I run away.

CHAPTER TWENTY-FOUR

LEWIS

Now

I pick up a smooth stone and feel its weight in my hand before sending it skipping across the water. Four bounces. Not bad, but I used to be better. I'm out of practice—it's been too many years since I last came here to while away time doing nothing in particular.

Half an hour ago, I was at the hotel, pacing around the office, humming and hawing over how to play things with Iona. I really wanted to nip across the road to see her, but I thought it might be weird to pounce on her the day after her split with Richard. Then again, I also thought it'd be weird not to acknowledge the split at all. I couldn't make up my mind about what to do until the solution hit me, and I grabbed a piece of paper, scribbled a message on it, and stuck it to my bedroom window: *Fancy a chat? Meet at our old place?*

Just like hanging out at the loch, leaving messages in my window is something I haven't done in a long time. This way, though, if she wants to speak to me, she knows where to find me. And if she doesn't want to speak to me . . . well, she doesn't have to show up. I've no idea if she'll come or not.

With a flick of my wrist, I send another stone sailing across the water. Three bounces—that's worse! Maybe it's not my technique that's at fault. I'm possibly not picking the right stones. Okay, this time I'll find a really good one, then I won't have any excuses.

I'm lost in my search when footsteps crunch on the pebbles. I look up, and my heart does a wee flip. It's Iona. Blonde strands have escaped her bun and blow across her face in the light breeze. God, she's beautiful, even in a cosy oversized knit sweater and a pair of well-worn jeans. She doesn't say anything as she approaches, just offers a tentative smile. My chest tightens with both hope and uncertainty.

"Hi." I consider hugging her then think better of it—that would probably be too much. Instead I sit on a patch of grass and pat the ground beside me. "Fancy chilling here for a while? For old time's sake?"

She glances at the tree. "What happened to the swing?"

"Oh, that went years ago."

She nods and tucks a few stray strands of hair behind her ear. "That's a shame. Kids always had fun with it, and today's teenagers could really do with a place to come when they need to escape everyone for a while. We liked coming here."

"Aye, we did." I make a mental note to get a new swing and put it up as soon as possible. Why didn't I think of that before? That might have impressed her.

She sits, leaving a bit of space between me and her, more than she would have when we were teenagers. She looks out to the loch, which glistens in the afternoon light. "A lot has happened since you and I last came here."

"It really has." I watch the loch too, my eyes following a few gentle waves until they break against the shore. "Remember when Bannock and the countryside around it were our entire world? Things were . . . simpler then. Life became more complicated when you went off to Glasgow."

She pushes her glasses up and glances at me, her lips curling ever so slightly. "More complicated, but also more fun, no? Don't tell me you didn't enjoy the things we got up to. When I asked you to put a glow-in-the-dark condom on your dick, you barely even hesitated."

Her bluntness takes me by surprise, but I drop my gaze and chuckle, rubbing the back of my neck. "Aye, those were definitely fun times. You always had the . . . *brightest* ideas about how to spice things up."

This earns a small laugh from Iona. "Good one." She pulls her knees up to her chest and wraps her arms around them. "You know, Richard was such a sweet guy, but he never was a fan of a dick joke. And frankly, if you can't laugh at a penis, you're taking life too seriously."

"Hmm, was it Confucius or Aristotle who said that? I always get the ancient philosophers mixed up."

"Neither. That bit of wisdom is an Iona Stewart original."

"Wow, really? You should print inspirational posters with those words. I reckon the Otter's Holt would stock them."

Jenny, the owner of Bannock's gift shop, typically sells much classier items. That being said, although my suggestion isn't serious, I could see her carrying a few of those for a touch of cheeky charm.

"You must have been living by that motto for a while now," I add. "The first time you clapped eyes on my penis, you laughed. A lot."

Given our history, I don't know if this is a brave or stupid thing to mention. Then again, it was Iona who brought up the glow-in-the-dark condom. I'm just trying to keep the giggles coming.

"Aye, well . . ." She holds her thumb and index finger a few millimetres apart.

"Bollocks! You never had any complaints about my size. You were in stitches because it looked like I'd dipped my cock in radioactive goo."

Another peal of laughter escapes Iona. Man, it feels good to make her laugh—even if the punchline is my dick. But I suppose, back when we were together, it always was, wasn't it? When it wasn't giving her pleasure, she was playing games with it.

"It really did look radioactive!" she agrees. "Ha, I can still picture it. And then I made you dance, and you shook it all about."

She giggles some more, and I chuckle along. I didn't expect for us to get onto this topic—and certainly not so quickly—but reliving the incident doesn't bother me. As Iona said, if you can't laugh at a penis, you're taking life too seriously.

"So . . ." Iona repositions herself, turning her body to face me. "Did you invite me here just to talk about dicks or was there another reason?"

"Another reason," I assure her. "In fact, discussing dicks wasn't on the agenda at all—consider that a bonus. I thought we could maybe talk about . . . things. In general. I, er, was sorry to hear about you and Richard."

"I bet you were devastated," Iona says drily.

I give a nervous grin then say, "Richard actually came to speak to me yesterday. He said he wants you to be happy, and . . . that's what I want too."

"Is it? That's funny coming from the man who shattered my heart into tiny little pieces."

And with these words, the mood changes. A palpable tension creeps between us, and it's really pretty uncomfortable—but that's okay. We need to talk about this if we're ever going to move past it.

"I don't expect you to forgive me, but I think we should discuss what happened that day."

"You mean when you broke up with me by text message then fucked another woman just a few hours later? An incident that hurt me so badly I gave up my plans to return to the Highlands after uni and stayed in Glasgow instead. You want to talk about that?"

It's impossible not to wince at the venom that's crept into her voice, even though she's perfectly entitled to speak this way.

"Aye, I do," I say quietly.

"All right. Whatever you've got to say is coming six years too late, but I'll listen to it. I'll give you my time, although I'm not sure you deserve it."

It's hard to believe we were laughing at dick jokes just a few minutes ago. This is already painful, and it's only going to get worse, but we have to do it.

"First, I want to be clear that I'll never try to justify what I did. It's beyond justification—I'm fully aware of that. And like I say, I don't expect you to forgive me. But maybe I can make you understand some of what was going through my head at the time."

Iona picks up a stone and traces its contours with her thumb.

"I know you were grieving, Lewis. I've *always* sympathised with your loss, but it isn't an excuse."

I hang my head. "Aye, I know. But . . . can I talk about it anyway?"

She gives a curt nod.

I wipe my hands on my jeans—my palms are already a little sweaty. "Looking back now, it's clear I was going through some sort of self-destructive streak. As we just discussed, it's not an excuse, but I missed Maw and Da. More than that, I felt guilty that I stayed home that night. They were killed and Jamie was badly injured, while I was . . . fine. Because I made up an illness so I could be with you."

Iona continues to fidget with the stone, watching me, waiting for me to go on.

"I didn't think I deserved to be happy, but you were so good to me. You came back to Bannock to see me as often as you could, and you called and messaged me every day. You tried so hard to help me cope, but I didn't *want* to cope. That was the problem. Just thinking was painful, so I tried to do as little of that as possible. I sacrificed my emotional health and went all in on physical health instead. The strain and burn of lifting weights became an obsession for me—the best way to escape my thoughts.

"But every day, you were there, in person or over the phone, so persistent, never giving up on me. You tried to make me see that, as impossible as it seemed, I would get through it. Aye, I'd never not miss Maw and Da, but I *would* find it in me to be happy again. And . . . maybe I didn't believe you. Maybe I thought I deserved to suffer. I don't know, really—I wasn't myself back then. But in my twisted logic at the time, I came to believe that I had to cut you out of my life. Your unwavering support was like salt in the wound. It made me *feel*, and I was trying so hard not to do that."

I take a long breath in then out. "All right, with that intro out of the way, let's get on to that day."

Iona's steady gaze reveals nothing. When we were younger, I was pretty good at reading her face, but right now I've got no idea what she's thinking.

"There was this . . . lass." I close my eyes for a moment. God, this hurts, but I have to tell her everything. "Well, a woman—probably about the age we are now. Northern Irish, although I think she said she lived in Scotland—Ayrshire, maybe. In any case, she was doing a driving tour of the Highlands and was only staying in Bannock for a night. She thought the town was a bit boring . . . apart from me. She took a shine to me and was pretty flirty. She had no idea I was seeing someone, of course, and I . . ." I rub the back of my neck. ". . . didn't mention it."

Iona's brows knit together, her lips pressing into a thin line, but she still doesn't speak.

"By this point I'd been trying to push you away for weeks, but you wouldn't let me—you were too good a friend. You just wouldn't give up on me, and I knew you never would, unless . . . I hurt you. I had to do something so bad that even you, with your seemingly limitless empathy and patience, wouldn't be able to forgive me. So, aye, I messaged you saying we were through, put my phone on silent, and then . . . pursued this woman."

This really isn't easy, but I force myself to press on. "I knew, when I checked my phone again later, I'd have missed calls and messages from you. And I knew they'd all be telling me that I was being stupid, that I shouldn't end things. My plan was to call you back, or maybe message you, and explain that I'd slept with someone else. That would be the final nail in the coffin. It never occurred to me that you might skip uni and drive straight up to Bannock."

"But I did," Iona says coolly. "Lewis, this is more or less what I thought happened. Don't get me wrong, you've told me a few details I didn't know—like she was Northern Irish, for example. But I didn't need to know that! None of this changes my view of what you did."

I scratch my arm. "Aye, I get that. And like I've said a few times now, I don't expect you to forgive me. But . . . there are a few more things I should probably say."

Eyes narrowed, she tilts her head—a silent signal for me to continue.

"So, I invited her to my room intending to have sex with her. And that's terrible, obviously. I've been beating myself up over that these last six years. But . . . I didn't actually do anything with her."

Iona raises a brow. "What?"

I shrug. "I couldn't. She was hoping for some fun, and instead she got a moody, grieving guy who, when it came down to it, didn't want to be touched by her—or to touch her. We lay in bed, clothed, and she kept on trying to kick things off, but I wasn't interested. Eventually, after a fair bit of pestering, I let her take my T-shirt off so she could see my muscles. I shouldn't have done that, but just so we're clear about what happened, she reached out and felt my pecs, and I flinched away. That's the extent of what took place between us."

Iona's body stiffens, the colour draining from her face. She swallows hard.

"Anyway, before I could get her out of my room, there was a knock at the door and . . . it was you. I opened up knowing exactly what you'd think. I was such an arsehole, but at the time I thought everything was working out for the best. I was able to push you away without actually having to sleep with someone else. Of course, after you burst into tears and ran off, the poor woman I messed around left too. And . . . that's all there is to tell."

I let out a long breath. That wasn't easy, but it does feel good to finally get it off my chest.

Unfortunately, not only did I make Iona cry back then, but in telling the story now, I've done it again. Her eyes well up, and a single tear trickles down her cheek. Then, in a sudden flash of anger, she lashes out and slaps my arm.

"You bastard!"

Whoa! I deserve that—nah, I deserve far worse—but I'm not used to violence from her. It takes me by surprise.

"For the last six years, you've led me to believe you ended our relationship via text message then fucked another woman. Now you're telling me that didn't happen?"

"Well . . . I did end our relationship by text. And I did invite a woman back to my room. Sure, I didn't sleep with her, but—"

"You're acting like that's some minor technicality. It's not! It's a bloody big deal. It completely changes how I view what happened. You can see that, right?"

"I shouldn't have invited her back to my room full stop. It was a really, really shit thing to do."

"It was," she agrees. "*Really* shit. And I'd have been fucking furious with you at the time even if I'd known you'd only let her touch your chest. But the pain and hurt I've carried these last six years . . ." She covers her heart with her hand. "Six years, Lewis. Six fucking years!"

"I'm . . . sorry," I offer, fully aware of how pathetic this sounds given the torment I've put her through.

She presses her fingers to her temples, takes a few deep breaths, then yells out, "*Fuck!*"

The scream shatters the tranquil calm of the loch. I don't think I've ever heard Iona drop the f-bomb so many times in such quick succession. I suppose the situation calls for it, though.

"You . . ." Apparently, she can't think what to call me. Instead of a word, she lets out a strangled cry then clenches her hands into fists.

I'm fully expecting to be hit again and am quite happy to be her punchbag, but suddenly it's like the fight goes out of her. Her shoulders slump, and then the dam bursts. She removes her glasses and wipes at her eyes.

For as long as I can remember, I've hated seeing Iona cry. My instinct is to wrap an arm around her and comfort her. Back when we were younger, I'd have done that without a second thought. If she'd *really* been upset, I'd have gone off and baked a cake for her. But in those days, I wasn't the one responsible for her pain. Now I am.

Through sobs, she says, "For years I hated any visit to Bannock. After you lost your parents, Maw tried to look out for you, Ally, Jamie, and Cat, a bit like a surrogate mother. She kept the tradition of McIntyre and Stewart family meals going, meaning I had to share a table with you—eat with you—after what you did. Or at least, after what I thought you did. Even though I was hurting inside, I kept everything that happened between us a secret, out of some misplaced loyalty to my childhood friend. I didn't want other people to hate you the way I did.

"But now . . . now I learn my entire understanding of that event was wrong. I've carried so much needless pain, Lewis! Why didn't you tell me this before now?"

"I . . ." I clear my throat. "I didn't think I deserved to be forgiven."

"Jesus." Trembling, she swipes a finger beneath each eye. "I need to go away and think through all of this. It's a lot to take in." She gets to her feet, her movements shaky.

I stand too. "Shit. I'm sorry—again. You . . . do whatever you need to do. I feel so bad for making you cry."

She nods and, without another word, walks away, leaving me alone by the loch once more.

CHAPTER TWENTY-FIVE

LEWIS

IONA

Hi.

LEWIS

Iona! How are you doing?

IONA

I'm okay. How about you? Have you found the
last two days tough without so much as a
peep from me? Have you been thinking over
everything, and is your head ready to 🤯?

LEWIS

It's been a bit rough, aye. But I wanted to give
you time. I didn't want to rush you.

IONA

Wrong answer. The right answer was: "Two
days? That's nothing compared to what I put
you through. I didn't tell you the truth about
what happened for SIX YEARS!"

LEWIS

Shit. Sorry, that's what I should have said.

IONA

Yep, it is. Clearly, I haven't let you stew for long enough yet. I'll be back in touch in five years and 363 days. See you then!

LEWIS

Wait, don't go! At least let me grovel for a bit and beg for your mercy?

IONA

😔 Fine. Grovel away.

LEWIS

Okay, imagine me as a character in one of your historical romances. "Oh, most gracious and benevolent Iona! Take pity on this wretched soul. I can't sleep, eat, or think straight. Pray, forgive me for my transgressions!" . . . that any good?

IONA

Hmm, interesting approach, even if it doesn't sound like the dialogue in any book I've read. Also, do you remember what happens in my smutty historical romances after the heroine forgives the hero? They ALWAYS bang. Is that what you think is going to happen here?

LEWIS

Well, if you were up for it, I wouldn't say no . . . 😉

IONA

Bloody hell, Lewis! We're not teenagers anymore. Long gone are the days when, to score a handjob, all you had to do was stick a glow-in-the-dark condom on your dick. If you want to earn my forgiveness and repair the damage you've caused, you'll have to work a LOT harder than that before there's even a HINT of anything sexual.

I'm listening. BTW, are you at your maw's? Because I'm at the hotel. We could talk in person—I can pop across the road, if you like?

IONA

But isn't this how you prefer to have serious conversations? Are you forgetting how you broke up with me?

LEWIS

Okay, this is why I'd rather speak face to face. In texts, I can't tell whether you hate me or whether you think there's hope for us.

IONA

Seeing my face wouldn't help. I'm still very much undecided about you.

LEWIS

That's fair. Anyway, you were saying something about working hard to earn forgiveness? Tell me more.

IONA

Well . . . I was thinking of MAYBE letting you take me on a date. At some point. It's too soon after my break-up with Richard, but I'm not ENTIRELY opposed to the idea.

LEWIS

Really?!

IONA

Don't get too excited. Dating me is going to be a brutal, demanding process. Think of it like one of those reality TV shows. One wrong move, and you're eliminated. And if you DO get through the first date, the second will be even harder. The third, worse still. Up for it?

LEWIS

Of course. If it means winning you back, I'd do anything.

IONA

I was hoping you'd say that.

LEWIS

That sounds a bit ominous.

IONA

It is, but I'll come back to that later. First, let's talk about the date(s).

LEWIS

No need for the brackets. I'm confident I'll smash the first one.

IONA

Wow, you're cocky. I'm not nearly so sure. Anyway, here's the deal. Back when I was a student, we never did the dating part of relationships, only the sex part. Now I want to do the exact opposite.

LEWIS

Which means . . .

IONA

Fine dining, spontaneous getaways to exciting places, surprise romantic gestures. You'll be the perfect gentleman the entire time and will see to my every need. After, say, six months of impeccable behaviour, I MIGHT let you kiss me. On the cheek. Just a quick peck.

LEWIS

Okay. How long till I get to kiss you on the lips?

IONA

Hmm, another six months after that.

LEWIS

Jeez. And how long until we get to do other things?

IONA

Other things? Whatever do you mean? 😇

LEWIS

You know . . .

IONA

Oh, THAT stuff? That's YEARS away.

LEWIS

Ha! You'll never be able to resist me that long. I reckon you'll be stripping my clothes off me a few dates in.

IONA

Ah, but this is where my genius plan comes into play.

LEWIS

Care to explain?

IONA

Sure. So, over the course of YEARS, you will treat me as a lady, satisfying my every whim, while receiving, in return, no sexual rewards whatsoever. Not even a peek at my cleavage—I intend to start dressing VERY modestly.

LEWIS

Right . . .

IONA

But when it comes to YOU, things are completely flipped.

LEWIS

And that means?

181

IONA

I won't treat you like a gentleman. Nah, I'll be pretty rude to you and will look at you with mild disdain the entire time—while leaving you to pick up all the bills, of course. But here's my favourite bit. Whenever I ask you for a dick pic, you have five minutes to send one over. Fail to do so before the deadline and we're done.

LEWIS

LOL!

IONA

?

LEWIS

You are joking, right?

IONA

Lewis, the first time you got naked in front of me, I made you put on a glow-in-the-dark condom. Does this sound like a joke to you? Or does it sound EXACTLY like the sort of thing you'd expect me to say?

LEWIS

Shit, the second one. But really?

IONA

Aye. And consider this a formal request for the first picture. Your five minutes start now.

LEWIS

Whoa, slow down! I need to know for sure if you're joking or not. Sometimes I misunderstand humour when it's written down. The last thing I want to do is send you a photo of my cock, only for you to be like, "WTF did you send that? I was only pulling your leg!"

IONA

Not pulling your leg. Any time, day or night, I might message you, and when I do, you have five minutes. No more. And as a reminder, the timer for that first picture is already counting down . . .

LEWIS

But I could be in the restaurant or talking to a customer! I can't agree to this.

IONA

You're really taking the fun out of it. Okay, I promise not to make a request when the restaurant is open. And at other times, if you have a VERY good reason not to send a pic, I MAY—at my discretion—grant an extension. But there will be no leniency for this first photo. So what are you waiting for? 📷 🤳

LEWIS

Bloody hell, this is nuts. But okay, gimme a moment . . .

CHAPTER TWENTY-SIX

IONA

As the sun sinks towards the horizon, painting the landscape in warm shades of orange and pink, I ascend the stone steps that lead to the Glen Garve Resort's grand main entrance. Above me, the building's turreted silhouette stands tall against the twilight sky.

The concierge—Gregor, a local man—greets me with a friendly smile. He's dressed in a smart jacket and tartan trousers. "Good evening, Iona. Lewis is waiting for you inside." He holds open the door for me.

When I come here to use the gym, I go in via the leisure centre entrance, and there's no fanfare there. I could get used to this sort of treatment.

"Thank you, Gregor."

Inside, polished hardwood floors gleam under the light of crystal chandeliers. Elegant floral arrangements in large vases add a burst of colour, while modern art pieces hang alongside classic landscapes, creating an intriguing contrast.

It's been years since I was in this part of the building, and I'd forgotten how breathtaking it is. The small family-run Bannock Hotel has a special place in my heart, but the Glen Garve Resort operates on a different scale entirely and typically caters to a wealthier clientele. Tourists with money to spend come here for its luxurious facilities, respected golf course, and fine dining.

For most locals, a meal at the resort's restaurant is for special occasions only—it's not cheap. As a result, Lewis and I should be able to have a private conversation without Bannock residents constantly walking over to tell us how pleased they are to see us together. I don't even have to worry about the cost because tonight Lewis is paying.

I spot him over in the seating area, in a leather armchair beside a roaring fire. He rises and grins. The smattering of stubble he's sported since I returned to Bannock is gone. He's clean-shaven once more, as he always used to be. His chestnut hair is immaculately styled—short on the sides with just the right amount of tousle on top, as if he casually raked his fingers through it with just a touch of wax.

My gaze trails down to the charcoal tweed jacket that fits his broad shoulders perfectly, showcasing the strength beneath. His crisp white dress shirt is tucked into grey wool trousers that accentuate his long legs, while brown brogues complement the leather belt around his waist. Damn, he looks good.

It's perhaps a little silly that we came here separately, given we live opposite each other. Maw certainly made a few comments about it as she dropped me off, despite her delight that Lewis and I are *finally* going on a date. But, hey, a girl likes to make an entrance every once in a while. As Lewis sweeps his eyes over me from head to toe, taking in every detail, I'm confident I made the right call.

My mid-length wrap dress, crafted from stunning navy blue chiffon, drapes elegantly around my curvy frame. The fabric is adorned with shimmering stars and planets, creating a galaxy effect that sparkles with every movement. Sheer butterfly sleeves add an almost ethereal touch. I've teamed the dress with bright-green low-heeled ankle boots, which don't match the navy at all, but I love the bold clash.

Lewis takes in everything while striding over to greet me, but I notice he pays special attention to my cleavage. In my opinion it strikes the perfect balance—tempting yet tasteful.

"Iona. Wow. You look incredible." A mischievous sparkle dances in his dark-brown eyes. "And this isn't nearly as modest as you threatened."

"Is that a complaint?"

"Definitely not." He hugs me in greeting, treating me to a whiff of his enticing, spicy aftershave.

Over the last six years, there have been occasions I've had to give Lewis a quick, reluctant embrace. Coming home for Christmas, say, I'd hug Ally, Jamie, and Cat then have no choice but to hug Lewis too, so no one noticed the omission and thought it odd. This is different, though. I don't find it uncomfortable at all. In fact, I appreciate the solid wall of his chest pressing gently against mine.

As he holds me, he murmurs into my ear, "Given I've now sent you several intimate photos, I'm glad you decided to rethink your wardrobe."

His scent, his hushed tone, the heat radiating from his body . . . this is dangerous territory. I can't let myself forget that he's on trial here. He needs to prove himself to me.

And yet, after withdrawing from him, I can't resist engaging in a little teasing banter. "You've kept to the five-minute deadline so far. Well done."

His mouth curls into a lopsided smile that sends shivers down my spine. "I'm good at meeting deadlines," he replies smoothly, then he inclines his head towards the restaurant entrance. "Shall we?"

Through the open doorway, the soft hum of conversation mingles with the soothing melodies of a piano. The maître d' greets us then guides us past crisp white tablecloths, gleaming cutlery, and the gentle flicker of candle flames to the table that Lewis has booked. We're beside a tall window that offers a panoramic view of the glen. The hills are awash with a warm, ethereal glow that creates an almost magical atmosphere.

Lewis slips his jacket over the back of his chair, his muscles stretching the fabric of his shirt nicely. He dips into his jacket pocket and pulls out a flat, rectangular jewellery box, which he lays on the table as we take our seats.

"I saw this in the Otter's Holt. It's just a wee thing."

I draw the box towards me and open it, revealing a delicate bracelet with a small silver pig charm.

"I hope it's okay. I know pigs aren't renowned for their beauty, but I thought it was kind of cute, and it reminded me of that time when I dared you to—"

"—free Fergus Murray's pigs," I finish, smiling. It's adorable, with tiny legs and a round belly. "I love it. Thank you." I slip it on.

He beams, pleased. "So I've not been eliminated from the dating competition yet?"

"Not yet, but it could happen anytime. I'm going to be testing you all throughout this meal. Do you know Rudyard Kipling's poem 'If'?"

He nods.

"Well, I'm looking for someone who can walk with kings without losing the common touch. A bit like myself, I'd say. Yes, I enjoy smutty historical romances, but I can hold my own in discussions about current affairs or the latest innovations in veterinary science."

Aye, I *can*, but generally, after a hard day's work, all I want to do is let my hair down—not engage in anything highbrow. But I'm trying to challenge him here. And anyway, if I can't put on airs somewhere like this, where can I?

"As for you," I continue, glancing around then lowering my voice, "I'm aware you can send a dick pic on command, so that's the second requirement ticked off. But can you walk with kings, Lewis McIntyre?"

He leans back, steepling his fingers. "I'd like to think so, but how do I prove that to you?"

"The other day, at the loch, I said that if you can't laugh at a penis, you're taking life too seriously. I stand by that comment, but I also acknowledge there's a time and a place. And this"—I gesture around the posh restaurant—"is neither. This is a place for scintillating, clever conversation, and I need to know that you can take part in such exchanges. I'm not twenty-one anymore, and while I may still enjoy a dick joke, there are other facets to my personality. I want a partner who's the same—someone who can make me laugh but also stimulate me intellectually."

He scratches the back of his head. For the first time tonight, a flicker of doubt crosses his face. "Er . . . you know I never went to uni, Iona."

Damn it, there's something about this flash of vulnerability that melts my heart, just a wee bit. I'm trying to put him through his paces, not feel sorry for him. I warned him that dating me would be challenging.

Still, I soften my tone a little. "You manage a hotel, Lewis. I bet you know a lot about tourism and issues affecting the Highlands. You also help in the restaurant, and you've always liked baking. Plus, you're keen on health and fitness. Engage me with fascinating facts. Entertain me with witty anecdotes. I don't care that you didn't go to uni—that's not the point. With sex not on the cards for the foreseeable future"—I will absolutely *not* cave to his good looks anytime soon—"and with dick jokes off the table, prove to me that Lewis McIntyre, now aged twenty-seven, is still a fun and interesting person to be around."

In a flash, his uncertainty is gone. A confident smirk lifts the corners of his mouth. "Oh, I can do *that*."

And he does. Well, his stories are more entertaining than intellectually stimulating, but that works for me. I hadn't *really* wanted an in-depth discussion about Scottish tourism—amusing tales about funny things guests have done or said are far better. But we keep it clean. We engage in wholesome conversation that wouldn't make my maw blush, and I have a really good time.

When we were younger, we could talk for hours and hours, day after day. As the wine flows, we gradually slip back into the effortless rhythm we once had. Soon we're chatting as freely and easily as we did in our youth.

I don't make Lewis do all the talking. I amuse him with a few of what my brother, Aidan, calls my "Bridget Jones moments". Like the episode where, as a newly qualified vet, I tripped and fell into a sheep's water trough. I was so embarrassed I told the farmer I'd been head-butted into it by the ram.

For some reason I have a whole catalogue of such stories—I honestly don't know how I get myself into these situations. As I work my way through them, Lewis grins and shakes his head, those dimples of his making an appearance.

The food, of course, is incredible. We both start with seared scallops—tender and succulent, with a buttery richness that melts in my mouth—then I have the truffle parmesan risotto, while he opts for the crispy orange duck breast. The risotto is a symphony of flavours, each mouthful a decadent experience.

After finishing our main courses, a somewhat mischievous idea comes to me. It's not at all appropriate for this setting, nor in line with how I told Lewis tonight was going to go. But then I have to keep him on his toes, don't I? I can't let him get too comfortable.

Lifting my phone as though to check a message, I tap it a few times, bringing up a certain image. Then, after glancing around the restaurant to ensure no one is looking our way, I turn the screen to him, just for a second.

His eyes widen, and a deep crimson flush colours his cheeks. "Bloody hell, Iona!" he whispers, squirming in his chair. "Someone might have seen that."

"Relax, I made sure no one was looking." Leaning closer to him, I add, "I call that one *Dick at Dawn*."

Despite being visibly flustered, he lets out a nervous laugh. "You named the pictures?" His mouth tugs upwards ever so slightly.

"Of course."

I requested that image after I woke early one morning and couldn't get back to sleep. He took a rather naughty snap by his bedroom window, and the hills and the sky are really quite beautiful in the background—almost pretty enough to draw the eye more than the main attraction. What frustrates and excites me most, though, is my curtains are visible in the picture. Had I thought to open them, I might have seen him take it. Instead, I was still lying in my bed when it came through.

Lewis inches closer to me, a conspiratorial glint in his eye. "This whole thing is pretty cruel, you know. I mean, I have to get into a certain state to snap these pics, and then I'm all worked up afterwards, and I have to try and calm down again."

"Don't blame me for that. I never specified that the pictures had to be of you when you're erect. You decided that yourself."

He raises an eyebrow. "Bloody hell, I'm not taking photos of my cock when it's soft. That'd be fucking weird."

I don't know why he feels so strongly about this point, but the forcefulness of his statement makes me laugh. I've seen his penis when it's soft—not for a long time, admittedly—but I remember it being really quite lovely.

"Anyway," he says in a low voice, "you were always the one who took the lead in the teasing, but when we actually . . . you know . . . *I* was in control. You said sex was *years* away"—he smirks, not believing me for a second—"but just so you're aware, when I've been taking these pics, I've been thinking very carefully about what I'm going to do to you when it finally happens. I've got it all planned out, and trust me, it's going to make every fantasy you've ever had seem pretty fucking tame."

He holds my gaze, and my pulse quickens at the raw hunger I see there.

"You're right to keep me waiting, but the longer you put it off, the more worked up I'll get, and so the more details I'll add to my plan. It's already pretty extensive. If you resist for too long, there'll be so much we need to fit in, we won't be able to leave the bed for days."

His words send a wave of heat straight to my core. The wine has loosened me up, and this promise turns me on more than I care to admit. I can almost feel his hands on me already, guiding me through every wicked scenario he's imagined. My heart races at the thought of him pushing himself inside me, filling me completely. I clench my thighs together and bite my lip, desperately trying to focus on something else, but it's impossible with him looking at me like he wants to devour me.

God, given our history, I absolutely *cannot* cave to Lewis any time soon. Like I said to him by text, we *have* to work on the other parts of our relationship—the romance, the bits we didn't explore enough when we were younger. But for how long will I be able to resist him? On future dates I really must go easier on the wine. Because the way I'm feeling right now, it would be all too easy to let him do what he wants to me.

Lewis lifts his water and takes a very long sip, staring out the window as he does so, like he's trying to calm himself down. When he eventually lowers his glass, he meets my gaze again and winks. "Anyway . . . shall we look at the dessert menu?"

CHAPTER TWENTY-SEVEN

IONA

Perched high on its rocky throne, Edinburgh Castle stands proudly above Scotland's capital city, watching over the bustle of people and cars on this crisp late October morning. For the past ten minutes, I've been convinced that it's to the historic fortress that Lewis is leading us—but no. We walk on past it and continue along one of the Old Town's picturesque streets, lined on either side with tall, narrow buildings made of weathered stone.

"So . . . our mystery date isn't at the castle."

"Nope." Lewis grins. "And I'm not giving you any clues, so stop fishing."

He's ridiculously upbeat, considering we left Bannock at six this morning. Then again, he's used to getting up early. Me, less so. I've only just finished my second coffee of the day, but I'm still sleepy. I don't want to come across as ungrateful, given he's whisked me away for the weekend, but to justify the early start, this surprise—whatever it is—better be bloody good.

We've left our overnight bags in the car for now, but Lewis has a large—and heavy-looking—rucksack on his back. He's being tight-lipped about its contents, so it must relate to the date somehow, but I can't think what could be in there.

"Are we going on . . . a picnic?"

He laughs. "You'll never get it, so there's no point guessing. But trust me, you're going to love it."

There's a boyish energy about him today, and tired though I am, there's something infectious about it. I think he's excited because he has a Saturday and Sunday off from the hotel—the others are covering for him. He's a bit like a kid on the first day of the summer holidays, with no more school for weeks.

Or . . . maybe there's another reason he's buzzing.

"I'd like to make clear, once again, that you will *not* be getting lucky this weekend, Lewis. As I told you, sex is years away."

It's been a month since we went to the Glen Garve Resort for dinner, and since then, I've insisted that Lewis dial down the romance when organising dates. We need to focus on re-establishing our friendship, and at the resort we got *way* too hot and bothered. I blame the wine. And the fact we were both dressed up and looked so damn good. The orgasmic food and opulent surroundings didn't help either.

"Don't worry, we're not sharing a bed tonight. We've each got our own." He nudges my shoulder playfully.

We've not yet kissed, but he's not above trying to fit in a bit of physical contact where he can. To be fair to him, though, it's always innocent.

"I know the rules," he adds. "Nudity is strictly for photographs only."

By now I have enough images of Lewis's penis that I could, if I wished, compile a rather risqué coffee-table book. It'd certainly be a conversation starter. I think I'd call it *Dick Pics: A Visual Journey*.

Much like our dates, the sending of such photos has become less overtly sexual and more playful—if that's not too odd a thing to say. I tweaked the rules because, really, how many "regular" pics do you need to see of a guy's dick? Once you've seen a few, you've seen them all, right? That's why I now give Lewis a little more time along with a challenge, like *Make it look like something else* or *Include a prop I wouldn't be expecting* or *Take it with your kilt on (but no boxers, obvs)*.

And you know what? It's so *fun*! I always look forward to seeing what he comes up with, and wow, he has quite the creative streak. Now that we're both over the initial naughtiness of the game, I find I mainly giggle at the pictures rather than being turned on by them, but Lewis is okay with that. He sees the funny side too. I love that he's never taken himself too seriously in front of me that way. I can't imagine many guys are as uninhibited.

We continue walking, leaving Edinburgh's Old Town behind us and entering the more modern area of the West End.

"Whatever you've organised, I doubt it'll top the last date," I comment.

"Oh, I wouldn't be so sure."

I give him a sceptical look. "What could possibly beat puppy yoga? The cutest cocker spaniel puppies clambering all over us and nibbling at our toes, while Grace attempted to talk us through our Sun Salutation and get us into Downward-facing Dog . . . it was one of the greatest hours of my life."

Lewis set up the class himself, arranging it with Grace and a local breeder and running it in the hotel's function room. It was a hit with everyone who attended, and there are already talks about putting on another session. The puppies were just so adorable! Aye, I love my wee niece, Callie, and Lewis's nephew, Ru, but I could play with a baby all day long without feeling the slightest urge to become a mother any time soon. But after one hour with those puppies, I was *desperate* to get a dog. Still am.

The yoga was incredible, but to be fair to Lewis, all the dates he's arranged so far have been a success. Some other highlights include a baking class in Auchenford, a pottery-painting session at the Coffee Bothy, and a comedy show in Inverness, where I laughed so hard I thought I was going to pee myself. If Lewis thinks this date is going to be better than everything we've done so far, it must be bloody special.

Before too much longer, Lewis nods to a sleek, modern building. "That's where we're headed."

It's a conference centre, and as I take in the banners hanging outside, my heart skips a beat. "Are we . . . are we going to a romance book event?"

He beams proudly, both dimples showing. "Aye, we are. Good, eh?"

"Oh my God, Lewis!" I clap my hands together and bounce on my feet like a wee kid who's just been told they're going to Disneyland. And then, because I don't know what else to do with this exhilaration, I fling my arms around him. "Thank you!"

"You're very welcome," he says, chuckling. He wraps an arm around me and draws me a little closer to him—any opportunity, the sneaky devil.

But I don't object. The man has earned a hug. I'm not going to take that away from him.

Inside, Lewis shows our tickets and we collect wristbands. The centre is buzzing with excitement. No one I know is as obsessed with romance novels as I am, so to come here, to a place filled with like-minded people . . . wow!

It'll be nice to chat with other readers, but what sends a shiver of pure joy down my spine is that, according to a sign I spot, over two hundred romance authors from across the world are in attendance today. And when I take in some of the names . . . oh my! I can hardly believe this. I didn't have any idea this event was taking place. I could have missed it! Lewis has surpassed himself.

The conference centre is *huge*. There are multiple levels, and each has several rooms. Apparently, there are authors to visit in all of them. There's also a pop-up bookstore. I don't know where to begin!

Unsure if there's a better way to plan our time, I suggest we start off in the nearest room. Around the hall, authors sit behind tables on which their latest books are displayed, along with swag such as bookmarks. Their names are emblazoned on colourful tablecloths or vertical banners. Straight away I notice several big-name authors, easily identifiable by the long lines of readers waiting to meet them. But with equal excitement, I spot a writer whose debut I enjoyed a few months ago and who seems to be free at the moment.

"How does this work?" I whisper to Lewis. "Can I just go up and . . . speak to people?"

"Aye," he confirms. "Ask them questions, get them to sign things, take a selfie with them. There's no charge for any of that stuff—it's all included in the ticket price."

"This is incredible." My voice is tinged with awe.

I'm about to approach the debut author when another attendee walks by us, wheeling a suitcase behind her. My initial assumption is that she can't have checked into her hotel yet. But then I realise she's far from the only person to have a case with her—a lot of readers have brought them. I ask Lewis if he knows why.

"Aw, shit. Aye, I almost forgot." He drops his rucksack. "I

nipped into your maw's yesterday and went through your, er, *extensive* romance book collection, comparing it to the list of authors who are here today. I then packed up some books so you could get them signed."

He unzips his bag, and when I look inside, I . . . well, I know it's silly, but I actually get a tad emotional. He's brought some titles I absolutely adore, which must mean their writers are here—and I'm going to get to meet them.

Tears threaten to spill. I have to wave at my face and take a few deep breaths. "This is a little overwhelming, Lewis. It would have been one thing had I bought a ticket for this months ago and been eagerly counting down the days, but I didn't even know this event was happening. Bringing me here and surprising me with this . . . it's too much happiness all at once! I can't cope with these emotions."

He chuckles. "Well, any time you think you might need a hug, just let me know. I'm right here."

"Yes!" I open my arms for him. "I'll take another hug, please."

He draws me in and holds me to him, his body warm against mine.

"In the entire history of the human race, I think this is probably the greatest date a man has ever taken a woman on." My voice comes out squeaky because I'm so overcome. "I'm being serious."

"Really? Wow! I was about to say if you see any new books you want to pick up, just let me know and I'll buy them for you. But if it's already the best date ever . . ."

I draw back from him and gaze at him seriously. "Lewis, be very careful. Do *not* tell me to grab any new books I want. I'll bankrupt you—you'll lose everything. We need to agree on some limits. How about this? I'll only buy five new books." I think this through. "Actually, that's rubbish. Okay, ten. In fact . . . maybe fifteen."

He smirks. "How about I just warn you when my funds are getting low?"

So we work our way around the room, and I lose myself in a sea of books and authors. There's an incredible mix of folk here, with writers from every subgenre I can think of: billionaire, romantic suspense, cowboy, paranormal, mafia, sports . . .

There are historical authors too, of course. Those stories remain my favourite—I think they always will—but I've cast my net more widely in recent years and dipped into contemporary stuff. It's really amazing to see such a wide range of books represented, with love being the one unifying theme across these tales, no matter what else may be different.

"What's monster romance?" Lewis asks, adding yet another new purchase to the rucksack.

I follow his gaze to a table that's apparently very popular with readers. The author's covers all show a human woman in the embrace of a green-skinned orc.

"Isn't it self-explanatory? I've actually never read a monster romance before, but maybe I should. After all, the first dick I ever saw was green—and monster-sized."

Lewis smiles cockily and puffs out his chest. "Well, the colour was from the condom, but the size? All me."

A nearby group of attendees burst into giggles, and I realise we weren't speaking as quietly as we should have been. Thankfully, they're not offended in the slightest, but Lewis's cheeks redden.

He rubs the back of his neck, his cockiness melting into a sheepish grin. "Sorry. Guess I need to work on my indoor voice."

Being one of the few men here, he attracts a lot of attention.

As we continue around the hall, he receives admiring glances from more than a few readers, as well as from a number of authors. I don't know what impresses them more—the way he looks or the way he carries my books for me without so much as a peep of complaint.

The rucksack soon fills up, so I have to deposit new purchases straight into his arms. Finally I understand his obsession with the gym. Clearly, all his efforts over the last six years were leading up to this moment. He needed the strength so he could lug around a crazy number of romance books for me.

We spend a full hour going around the first room before moving on to the second. I'm not sure how many rooms there are, but we're still just on the ground floor. The event goes on until five, and I think it's safe to say we'll be spending the whole day here.

In the new hall, I do an initial check of author names to see if there are any that catch my eye. Oh aye, there are a few people here I really like. This is great. But then I catch sight of a certain name, and it's like the world stops. I can't quite believe what I'm seeing. My heart flutters, and I feel a little weak in the knees. I grab a hold of Lewis's arm to steady myself.

Wow, he really *has* put on a lot of muscle over the years—but no, I can't think about that right now. Because . . .

"Lewis," I say, breathing heavily, "is that . . . who I think it is?"

At a table nearby are the words AURORA MCKENNA.

I squeeze Lewis's arm even tighter. "Is the author of the *Highland Hearts and Hidden Treasures* series really here? Oh God, I think I might faint."

I always thought it a little silly that, in a certain type of historical romance, there'd invariably be a moment when the heroine would faint. Now I realise it's an entirely reasonable response to intense emotion.

"Don't go fainting," Lewis says. "If you do, I'll have to drop all these brand-new novels to catch you."

"You're right." I nod bravely. "I'll pull myself together. For the sake of the books."

There's quite the queue at Aurora's table, as I'd expect, but the nice thing about that is I get to chat with other fans while we wait. And the more we all fangirl over how much we utterly adore her, the more excited we all become about finally meeting her.

By the time I make it to the front, I'm so buzzing with energy I don't know where to begin. Words fail me. Eventually I blurt, "May I shake your hand?"

Aurora smiles kindly, her emerald-green eyes sparkling. "Of course, sweetie."

Eagerly I reach out and clasp her. "It's no exaggeration to say that this is the single greatest honour of my life," I gush.

She lets out a rich, warm laugh. "Oh, that's such a lovely thing to hear. It's an honour for me to meet such a passionate reader."

Although many of her books are set in Scotland, she's American, and her voice has a smooth, melodic quality that draws me in.

Lewis, who's taken *Rival Clans, Secret Riches* out of his rucksack, passes it to me to present to Aurora.

"Would you mind signing this for me?" I say.

"I'd love to."

She raises her pen, and I desperately try to think of something more to say, but my brain is empty. What's wrong with me? There are so many things I'd like to ask her. I blurt out the only thing that comes to mind before thinking it through.

"My boyfriend and I once acted out a scene from that book." I gulp and then, for some odd reason, continue rather than shutting up. "The one where Eilidh tends to Douglas's wounds by the campfire . . ."

For the second time since arriving, Lewis's cheeks flush red. On this occasion, mine do too.

But Aurora just chuckles. "Did you now?"

My embarrassment is short-lived because I notice a pile of books on the table, and I can't quite believe what I'm seeing. "Is that a new story in the *Highland Hearts and Hidden Treasures* series? I thought you wrapped up that series years ago?"

"I did, but it's always been my most popular, and I thought perhaps there were a few more stories to tell. It's a novella, a bridging story between the original books and a new set of novels that'll start coming out next year."

"Oh. My. God."

Lewis doesn't have to be told to buy a copy—he just does it, transferring the book pile to one hand to do so. I ask Aurora to sign the new novella too, then I get a picture with her because . . . well, of course I want a photo with Aurora McKenna.

By the end of this event, I'll have a whole series of snaps of me posing with the most amazing authors. I can't imagine I'll be interested in receiving any more images from Lewis. Why would I be when I can look back through my memories of today? Dick pics were *so* yesterday.

After saying a reluctant goodbye and leaving the table, I say to Lewis, "I can't believe that just happened. We actually met her!"

"Do you realise you referred to me as your boyfriend when you were speaking with her?" He seems pretty chuffed about it.

"Did I? Oh, don't read anything into that. I was overwhelmed—I wasn't thinking straight. Besides, it would have taken too long to explain our actual relationship."

Lewis's grin doesn't waver in the slightest, but I don't have time to worry about that. I need to replay every second of that meeting and relish it all. I don't even know what she wrote in my books! I open my copy of *Rival Clans, Secret Riches* to see.

To Iona,

I was pleased to hear this book "inspired" you and your boyfriend!

Aurora McKenna x

Lewis glances over my shoulder and reads the inscription. "Ha! 'Boyfriend'. If your hero thinks that's who I am, why don't we just make it official?"

"Nice try, but don't go getting any ideas. You're only my literary packhorse, not my knight in shining armour. Now, giddy-up! It's time for you to trot along to the next table."

CHAPTER TWENTY-EIGHT

IONA

"I don't see what the problem is. We've each got our own bed." Lewis sets down our overnight bags.

"The problem, Lewis, is that they're in the same room."

He's booked us into a luxury hotel with an incredible view of the castle. I can see it through our window, illuminated in soft golden light, standing majestically against the night sky. The room itself radiates extravagance and, yes, there *are* two beds, each adorned with crisp white sheets and deep burgundy throws. But when Lewis reassured me about the sleeping arrangements, I'd pictured two separate rooms—not this.

"It might be fun, no? Means we get to hang out a while longer. Remember when we were young and had sleepovers?"

I cross my arms. "Those stopped when we hit puberty, Lewis. Presumably because our parents didn't trust us in a room together."

"True, but we're twenty-seven now—mature enough to control our baser instincts, right?"

I drum my fingers on my arm and narrow my eyes.

He stuffs his hands into his pockets then rocks back on his

heels. "Shit, Iona, I don't want to bring money into this, but . . . this place wasn't cheap! Two rooms would have been a stretch—especially after the number of books you bought today." He grins, attempting to lighten the mood, but when I don't reciprocate, his smile falters. "Crap. All right, I'll go down to reception and see if there are any other rooms going. If not, I should be able to find something nearby."

He hoists his bag back up. "You stay here. I'll, er, see you in the morning, all right?"

A pang of guilt hits me. "Wait! You *have* spent a lot on me these last few weeks, and . . . well, I appreciate you're not some hero from a billionaire romance. I suppose I should leave you with *something* in your bank account. You're right, we're old enough to be able to keep our hands to ourselves."

His face brightens again. "It's really not a problem for me to go, if you'd rather that. I don't want you to feel uncomfortable."

"Stay. I trust you can behave yourself. And you're right, maybe it will be fun to have a sleepover. Besides, I'm not ready for sleep yet, but after being on my feet all day, I don't have the energy to go out again. It'd be a shame to cut things short and go to different rooms."

"If you're sure, that'd be amazing because I don't think I can walk any further anyway." He collapses on a high-backed chair by the window and leans back with his hands behind his head, stretching out his long legs.

When we picked up our overnight bags from the car, we left my purchases there. Lewis didn't complain once all day about having to carry my books around, but even with his strength, it must have been tiring. Perhaps a suitcase with wheels would have been a better idea.

I lay claim to the bed on the left and, sitting, kick off my shoes and rub my aching feet.

"This is the life, eh?" Lewis murmurs. "No annoying wee brothers, no guests to look after . . ." He sighs contentedly. "I can't wait for breakfast in the morning. Not only do I get to sleep in—for once!—but I get to sit and enjoy food that someone else has made. I definitely owe your maw for covering for me."

"Och, you know what she's like. She was delighted to help out if it meant you and I could come here on a date."

While it would have been nice to have taken another look through all the books I bought today, even Lewis couldn't carry both them and our bags from the car. I did, however, grab one to bring with me: *His Highland Treasure*.

"I still can't believe Aurora McKenna is continuing the *Highland Hearts and Hidden Treasures* series. Since this one is a novella, it'll probably only take me a few hours to get through. That's a pretty good way of spending an evening, if you ask me." I swing my legs up onto the bed, adjust the pillows, then rest back against the headboard.

Lewis yawns and stretches. "If you're happy here, I think I'll grab a shower."

I gesture to the bathroom. "Go for it."

A minute later, water hisses and splashes against tiles, and I try not to be distracted by the thought of Lewis standing under the hot spray, droplets of water tracing every line and curve of his body.

I open *His Highland Treasure* to the title page.

To Iona,

I hope this story sends you and your boyfriend on another thrilling "adventure"!

Aurora McKenna x

I chuckle softly at the message. I made it clear to Lewis that I wasn't best pleased with the sleeping arrangements, but *is* it too soon to be thinking of bedroom adventures with him? I told him he'll have to wait a *very* long time, and yet I've simultaneously been asking him to send me rude pictures. A bit of a contradiction? Sure, but a fun one.

Yes, he hurt me once—badly—but he *was* struggling at the time. That doesn't excuse his behaviour, but it at least helps me understand it. The question is: am I genuinely worried he may one day do something like that again?

No. Not at all.

I know this man inside out. Sure, our friendship was on a break for a number of years and we're only just now rekindling it, but I *know* he has a good heart. The event that drove us apart . . . it really was just a blip.

Could I keep him waiting longer? Of course. But what was the epiphany I had at the top of the wind turbine? Life is short, and I have to be brave.

We've already lost six years. How much more time should I let go by? And what's the point of it? Because, in my heart of hearts, I'm sure it's Lewis I'm meant to be with. It's always been him.

I pick up my phone. I'm sitting here with a brand-new book in the *Highland Hearts and Hidden Treasures* series, and in my photos app there are wonderful pictures of me posing with

Aurora McKenna and many other authors. Nevertheless—and despite my earlier verdict that dick pics are *so* yesterday—I instead flick through the images that Lewis has been sending me. And yes, I giggle. Is it odd that I find it kind of sweet that he'll drop what he's doing and send me a pic when I request it? He always has been eager to please.

The picture I linger on the longest is the one of him in his kilt. Naturally, I dubbed it *Braveheart's Boner*. While I now mainly find Lewis's photos amusing, there's something about this image that really does it for me. It's so hot.

Out of the corner of my eye, I glimpse *His Highland Treasure*, the cover of which features a topless, muscular, kilted man. Ah. I think I know why I like *Braveheart's Boner* so much. I've always had a thing for kilts.

With horror, it occurs to me that, over the three years we were together, never once did Lewis make love to me while he was in a kilt. In fact, I've never had sex with any man while he was in a kilt. I'm twenty-seven and I live in Scotland. What have I been doing with my life?

When the bathroom door opens, I hurriedly get Lewis's erect penis off my screen. He emerges with a towel wrapped around his waist, his body otherwise bare. I look from him to *His Highland Treasure* and back. A towel . . . a kilt . . . they're not so very different, right?

I may be delighted by what I see, but I have to at least pretend to be outraged. "Lewis! Do you think it's appropriate for you to waltz around without a top on?"

We did agree nothing would be happening between us, and if *I* change my mind on that point, fine. But he doesn't get to test the boundaries.

"Er, sorry, is it a problem?" He seems genuinely taken aback by my indignation. He glances down at himself then meets my eye again. "I'm just quickly grabbing a change of clothes—I'll be putting them on in the bathroom, obviously. I go swimming at the Glen Garve all the time, and I have my chest out there. I didn't think it was an issue. A guy's chest isn't really a sexual thing the way a woman's is, right?"

Isn't it, Lewis? What about the night you broke my heart— why do you think that woman took your T-shirt off? Are you playing with me or are you really this clueless?

"If he's built like you, it's definitely a sexual thing." I hold up *His Highland Treasure*. "Why do you think the model doesn't have his top on, Lewis? Because he's sexy without it on, and sex sells."

"Ah. I see." He nods, a cheeky smile tugging at his lips. "So . . . you're saying I'm sexy, are you?"

"I did not say that, no." But I can't stop my eyes from trailing downwards to take a proper look at him. I mean, if he's not going to hide it . . .

The last time I saw Lewis topless was on that awful day, standing in his doorway in nothing but his joggers. Back then, his body was in its chrysalis stage, but now it's fully transformed, and it is a sight to behold.

His chest is a landscape of chiselled perfection. His pecs are broad and powerful, and they glisten with droplets of water he must have missed when drying himself. These trace pathways down to the grooves and ridges of his abs—a perfect set of six. Then there's his V-line, which is basically an arrow pointing under his towel, loudly proclaiming where his dick is, just in case I needed directions. His arms, meanwhile, are thick and veined, his dampness accentuating the contours of his biceps and triceps.

Hmm, maybe those muscles aren't *just* for carrying around

large numbers of romance books. I mean, I'm a curvy woman, but seeing him like this, I'm confident Lewis could get me into any position he wanted with ease. When we were younger and the lust took a hold of him, he'd always take control of our lovemaking, and I loved that. Now, though, he's got a strength he didn't have then, and it's hard not to wonder what possibilities that might open up.

As I take him in, he retrieves some clothes from his bag. He's about to head back into the bathroom when I tease, "Are you a true Scotsman under there?"

He smirks. "Obviously. Who wears underwear under a towel?"

"All right, well, before you get changed, give me a quick flash."

His eyebrows shoot up. "What?"

"Don't look so surprised. You've sent me a lot of pictures of your dick recently. Besides, you're adamant you won't take a photo of it when it's soft, so this is the only way I'll get to see it in its relaxed state. Go on."

"Er . . ." He shifts his weight from foot to foot. There's a smile playing on his lips—he's certainly not offended by my request—but he's unsure. "You're sending me mixed messages here. I thought we were just friends sharing a room?"

"We are. But friends can have a laugh, can't they? I just want to see it. It won't lead to anything."

"Right . . . er . . ." He makes no move. He doesn't do what I've asked him to do but nor does he retreat into the bathroom.

"Oh, for goodness' sake. *I'll* do it, then."

I stand and walk over to him. Lewis shrugs as if to say, *Whatever*. So I bend down, take a hold of his towel, and lift it up, just having the quickest glimpse underneath. I can't help but giggle. He chuckles too.

"All right, that was all." I drop the towel again. "You may get changed."

Shaking his head but still smirking, Lewis disappears into the bathroom. He comes out shortly later in a grey T-shirt and loose navy shorts. There's a strange juxtaposition between his toned arms and legs and something adorably boyish about the outfit. When we were hooking up between the ages of eighteen and twenty-one, he'd sleep in his underwear—or, more commonly, naked. I don't remember him ever wearing jammies, but he's really kind of cute in them, like he's just begging to be snuggled up to.

"Looking comfy," I say.

"Aye, I am." He grins happily. "It's chilling time." He hops onto his bed and picks up the TV remote. "Are you okay if I see what's on?"

"Go for it. I'm going to wash as well. Is there a bath?"

"Aye, but just to let you know, there's no lock on the door. Not to worry, though. I'm a gentleman."

I give a curt nod. "Good. Because the last thing I'd want is for you to burst in with me lying there, naked, my body covered in soap suds, rubbing my hands *all over* as I wash myself . . ."

"Jesus." He glances away from me for a moment.

"If I looked at your dick now, would I notice any changes?" I tease. "Might it be starting to stiffen up?"

"Bloody hell, there's teasing and then there's this. You're *really* winding me up." He shifts slightly. "I know we said no sex, but you're testing my self-restraint here. I'm going to watch TV and try to clear my head of all the filthy images you're putting in it. Don't get me wrong, if you change your mind about things, just let me know. Until then, even if you're lying naked just a few metres from me, in an unlocked room, rubbing your hands all over yourself, I won't be doing anything."

"Understood." I take off my top.

His eyes widen in shock. "What the fuck are you doing?"

"Er, getting ready for my bath?" I tug my jeans off. "What's the problem? You thought it was fine to be in front of me in a towel because, at the pool, you're in nothing but shorts. Well . . ." I glance down at my bra and knickers. "These cover about the same as a bikini, don't you think? And what we can't have is one rule for you and another for me."

A flush creeps up Lewis's neck. He's put the TV on but is paying it no attention. His gaze is on me.

He wipes a hand over his face, and—oh! Was that a twitch in his shorts? Ha, he really is too easy to toy with.

"Enjoy your chilling," I say, then I head into the bathroom.

I twist the hot water tap and steam begins to rise, filling the room with a warm, misty haze. After I add a generous amount of bubble bath, the tub soon froths up. I slip out of my remaining clothes and sink into the blissfully warm water, its heat seeping into every muscle. Heavenly.

Minutes pass in sheer relaxation, but then I get a little bored. I could do with something to pass the time. Like a book, for example.

"Lewis?" I call. "Could you bring through *His Highland Treasure*? I'd like to read it while I soak."

There's a pause. Then, "Er . . . aren't you naked in there?" His voice wavers—with hesitation, but also with a hint of something else. Desire.

"The bubbles are covering me. Don't worry, you can't see anything naughty."

A second pause. "I don't know that this is a good idea, Iona."

"Oh, stop being such a prude! Just come in, hand me my book, then you can leave again."

He mumbles something under his breath and then the bathroom door opens. He glances at me, then quickly up to the ceiling, then back to me—and this time his gaze lingers, roving over me, taking in the bits of my body that rise from the bubbles, and perhaps also imagining those parts hidden from view. I'm impressed he *tried* to look away—he gets a point for that. But I'm also glad he couldn't resist the temptation to ogle.

"Er . . ." He takes a step towards me and thrusts the book in my direction. "Here you go."

I make to take it but then snatch my hand away. "Oh no! I forgot. *I* can't hold it. My fingers are all wet, and it's a brand-new book—and signed. I don't want to risk it getting damaged."

"Right . . ." His gaze drops from my face to my chest. My nipples are hidden, but there's still plenty of boob on show.

"I've got an idea!" I point to the floor beside the bath. "Why don't you sit there? You can hold the book up for me so I can read it while I'm in here."

"Iona . . ." He gulps. "I know you think it's fun to tease me, but there are limits to what I can take."

"You're the one who insisted we share a room tonight and hang out, so why would you want to be through there watching TV while I'm here soaking in the bath? This is an opportunity for us to spend a bit more time together, isn't it?"

He runs a hand through his hair, saying nothing for some moments, then finally he shakes his head. "You're impossible." But despite this protest, he kneels beside the tub. He opens the book and holds it up. "Just don't blame me if I get distracted and drop it."

"Thank you. You can read the hero's lines—I'll be the narrator and the heroine."

"Wait, we're reading it aloud?"

"Of course. Otherwise, we'd read at different speeds and it'd be a pain."

"Right. I didn't realise I was going to be reading it at all. I just thought you wanted me to sit here and hold it for you while I suffer in sweet agony. But okay. Er . . . is this story likely to be as spicy as the one I read that time in your halls of residence?"

"Without a doubt—it's her trademark. It wouldn't be an Aurora McKenna book if it were closed door. Her fans would riot."

"Right. So . . . you're naked in the bath, and I'm to sit here, right next to you, and read a sexy story with you. And yet nothing is going to happen between us?"

"Correct," I confirm. "You assured me you'd be a gentleman, so I expect you to keep your hands to yourself. This is just two friends passing some time together."

He rubs the back of his neck. "Jesus. But all right, *friend*, let's do this. Seeing as you're the narrator, kick us off, please."

I do.

Like all the stories in the *Highland Hearts and Hidden Treasures* series, it's pretty formulaic, but that's not a criticism—far from it. I love the formula, and I'd have been upset had Aurora McKenna strayed from it.

The hero, Logan, and heroine, Marion, begrudgingly team up on their search for treasure, working their way through a series of clues, each one leading them ever closer to the riches. Although they start off on the wrong foot, sparks soon fly and desires flare.

Aurora never takes long to get to the good bits, but seeing as this is just a novella, it's no time at all before the characters are getting down to it. With their adrenaline high after a thrilling escape from rival treasure hunters, Logan and Marion take refuge in a small cave, and one thing quickly leads to another.

"The moment Logan's lips left hers," I read aloud, "Marion trailed her fingers down his chest, finally grasping his cock with a needy grip."

"Whoa, whoa, whoa!" Lewis protests, stopping the story. "What's going on? What happened to 'shaft'? Or 'claymore'? Or any of those other funny euphemisms she used to use? Aurora McKenna just said 'cock'!"

I was really getting into the scene so am a little upset by this interruption. "Sex scenes in romance books have changed over the years, Lewis. Tastes have evolved, and things that were once taboo are now accepted—expected, even."

"Oh. That makes sense, I suppose. The words and phrases she once used were pretty silly, but they did have an odd kind of charm."

"Anyway, let's keep going. It's your line next."

Lewis nods. "Marion, feel how hard I am for you. Every inch of me is aching to be inside you."

Out of curiosity, I peer over the edge of the bathtub. The outline of Lewis's impressive erection is unmistakable through his shorts.

I smile with satisfaction. "Wow, Lewis, you're *really* getting into character!"

His cheeks flush, and he scratches behind his ear. "Sorry, but this scene is hot—and you're naked and wet. I can't help it."

"Well, as you've been sending me pictures of the thing for the past few weeks, I suppose I can't pretend to be shocked by it. All right, take your shorts off."

"*What?*"

His surprise is understandable. My instruction comes out of nowhere, without preamble.

"Go on!" I encourage. "Logan's got his dick out. You should get yours out too. As we read on, it'll add a certain something to the scene if I can look at your penis and imagine it's Logan's."

Despite his surprise, a playful glint lights up Lewis's eyes. "Well, right now Marion is holding Logan's cock, so if you hold mine, I bet the scene will start to feel *really* real for you."

"Nope." I shake my head resolutely. "I won't be touching you tonight, and you won't be touching me. There will be no physical contact between us at any point."

I adopt a serious tone so he understands this isn't part of the game. This is me clearly stating boundaries.

"Fuck, okay, but . . . what's going on here, Iona? I mean . . ."

"You can't touch me, Lewis, but you're very welcome to touch yourself."

Under the bubbles, I slide my hand down, just to ease the ache there. Even though Lewis can't see, his sharp intake of breath tells me he knows exactly what I'm doing.

"Shit. Are you . . . ?"

"I want us to finish reading the scene." Carefully parting my folds, I find my clit and tease it gently. "I don't care if the book gets wet. Give it to me." I hold out my other hand for it. "I'll read the rest. You stand, remove your clothes, and hold on to your dick. I want to see what you do with it."

He hesitates—for all of a second. Then he gets to his feet, pulls his T-shirt over his head, and drops his shorts. As I take in the sight, I move my hand under the water more insistently, waves of pleasure washing over me.

"I much prefer seeing it in the flesh to on my phone," I admit. "Now grip it. Pump it!"

He doesn't need any more encouragement. "Can I . . . splash some of the bubbles away?" he asks, his breath hitching. "I want to see what you're doing down there."

"No." I shake my head. It thrills me to be able to see all of him while my own body is tantalisingly concealed.

"Fuck, you're such a tease!" But he accepts the rules and continues stroking himself.

As I watch him, I push a finger into myself, then two. I curl them slightly to hit that spot that always makes me see stars. I turn my attention back to the page, although it's hard to focus on it.

I continue reading the scene aloud. My breathing grows heavier, synchronising with the rhythm of my fingers. A moan escapes my lips, but I push on, narrating the joining of Logan's and Marion's bodies, their heated breaths mingling as they reach for that ultimate release. When Marion finally comes, my own orgasm surges through me, my body arching, my head falling back in a blissful daze.

The sight does something to Lewis because he works his dick even faster, and soon he too erupts in ecstasy. It's messy and raw, a sight that has me biting my lower lip.

"Fuck!" he moans.

"Good." I smile. "We both really needed to get that out of our systems. I think we'd have struggled to sleep in a twin room otherwise."

CHAPTER TWENTY-NINE

LEWIS

Following a lie-in and a hearty breakfast—one I couldn't fault—Iona and I are now packed up and ready to head downstairs to check out.

I lift the overnight bags. "Shall we?"

She nods then glances around the room as though capturing a mental snapshot of it. She has one last look out the window, taking in the view of the castle, then comes over to me by the door.

"After we spent all day yesterday at the book event, it'll be really nice to do some touristy things around the city with you today." She smiles. "Let's not head back to Bannock till late, all right? You hardly ever get a weekend off, so let's make the most of it."

I grin back at her. "That sounds perfect." I'm more than happy to spend as much time with her as I can.

"Oh, and just before we go . . ." She places her hands on my chest, rises onto her tiptoes, and kisses me.

At first, the unexpectedness of it freezes me to the spot, but then elation floods through me. For the longest time, I wasn't sure I'd ever kiss Iona again, but now it's finally happening. Her lips are so soft, and their warmth feels like coming home.

Dropping the bags, I cup her face, gently stroking her cheeks with my thumbs. Her hands slide up to my neck, her fingers weaving into my hair. I press my lips more firmly against hers, and she responds by pushing me against the door. A laugh escapes me even as our lips remain pressed together, but this quickly morphs into a groan when her mouth opens, giving me an invitation I can't refuse.

My heart racing, I deepen the kiss. Our tongues dance, and a symphony of moans and breathy whispers fills the air. Our kiss becomes hungry, fervent, years of suppressed emotions pouring out like water through a burst dam.

I draw her closer to me, the soft curves of her body moulding against mine. Her hands continue exploring, her fingers scraping lightly along my scalp, sending shivers down my spine. Through our clothes, I feel the heat radiating from her skin.

A surge of arousal rushes through me, and my cock hardens, pressing insistently against the denim of my jeans. The friction is both torturous and delicious. It makes me want more—no, *need* more.

My hands slide from her face down to her waist, then lower still, gripping her hips and pulling her even more tightly against me. She gasps into my mouth when she feels my hardness, and then a breathy giggle escapes her lips. She moves against me, rocking from side to side in a rhythm that sends shock waves through my entire body.

The tension between us builds to a fever pitch. Every movement, every touch, is amplified and significant. When our mouths finally break apart, we're both panting and flustered. I grin down at her, admiring her flushed cheeks and pink kiss-swollen lips.

I return one of my hands to her face, gently brushing her cheek, while my other remains on her hip, holding her firmly against me.

"Iona, this means the world to me." My voice wavers, rough with both emotion and desire. My words may be clichéd, but they're the truth. I wasn't sure I'd ever win her back, nor did I believe my life could be complete without her. For us to be taking this step . . . it means everything.

Aye, we've maybe not done things in the most conventional order. Some couples might have kissed *before* they did what we did last night. But hey, when we were eighteen, the kiss came first. It's nice to do things a little differently this time.

Dipping my head to her hair, I inhale deeply, the sweet strawberry scent filling my nostrils.

"When you showered this morning, you didn't use the shampoo the hotel provided, did you?"

"No." There's a hint of surprise in her voice. "I always bring my own. I've been using it for years—it works so well for my hair. I'd be so upset if they ever stopped making it."

"Me too." I play with a loose lock. "I have a lot of memories associated with that smell."

I plant a kiss on her neck. She shivers, and a soft, contented sigh escapes her lips.

"You know, maybe we don't have to wait *years* before sleeping with one another," she says. "I've thought about it, and . . . I've decided I'm ready now."

"Fuck, are you sure?"

She rolls her hips in a teasing motion, making me half gasp, half laugh.

"Aye."

My pulse quickens. My skin tingles with anticipation. "Well,

220

in that case, I guess the only question is . . . your bed or mine? Or shall I push them together to give us a bit more room?" I wiggle my eyebrows.

"Oh, wait a minute!" Iona glances over her shoulder and checks the clock on her bedside table. "Oh no! Have you seen the time? We've only got a couple of minutes to check out. We'll have to take a rain check." She feigns a pout, but her eyes twinkle mischievously.

"Iona, whatever the fine is for checking out late, I'll pay it."

"No, we can't do that. As everyone knows, I'm a bit of a goody two-shoes. I don't want to be fined."

"Bollocks! A goody two-shoes? You're anything but, and I love it."

"Okay, but you're a hotel manager. Imagine how hypocritical it would be if you were to be late for checkout when you expect your own guests to leave promptly. No, that wouldn't do at all. We'll just have to have sex another time."

"You like teasing me too much," I say gruffly. "You deliberately waited until we didn't have any time left, didn't you?"

She giggles. "Hey, you got a kiss."

"Aye." I smile. "I'll take that."

"We can do it tonight. Back in Bannock. Think you can wait until then?"

"If we head straight to the car now, and take just a short break for lunch, we could be in Bannock by three. What do you think?"

"Oh no, we can't do that. Remember what we agreed earlier? You hardly ever get a weekend off, so to make the most of it, we're going to stay in Edinburgh *all day*. No need to get home till late. I'd feel terrible were you to rush back on a rare day off, all on my account."

I sigh, and then chuckle. "Genuine question: doesn't all this teasing bother you too? I mean, I'm not the only one you're denying here."

"Of course it bothers me. Yesterday, when you were standing beside me, jerking off, I wanted you inside me so badly. But, unlike you, I'm okay with anticipation. It's part of the experience. I mean, where's the fun in immediate satisfaction? Delayed gratification is what it's all about."

"I've been waiting six years to have sex with you again. If we were to do it right here, right now, I don't think anyone on the planet would describe that as 'immediate satisfaction'."

"True, but if you've already been waiting six years, what's another ten hours or so, eh?" She flashes a smile. "All right, let's go. We don't want to be late for checkout!"

◆ ◆ ◆

It's after nine when we finally get back to Bannock. I had a really fun day with Iona: we visited Edinburgh Castle, walked the Royal Mile, and climbed Arthur's Seat. Was I distracted because I was desperate to take her to my bed? Maybe a little—okay, a lot—but I still appreciated getting to spend time with her. After so many years of things being strained between us, I'm now savouring every minute I get with her.

I park up outside her maw's and help Iona upstairs with her bag and her haul of books. We've got the place to ourselves—Elspeth must still be at the restaurant. On the drive up, Iona and I agreed she'd come over to my room, but if we're not going to be disturbed here . . .

Gently I place my hand on the small of her back and draw her closer to me, but she playfully pushes me away.

"Oi! You can wait another few minutes, you randy bugger.

Let me freshen up and get changed. I'll pop over to yours soon." She gives me a quick peck on the lips.

I suppose I *can* wait a few more minutes—just about. "All right, see you in a bit."

As I make for the stairs, she says, "Oh, just one thing."

"Aye?"

"Well . . . you've mentioned you have a lot of fantasies you want to try out."

"I do."

"And I've read a *lot* of romance books over the years. There are a whole host of scenes that live rent-free in my head. There are so many things I've wanted to try out but haven't been able to because past partners weren't open to experimenting or didn't have the strength. I'm confident I could try them with you, though. You and I have always been on the same wavelength about this stuff, and I reckon you're strong enough for us to try even the most adventurous positions."

I smirk. "I am." No point in being modest—I've spent a hell of a lot of time in the gym over the years.

"Anyway, my point is . . . with so many things we both want to try, how are we going to organise this?"

"Ah. You're right." I click my fingers. "We have to think of the *practicalities* of all the crazy, passionate sex we're going to have. Some people might claim sex should be spontaneous, and that being organised would take the excitement out of it, but I'm not convinced."

"Right? I think it'd be far sexier to take this *very* seriously." She places a hand on my chest. "We should act like we're researchers and give this the consideration it deserves."

A shiver runs down my spine. "Damn, there's something

insanely hot about the idea of you putting that brilliant mind of yours to our sex lives."

"Well, you run a hotel—you've got a head for organisation too. Between now and me arriving in your room, I want you to have a think about how we're going to tackle this project."

I grin. "Never have I been happier about being assigned a piece of work. I'll put my mind to it. See you soon."

I move the car around to the back of the hotel, grab my bag, and head inside. Finally, after a month of teasing, the exchange of I-don't-know-how-many rude photos, and a day of intense sexual frustration, I'm about to take Iona to my bed. Pure, unfiltered excitement courses through my veins.

Inside, Jamie is tidying up in the restaurant, but he stops when he spots me. "Lewis, thank God! While you were away, three customers got food poisoning, and the bathroom in room five flooded. It's been a disaster!"

My heart sinks. When it comes to the hotel, I'm normally extremely conscientious, but I just don't want to have to deal with this. All I want to do is take Iona upstairs. And bloody hell, food poisoning? How did *that* happen?

"Ignore your wee brother, the little troublemaker. None of that is true." Elspeth emerges from the kitchen and smiles at me. "We got on just fine. No incidents to report."

"Ha! Your face, though!" Jamie grins and does a wee dance. "You're so easy to wind up."

I shake my head but can't bring myself to get annoyed with him. I'm just relieved I don't actually have to deal with any of that stuff. After all Iona's teasing, it would have been awful if something else had delayed our date in my bed.

"Well, how did the weekend go?" Elspeth asks, tilting her head.

"Aye, it was really good. Iona loved the book event, and today we did the castle and a few other touristy things."

"Come on, tell us the good stuff!" Jamie leans in closer, lowering his voice to a whisper. "How was the sex?"

"*Jamie!*" Elspeth rebukes.

He really is the absolute worst. Why would he say that in front of Iona's maw?

"We slept in a twin room, in separate beds, and there was no sex," I report. It's the truth. There *was* a pretty hot scene in a bathroom, but no contact was involved.

"Bloody hell, you and Iona are so *boring*!" Jamie complains.

"Thanks, Jamie."

"Is Iona back in the house?" Elspeth asks.

Her smile has tightened almost imperceptibly. I get the strangest impression she's disappointed by my announcement that I didn't sleep with her daughter. Maybe I'm misreading her. No doubt she's just anxious that everything goes well between me and Iona, but even so, I'd rather she didn't have opinions about our sex life.

"Er, aye, she's across the road," I confirm.

"Great, I'll just finish up in the kitchen then go over and chat with her. Hopefully, I'll get more out of her about the weekend than I'm getting out of you!"

"Oh . . ."

Shit, while I've no desire to talk about anything sex-related with Elspeth, the days of sneaking Iona up to my room are gone. Iona and I discussed this on the drive up and were in agreement about it. We're adults, and if she's going to be spending the night with me, we're not going to hide that from anyone.

I need to set the record straight about what's going to be happening—tell Elspeth that Iona won't be available for a chat tonight—but I've no wish to have an extended conversation about the matter. That's why I casually make my way towards the stairs. With one foot on the bottom step, I say, "Er, maybe you could catch up with Iona tomorrow? The thing is . . . she's going to be staying in my room tonight."

A spark of surprise—and then, I think, delight—flickers in Elspeth's eyes, while Jamie whoops enthusiastically. He says something about knowing for a fact that my room isn't a twin room, but I ignore him and set off upstairs.

I've barely closed my door behind me when my phone pings. I check it. It's the McIntyre Clan Group Chat.

> JAMIE
>
> Cat, Ally, I have some BIG news about Lewis and Iona!

Bloody hell, he didn't wait long. Shaking my head, I choose to ignore the barrage of subsequent pings. It seems Ally and Cat are just as interested in the news as Jamie.

Going over to close my curtains, I glance across the street and notice that Iona's are already shut, although the subtle glow around her window tells me her light is on.

I leave my curtains for the moment and lift my phone. Ignoring the messages that have come in from Ally and Cat, I send one to Iona.

> LEWIS
>
> A spreadsheet. On the cloud. I'll add my fantasies, and you can add the scenes from your romance books.

> IONA
>
> Perfect! We can have columns for recording your rating, my rating, any comments/observations . . .

> Nice, I like the idea of rating each entry.
> That's hot.

All this chat about sex is amazing, of course, but this relationship is about so much more than that. This is my best friend, the only lass I've ever loved. She wanted to put off sex until we'd re-established the strong friendship we once had. I'm delighted she thinks we're ready to take the next step, but I hope I haven't been too sex-focused today. It's important she knows just how much she means to me.

LEWIS

> Open your curtains for a moment.

Across the way, Iona appears and smiles at me. I lean close to my window and blow hot air at it, steaming it up, then I draw a heart. It's a small gesture, but I hope she gets the message.

Iona draws one too then glances down and taps at her phone.

IONA

You're so sweet, Lewis. xx

But . . .

Back to our sex plan. We'll make a start on the spreadsheet tomorrow. For tonight, please put your kilt on (and nothing else) and get into your bed. I'll be over in a few minutes. x

CHAPTER THIRTY

IONA

The days have shortened and the nights lengthened, and the first hints of snow now dust the hilltops around our quiet town. Helpfully, Lewis knows exactly how to ignite a fire deep within me, chasing away the Highland chill.

Most of my things remain in Maw's house, and I nip back there all the time, but I haven't slept in my own bed for close to a month. Lewis and I have been hard at it, working our way through the sex spreadsheet. We've made a lot of progress, but there's still a way to go. The problem is, he's *very* imaginative when it comes to these things, and I've read a lot of romance books. As a result, there's a seemingly endless list of things we're keen to try out.

"Are you ready?" he says to me now.

I nod, my back to the wall. "Aye. I would ask if you are, but I don't think I need to." With a giggle, I glance down at his dick, which is rock hard and raring to go.

Recently I've grown accustomed to catching only tantalising glimpses of Lewis under his kilt, something I find incredibly hot. It's an interesting subversion of our dynamic that night on our Edinburgh trip. Now I'm the one who's typically completely naked, while his most private parts are often just out of sight.

Tonight, though, we're both as nature intended, and every inch of his formidable erection is on display for me to admire. For the position we're about to try, we agreed his kilt would only get in the way.

"I'm really looking forward to this one," Lewis says, bending to lift me, his eyes ablaze with anticipation, his muscles taut with excitement.

"Stop!" I blurt out.

He does, standing up straight again and raising an eyebrow. "Everything okay?"

"Are you *sure* you'll be able to support me? Because imagine you tire midway through, drop me, and . . . well, you know . . . *that* snaps." I point down, and Lewis's gaze follows my finger. "I love it, and I'd really hate for something to happen to it."

He shudders, and I can almost see the wheels turning in his head as he processes what I just said. "Thanks for that thought," he manages finally, rubbing the back of his neck. "I'm pretty attached to my cock too. But you don't have to worry—I can carry you, no problem."

"Okay. I suppose, if there *is* a disaster, we at least have plenty of photos to remember it by."

He blows out a puff of air. "Jesus, Iona! Could you *please* cut this chat out? You're giving me the chills, and you're worrying over nothing."

I nod but wordlessly take some moments to study his penis, etching every detail into memory, just in case. It helps that he doesn't have to cover it with a condom nowadays. When we were younger, I hadn't yet had the coil fitted, so we always used them.

It's been incredible these past weeks to explore our sexual fantasies without any barrier between our bodies.

"Oi, I know what you're doing!" Lewis says. "You don't have to take a mental snapshot of it. It'll be fine."

I look up and bite my lip. "Sorry!"

"Relax. The only thing happening to my cock tonight is that it's going to be deep inside you, driving us both wild." A devilish grin lights up his face.

Heat blooms between my thighs at his words, and I nod. "Aye. Okay, let's do this. I'm ready."

My back still to the wall, I clasp my hands behind his neck. He takes a moment to trace the outline of my lips with his thumb, then he gives me a cheeky wink, bends, and—gripping me where my thighs meet my arse—scoops me up. Held aloft by him, I wrap my legs firmly around his waist.

Lewis positions me so that his tip nudges my entrance, then he fixes his gaze on me and wiggles his eyebrows in a silly way that makes me chuckle. Slowly he lowers me onto him, guiding my descent with tender care, and my laugh becomes a gasp as he fills me, inch by inch. There's a delicious pressure as my inner walls accommodate him, sending waves of pleasure radiating through my body. I cling tighter around his neck, my breath hitching.

He watches me with fascination and is careful to ensure I take in all of him until there's no space left unclaimed between us.

"Mmm, your pussy always grips me just right. Does it feel good for you?"

"So good."

I clench my inner muscles to squeeze him even tighter. His eyes widen and he groans, the sound vibrating through both our bodies.

"Bloody hell," he says. "I love being inside you so much. All right, let's move away from the wall . . ."

Carefully he steps back a few paces, his body now taking my full weight.

"There we go! Freestanding. Not bad, eh?"

His ability to effortlessly carry me this way makes me feel secure and excited all at once.

"Lewis, I love you," I say earnestly. "I really, really love you."

It's not the first time I've made this declaration in recent weeks. After fully forgiving Lewis and making peace with our past, the floodgates opened and love poured back into my life faster than I could ever have imagined.

"And I love you, Iona. You're utterly perfect in every single way."

He lowers his head to capture my lips in a kiss. It's both tender and passionate, filled with promises of forever.

"Are you ready for me to start moving?" he murmurs.

"More than ready."

Lewis starts slowly, thrusting his hips with a gentle rhythm that quickly builds in intensity. I watch as his expression shifts—his eyes darkening, his jaw clenching. I know the look well. His passion is consuming him. This transformation from kind, loving man to primal lover is one that never fails to send shivers of excitement down my spine.

In this position—suspended congress—he rules our movements completely, which is just how he likes it, and I wouldn't have it any other way either. His pace quickens, and he begins to move me on him, lifting me then pulling me back down in sync with each of his upward thrusts. Our gasps and moans fill the room, a symphony of raw passion.

"Oh God, yes!" I exclaim. "Don't stop! Just like that!"

The pressure builds inside me, spiralling higher and higher until I can't hold back anymore. My orgasm crashes over me.

"Yes, that's it! Come for me, Iona!" Lewis commands.

He lasts another few thrusts before emptying himself into me, the sensation triggering another ripple of pleasure that makes my toes curl and my breath hitch. Lewis takes a moment to catch his breath and then devours my moans with eager kisses.

Soon after, we lie beside one another on his bed, Lewis with his head resting on my breasts. He's always liked relaxing like this afterwards, while I've always been fascinated by the contrast between his intensity when he's in the throes of passion and his gentleness after he's sated.

"Well? Your rating for the spreadsheet?" I prompt.

"Hmm . . . a ten."

"Aw, c'mon, Lewis!" I tease, running my fingers through his hair. "You can't give them all a ten. I need a bit more discernment from you. What's the point of rating them if you give them all the same score?"

"I've come every time, haven't I? Sex with you is always amazing. When I'm inside you, I'm happy—I don't know what else to say. What would *you* rate that one?"

"Well . . . okay, I'm going to give that one a ten too because it *was* phenomenal. But unlike you, I *have* given a few of the things we've tried a lower rating."

"But . . . never a score below nine, eh?"

"Well, no, but—ugh! You're right. Everything always feels so good."

These last few weeks haven't just been about the sex, of course—although that has been great. Lewis and I have been continuing to catch up, and now that we've rekindled our special friendship, Bannock truly feels like home again. As time goes on, I wouldn't be surprised if the six years when we barely talked become pretty irrelevant in the grand scheme of things. For the first twenty-one years of our lives, we were best friends, and I'm confident that's how we'll be for the rest of them.

"You know," I say, "I'd ideally like to tick something else off the spreadsheet tonight. Will you be good to go again soon?"

"Bloody hell!" He laughs. "I'm absolutely loving this, but these last few weeks . . . there's been no recovery time. We've been at it like rabbits."

"Is that a complaint?"

"Absolutely not. I wouldn't have it any other way. But . . . why don't we watch an episode of something before getting back to it?"

I sigh. "Okay, fine. But I'm not watching some hour-long programme. Put on something short. I want you again soon, Lewis."

He sits up, gives me a sweet kiss, then winks. "Understood."

CHAPTER THIRTY-ONE

LEWIS

I'm checking through recent online reviews of the hotel—all pretty good, thankfully—when Emily wanders into the office, carrying Ru and Callie, one on each hip. They're both now seven months old. She sets Ru down in the playpen that sits in the corner of the office—a new addition to our workspace—then takes a seat and bounces Callie on her lap. Ru immediately reaches out towards Callie with tiny, curious hands, and in response Callie giggles and kicks her legs.

It's impossible not to smile at the pair of them. They already seem to be developing a sort of friendship. Of course, they remind me a lot of me and Iona. We became friends as babies, and our maws were best friends before us—just like Emily and Grace are. Even though it's a silly thing to think, given they're so wee, I can't help but wonder if, in his teenage years, Ru might find himself developing certain feelings for Callie, just as I did for Iona.

"Was there a good turnout for Grace's yoga class?" I ask Emily.

Emily and Grace have an arrangement where they help each

other out as working mothers. Emily looks after both babies whenever Grace is running a class in our function room, while at other times Grace cares for them when Emily needs to get things done around the hotel.

"Yeah," Emily confirms, her voice a little flat.

Her usually vibrant eyes seem duller today, and she's clearly distracted. I'm aware that being a mother to a young baby can't be easy, and there must be days where she feels utterly exhausted. But having now worked with Emily for eighteen months, I know her well enough to be confident something else is up.

"What's wrong?" I ask.

"Oh, nothing." She forces a smile but it's unconvincing.

"Bullshit. You can tell me." I stand. "Can I make you a tea? Coffee?"

She shakes her head and waves me back into my seat. "No, I don't need a drink. It's just . . ." She sighs. "Can I ask you something? In confidence? In other words, you won't tell Ally?"

I frown, surprised by the question. "Aye, of course. Is . . . everything okay?"

"Oh, it's nothing to do with your big brother. He's perfect, in every way. It's just . . ." She blows out. "Do you ever feel this is all a bit . . . much?" Cradling Callie with one hand, she gestures vaguely with her other. "Working here, living here, no separation between home life and working life?"

"Er . . ." I scratch my head. "Honestly? I grew up in the hotel, so it's all I've ever known. I'm used to having guests around constantly—I feel pretty relaxed around them. But for someone who didn't grow up the way we did, I can see that it might be a bit . . . draining to constantly feel like you need to be on your best behaviour."

"That's it exactly!" Emily says. "It's *draining*. Don't get me wrong, I love the hotel and I love working here with you. Moving to the Highlands is the best thing I've ever done. But . . . whenever I go to Grace and Aidan's adorable little cottage by the river—or David and Johnny's, just a few homes along from them—it's hard not to feel a *little* envious. I wouldn't mind living in a place where I can nip to the kitchen to sort Ru a snack without having to make polite conversation with a guest or answer a question."

Ru is now stretching his wee arms out towards me, so I lift him out of the playpen then place him on my knee. I bob him up and down, occasionally tickling his tummy to elicit adorable wee giggles.

"I can see where you're coming from," I say to Emily. "And the truth is, Ally is probably like me on this. It's what he's always known so he might not appreciate how difficult it is for you. I reckon you should just talk to him. I can't imagine him being upset with you about this. You know how he dotes on you."

This time, Emily's smile is genuine. "You're right. I suppose the only reason I've not brought it up with him is because this isn't just any building—it's his childhood home."

I glance down at Ru, checking he's comfortable, then return my attention to Emily. "Since you opened up to me, can I confess something to you?"

"Sure."

"Well . . . even though Ally isn't responsible for the hotel anymore, he still likes to give me his thoughts on things every now and again, and I think that's because he still lives here. He just can't help himself."

"Yeah, he does do that, doesn't he?"

"It's not a big deal. I don't mind, really. But the other thing is . . . hmm, how to put this? Er, let's say you and Ally have more kids. I'm not sure what your plans are! I'm just talking theoretically. Equally theoretically, and I know it's pretty early to be talking about such things, but . . . let's say Iona and I have kids at some point."

At this, Emily's tired eyes light up with a spark of excitement.

"Not any time soon!" I hurriedly add. "I'm talking somewhere down the line. Maybe. Or maybe it'll never happen and Iona will just get a puppy. Like I say, this is all theoretical! The point I'm trying to get to is about . . . space. I mean, it seems incredibly unlikely, given his personality, but even Jamie might find a lass one day. If so, would she move in here with him? And Cat is in Wick at the moment, but she's determined to get a job closer to home next year. Is she going to be moving back into the hotel? And what if she meets someone?

"Do you see what I'm getting at? This place was a great family home for my maw and da and four young children. But as we McIntyres start to fall in love and have children of our own . . . well, there just isn't space for all of us, unless we convert all the guest rooms into family rooms, but then there'd be no business— and that's how you, me, Elspeth, and Jamie make a living. Of course, I've no more right to this building than Ally, Jamie, or Cat, but . . ."

"Of the four siblings, you're the one who's always been the most passionate about the hotel, and so if anyone has to leave, you don't think it should be you," Emily finishes. She's not being unkind—just stating what we both know to be a fact.

"Well . . . aye. I can't imagine ever living anywhere but here. Ally, though? He's never felt about the hotel the way I do."

"So what you're saying is, I'm not the only one who quite likes the idea of me, Ally, and Ru having our own place?"

"Not that I want rid of you!" I clarify. "You and I work really

237

well together. But if, rather than *living* here, you'd prefer to live somewhere else—somewhere nearby, of course—and simply come here to work . . ."

Emily nods then gives me a small smile. "Yeah. Why don't I have a chat with Ally, at least to float the idea?"

"Aye, like you say, to float the idea. In the meantime, though, I've got a suggestion for you."

"Yeah?"

"You always loved doing yoga with Grace, but because you look after the babies while she's running classes, you never get a chance to go anymore. I reckon a session would do you a world of good. Why don't you go join in while I look after these two?"

She frowns. "You really think you can look after two babies *and* run the hotel?"

"Well, Jamie's about too. And it's not like you'll be far—just in the function room. The class is only an hour, right? I'm sure I'll manage."

◆ ◆ ◆

The babies will not stop crying. Rocking and singing to them hasn't helped. I've tried my best—Jamie too.

I know they've both been fed recently, and as far as I can tell, their nappies are dry. If I don't do something soon, Emily is bound to come through to see what all the fuss is about, and I really don't want to disturb her yoga class. I reckon she needs it today.

That's why, with Jamie's help, I get the babies wrapped up for going outdoors. He secures Ru in the sling on my front, then we place Callie in her pram.

I'm going to take them for a walk. I can do this.

"You're in charge," I say to Jamie before setting off outside.

It's a brisk November day but bright and dry. I'm fully expecting this to be a disaster, and to have to run back into the hotel and straight to Emily, conceding defeat. But actually, once I start walking along Main Street, both babies calm relatively quickly. I don't want to get cocky, but . . . am I a natural at this?

I head down to the river and go along the riverside path for a while. The water glistens in the sharp sunlight filtering through bare branches. Ducks paddle serenely, leaving gentle ripples in their wake as they drift downstream.

When I come to a bench, I snap a photo of me and the babies and send it to Iona. She's working, but she obviously has her phone on her because she messages back almost straight away.

IONA

Oh my God! I honestly didn't think babies were as cute as puppies. But now that I see YOU with some, I think I may just have started ovulating.

Chuckling, I check how long I've been out for then decide to head back, taking my time. I'd rather not continue along the path any further, just in case the crying starts again. I don't want to take Ru and Callie too far from their mummies.

I retrace my steps. As I approach the old stone bridge, by which I got down to the river, voices reach me from up on top of it. Well, I say "voices", but it's mainly Morag the baker I can hear. Whoever she's talking with can barely get a word in edgeways. Morag is a lovely woman, but a chatterbox and quite the gossip.

It's only when she says my name that I come to a stop and listen to the conversation more closely.

"I'm glad Iona has finally seen sense," Morag says. "For years, every time she came back to visit, he'd run up to greet her, happy as anything, but she had no interest in him whatsoever. And yet just look at the lad! What a specimen. How could anyone say no to him? Iona, meanwhile . . . well, yes, she's certainly pretty in her own way, but he's clearly the more attractive of the two."

What? I think. *She's fucking gorgeous.*

"She's very lucky," Morag continues. "Very, *very* lucky. Playing hard to get obviously worked for her in the end."

I'm completely caught off-guard. Is this what people around Bannock actually think? Hell, even if it's only what a few of them think, that's not good enough.

It's not the case that Iona is "lucky" to have me. Instead, it's a bloody miracle that, after the way I hurt her, I've somehow managed to win her back. People don't know the truth about what happened between us in the past, so obviously they're creating their own narratives.

I'm about to head up to the bridge and confront Morag when I stop myself. No, correcting one person won't nip the gossip in the bud. I need to go bigger. It's not okay for *anyone* around town to think Iona is the lucky one. I need everyone to understand that *I'm* the luckiest man alive.

I have to set the record straight.

CHAPTER THIRTY-TWO

IONA

"Hello, Maw!" I call, letting myself in.

Her front door wasn't locked, which means she's about. It's a sunny, albeit rather chilly, Saturday afternoon, and so I'd thought she might be out for a walk. She often enjoys a bit of air in between lunch and dinner service at the restaurant.

I find her in the living room, watching TV.

"Iona! Hello." She smiles widely. "Is anything the matter?"

That's an odd question. Why would she assume something is the matter? I've not slept over in a while, but I pop in frequently to pick up things from my room. This is the first time that Maw, upon seeing me, has immediately concluded that something is wrong.

"Er, the shower in Lewis's room has stopped working, so I came over here to wash. He was oddly insistent I should do so, even though I don't normally shower in the middle of the day. I might have been offended had I not suspected he was planning something and wanted me to look my best for it."

I eye her suspiciously. "Now, though . . . I'm not sure there even was a problem with his shower. I'm beginning to suspect he just wanted to get me over here for some reason. Whatever is going on, it involves you, doesn't it?"

She can't hide the sparkle of mischief that dances across her features. "I have no idea what you're talking about, Iona. But by all means, go upstairs and have a shower. And afterwards, why don't you put on something nice?"

I place a hand on my hip. "You're a terrible actor, Maw. But fine. How nice are we talking?"

"Pretty but not ballgown fancy. Oh, and you'll want to wear boots with it."

Shaking my head at her complete lack of subtlety, I head upstairs.

A short while later, I come back down wearing a long-sleeved cowl-neck tunic dress patterned with autumn leaves. I've paired it with cosy leggings and have brushed my hair out so it flows in a soft cascade over my shoulders.

"Oh, beautiful!" Maw praises. "Funnily enough, there was a delivery for you while you were upstairs." She hands me a purple paper heart on which a message has been handwritten.

Where the pigs refused to flee,
Your next clue waits for thee.

A small smile tugs at my lips. Is this a treasure hunt, like something out of the *Highland Hearts and Hidden Treasures* series?

"I suppose I'll be heading off to Fergus Murray's farm, then," I say. That's where, aged eleven, I opened a gate to free some pigs, only for none of them to move. "Will you be tagging along?"

"No, no. This adventure is for you alone, dear. Although . . . I may see you again at the end of it." She winks.

"Okay. Love you, Maw." I give her a kiss on the cheek.

As I head to my car, I wonder what exactly Lewis has planned for me, and just what treasure I might find at the end of this.

At the farm, Fergus greets me with a piglet tucked under one arm. "Iona! I've got something for you." He passes me a second purple heart.

Head to the place where our first kiss was shared,
Where dreams and confessions were openly bared.

"You know," Fergus says, "I've never forgotten the way Lewis tried to take the blame when I caught you opening my pigsty gate. Even then, it was plain to see how much he cared for you."

Thanking Fergus, I give the piglet a wee scratch behind its ears then take my leave and head to Loch Bannock. That's where Lewis and I shared our first kiss, the night before I left for university.

By the shore, a swing once again hangs from the tree, and on it is Archie, my half-brother, now sixteen years old. He uses one foot to kick off the ground and maintain a slow, steady sway, just as I'd do when I was a teenager. He's with Da and Da's new partner, Kirsty. Lewis has really gone to some effort if he's invited them through from Inverness.

There's a fourth figure with them—Jamie—and when he spots me, he does a slow-motion run across the pebble beach, his arms spread wide, like something out of a film. "Well done!" he proclaims. "You found me!" Reaching me, he closes his eyes and puckers his lips, ready for a kiss.

I walk right past him and go see my da and his family, who I'm overdue a catch-up with.

"He always was a joker, that one." Da nods to Jamie. "Anyway, good to see you, Iona." He wraps me in a hug.

"You too, Da."

I hug Archie and Kirsty as well.

Archie says, "I was telling Jamie about the time me and Da met up with you and Lewis in Inverness, at that burger place. I still remember it. *We* first knew there was something going on between you *years* ago. These Bannock folk, though"—he teasingly gestures to Jamie—"they only found out about it a few weeks ago, right?"

"Not true!" Jamie protests. "I've been making sex jokes about Lewis and Iona for close to a decade! Haven't I, Iona? Tell him!"

Wow. These two barely know each other, but it seems they're getting on just fine. They both enjoy winding people up.

Ignoring them, I turn to Da and Kirsty. "Does one of you happen to have a clue for me?"

Kirsty, smiling kindly, hands me a third purple heart.

Visit the spot where you broke the mould,
And your image turned from shy to bold.

This one is a little more cryptic than the first two, but the answer still comes to me pretty quickly. It's a reference to the night at the Pheasant when Lewis and I sang "Comin' thro' the Rye". Lewis thought that'd be a good way for me to reinvent myself in people's eyes.

"I suppose I should continue this treasure hunt," I say to Da, "but I want to catch up with you properly. Will I get to see you again before you head back to Inverness?"

"Aye, we'll be waiting for you at the end."

We hug again, and he squeezes me tight.

"I always did like Lewis," he says. "I'm glad you two have sorted things out."

A short while later, I walk into the Pheasant and am immediately pounced on by Maisie, who's buzzing with excitement. Her hair is a bright pink nowadays, and the colour is quite the contrast to the dark outfit she's wearing. Since that first girls' night, she and I have been meeting up regularly, and I now consider her a good friend.

But there's another figure here I wasn't expecting to see.

"Cat!" I exclaim.

She bounces on the balls of her feet then takes my hands, beaming at me with dimples that remind me so much of Lewis's. "This is so exciting! And just look at us: the Scottish Sirens together in person!"

I chuckle, remembering the name Cat picked for our group chat.

"We *so* need a proper girls' catch-up," Maisie says, "but we can do that later. Lewis specifically warned us not to keep you— you've got a treasure hunt to complete, after all!—so here's your fourth clue." She passes me yet another purple heart.

Go seek a MacDonald, where the food is a delight,
It's the place we admired a dawn photo at night.

I can't hold back a giggle at this one. The manager of the Glen Garve Resort is called Craig MacDonald, and so it's clearly to the resort that I'm meant to go. But it's the "dawn photo at night" bit that amuses me. During the fancy dinner Lewis treated me to, I briefly flashed up his *Dick at Dawn* picture on my phone. He's rather cheekily worked that moment into a clue.

"What's so funny?" Maisie asks.

If it were just me and her, I'd probably tell her, but I doubt it's a story Cat wants to hear—not about one of her brothers.

"Oh, nothing," I say vaguely. "Right, I should push on. See you later!"

The Glen Garve Resort is a vast place—complete with, among other things, an eighteen-hole golf course—so it's helpful that Lewis's clue directed me to seek out a MacDonald.

No sooner do I arrive in the car park than I spot Robbie MacDonald tinkering with his motorcycle. He's Craig's elder son and is the same age as Aidan and Ally, although, as lads, they did *not* get on with him. With tattoos, an eyebrow piercing, a leather jacket, and a bit of an attitude, Robbie is Bannock's "bad boy"— or at least, that's his reputation. I've never been convinced, possibly because I've read too many romances where the bad boy ends up having a heart of gold. But I suppose reality doesn't always match fiction.

"Hi, Robbie!" I say. I'm a little surprised he's getting involved in the treasure hunt—it doesn't seem like his kind of thing.

He looks up, puts down a spanner, then rises to his feet. He's tall—exceptionally so—and his icy-blue eyes match his generally frosty demeanour.

"Iona. Hi. How can I help?" His voice is low. Gruff.

"Do you, by any chance, have a clue for me?"

His brow furrows, a shadow of confusion passing over his face.

"Iona!" a voice calls from behind me. "Over here!"

I turn around to see Johnny, Robbie's brother, waving as he comes down the steps of the resort's main entrance. Johnny is, in many ways, the polar opposite of Robbie—approachable, sweet, smiley, occasionally a little shy. With Johnny is his boyfriend, David, who's dressed—as always—in bright colours, today a vibrant orange coat. David is carrying Callie, his gorgeous wee niece, who also happens to be my gorgeous wee niece. Behind him are his sister, Grace, and my brother, Aidan.

"Sorry!" Johnny calls as the group makes their way over. "Lewis asked us to wait inside, at the spot you met him when you went for dinner together. It was Grace who noticed you out here chatting with Robbie."

I glance over my shoulder and flash Robbie an apologetic smile. "Sorry! Wrong MacDonald!"

I head over to meet the others and give everyone a hug, except for Callie, who I give special treatment. I squeeze her hands and kiss both of her adorably chubby cheeks.

"You've almost reached the end, Iona," Grace says.

"Aye. This is your last clue, sis." Aidan passes me a purple heart then wraps an arm around Grace and draws her closer to him. Before meeting Grace, Aidan was something of a player, but now he only has eyes for her.

Where laughter rang and memories grew,
Seek the spot where home feels true.

"Have you figured it out?" David asks eagerly. "And by the way, it is *so* romantic that Lewis organised this for you. I would *love* it if someone planned something like this for me."

Johnny, standing right next to him, rolls his eyes good-naturedly.

"It's the Bannock Hotel, isn't it?" I guess.

That place is the setting for so many happy memories, of joint dinners between the Stewarts and the McIntyres, of party games and laughter. Growing up, it always felt like a second home. I was as comfortable there as I was in my actual home across the street.

"Well done." Smiling, Grace touches my arm. "You figured it out."

"So . . ." I think this through. "Lewis kicked this whole thing off by pretending the shower in his room was broken and sending me over to Maw's. I've spent the last hour driving around Bannock and the surrounding area, and now I'm to head back to the hotel, which is where I started?"

Aidan winks. "Well, he had to get you out of there and keep you busy so he could get things organised, didn't he?"

Ah, I get it now. There's a surprise waiting for me back at the hotel.

Aidan collects Callie from David then says, "Anyway, we're going to go to our cars now. Could you give us a few minutes' head start? We want to get there before you do."

I wave them off, wait a couple of minutes, then get in my car and drive to the hotel.

At reception, Emily beams at me from behind the desk then comes out and gives me a hug. "You found your way back here!"

"Aye. I'm starting to feel a little nervous. I've no idea what's about to happen."

Emily squeezes my shoulder. "I think you're going to like it."

Ally emerges from the office, gently bouncing Ru and blowing raspberry sounds to make him giggle. I wrap an arm around Ally in greeting then kiss Ru's forehead.

"Auntie Iona is hunting for treasure," Ally says to Ru. "Just like a pirate. Arrr!" He does his best Long John Silver impression.

Of course, I'm not really Ru's aunt. "Auntie" is just a term of endearment since our families are so close. Growing up, I referred to Mairi as Auntie Mairi and Angus as Uncle Angus. But I suppose, if Lewis and I were ever to marry . . . well, I'd become Ru's aunt for real.

"Are you ready?" Emily asks me.

"Er . . . I think so?"

"Great. I'd say you're ready—you look amazing. Let's go."

She leads me into the function room, Ally and Ru following close behind. At the far end of the room are French windows that look out into the hotel's garden, and . . . wow! There are a *lot* of people gathered out there. It almost looks as if Lewis has invited the whole town—or at least, as many folk as he could fit.

As I step outside, I take in faces. Everyone I've already seen as part of the treasure hunt is here, from Maw, who gave me the first clue, to my brother, who I saw at the last location. But there are plenty of other people here too: Morag from the bakery, Tom from the Coffee Bothy, Jenny from the Otter's Holt . . . oh, and there's Donald, the senior vet at the surgery.

Every single set of eyes is fixed on me, which is . . . somewhat intimidating.

Awkwardly I raise a hand and give a small wave. "Er, hi, everyone! Nice of you to come along to"—I flap vaguely—"whatever this is!"

Chuckles fill the air.

One person stands quite literally head and shoulders above everyone else. At the far end of the garden, the ground slopes up, and at its highest point is Lewis. It's as though he's on a natural stage.

I don't need anyone to tell me that I'm supposed to go to him. That's what everyone is expecting, and it's what I want to do. It's just . . . suddenly this all seems incredibly nerve-wracking. Whatever is going on here, it's clearly a big moment, and . . . I don't know that I *am* ready for it.

I remind myself of the resolution I made atop the wind turbine—to be brave. And so, squaring my shoulders, I squeeze my way through the crowd towards him. People greet me and pat my back as I pass.

When I reach Lewis and get a proper look at him, I see he's in his sex outfit—by which I mean his kilt, of course. But he's put on all the other bits and bobs that I'm less used to seeing, like a white shirt, a black jacket, and tall white socks with garter flashes in the same muted greens and blues as the kilt. I'm a huge fan of his usual, minimal, bedroom attire, but I've got to admit, he looks pretty bloody smart when he dons the full ensemble.

November sunlight glints off his chestnut hair, bringing out the reddish strands. He stands with one hand on either side of his sporran, strong emotion playing in his dark-brown eyes. One of his hands now reaches out to me, and I take it. He guides me to stand beside him, his gaze roving all over me.

"You look incredible," he whispers so only I can hear.

"You're not so bad yourself." I bite my lip then, glancing around me, lower my voice even further. "But quick question: is this a proposal? Because . . . you're kind of putting me on the spot here. I do love you, but we haven't been back together *that* long . . ."

He smirks. "It's more of a . . . declaration. Of your amazingness. No rings involved, I swear. One day I'll go down on one knee—just try and stop me—but not today. No, today there are just a few things I want to say that I want everyone to hear. And don't worry, they're all good."

His mouth curving into a dimpled smile, he inclines his head towards the crowd. "Literally everyone is watching us, so . . . would it be okay if I start?" He gives my hand a wee squeeze.

I squeeze his right back. "Well, if you're just going to tell everyone how amazing I am, then yes, don't let me get in the way. You may begin."

With a wink, he turns to address those gathered. "Here she is! The one we've been waiting for, and the most beautiful person I've ever laid eyes on."

These words are met by a cheer, and my face warms. Despite my outward embarrassment, my heart swells at the compliment. It's a pretty good start, I'd say.

But then Lewis rubs the back of his neck, and his smile falters slightly. "I'd like to thank you all for coming here. There's something I want to say, and . . . it isn't easy. But it's important, so I'm going to say it."

A hush falls, and glances are exchanged. People were expecting a celebration, but Lewis's tone is suddenly serious.

"I think you all know that, as children and teenagers, Iona and I were best friends—utterly inseparable. At some point, though, things became . . . strained between us. I won't go into details, but it's important I confess that . . . I messed up. I pushed her away—hurt her—at a time when she was trying to support me."

There are murmurs of confusion, and a few people shift uncomfortably. I've no clue what to think or where this is going, but I wasn't expecting this.

"Here's the thing, though," he continues. "Even when I did that—even when I drove a wedge between us—Iona continued to show me a loyalty I didn't deserve. Rather than tell everyone what I did, she kept quiet about it so you wouldn't judge me harshly. Because that's the kind of person Iona Stewart is: loyal, compassionate, and much more besides. I think this woman deserves some recognition for being so wonderful, so . . . I'd like to tell you all about a wee treasure hunt I just sent her on."

With these words, Lewis's lips curl up, and it's as if the air itself lightens. Everyone visibly relaxes—myself included—and the tension melts away.

Turning, he addresses me, although his voice remains loud enough for all to hear. "Iona, each of the locations I sent you to says something about your personality. First, you're caring, which is why you work as a vet—a calling you discovered at Fergus's farm. Next, you're funny—no, hilarious. When we'd hang out at the loch as teens, you always kept me entertained. It didn't matter whether you were talking about goings-on at school or . . . I don't know, telling jokes about *Star Wars* and lightsabers."

He shoots me a quick wink. Oh, cheeky! Fitting in an in-joke about glow-in-the-dark condoms in front of friends and family? Naughty, Lewis! But I like it.

"You also have a bit of a wild side, and you proved that at the Pheasant when you and I sang 'Comin' thro' the Rye'. When we were younger, we always denied there was any sort of romance between us, but . . . well, I reckon the cat is out of the bag now."

"It was never in the bag!" Jamie calls from somewhere. "It was out purring in plain sight for us all to see!"

A chorus of laughter breaks out at this.

Lewis grins. "Aye, well . . . anyway, when we were younger, 'Comin' thro' the Rye' used to be a theme song of sorts for me and Iona. We didn't think it was anyone else's business if we, er, *kissed* in the rye."

He's getting even cheekier! Stressing the word "kissed" like that in front of everyone? He really is being a naughty man today. *We* both know there's an alternative version of the lyrics in which *kiss* is replaced by *fuck*, but other people might be aware of that too.

"Nowadays, I want *everyone* to know that I kiss you," Lewis says, "and that only I get to kiss you."

These words send a shiver down my spine. Is it kind of primitive and backwards for a man to lay his claim on a woman like this? Aye. But is it also kind of hot to hear Lewis do it in front of everyone? Absolutely.

"Finally, on our first formal date, which was at the Glen Garve Resort, you talked to me about being able to walk with kings without losing the common touch—words from Rudyard Kipling's 'If'. I think they describe you perfectly, Iona."

Faces light up at this. Maw—who's squeezed her way to the front row—clutches her hands in front of her chest as though never before in her life has she heard anyone say something so sweet. It's probably a good thing Lewis didn't mention the context of that conversation. I'm pretty sure we were talking about smutty historical romance books and dick pics at the time.

"Anyway, the final clue brought you here, so without further ado, I'd like to present you with your treasure." One of his hands still clasping mine, Lewis opens his sporran with his other. "And just to warn you, it's . . . er, more of a symbolic kind of treasure, rather than a literal one."

He pulls out an old brass key and holds it out to me. I take it, curious.

"That's a key to the hotel. Not that you need one, really—you've always been welcome inside. Plus, this last month or so . . . well, you've slept in my room every night."

Chuckles ripple through the crowd. Even the oldest and most conservative of Bannock's residents are no longer shocked by the thought of sex before marriage.

"This, Iona, is about making it official, if you'd like to do that. I'm asking you to move in with me and to make the hotel your home. If you accept, I'll move all your things over from your maw's. No doubt I'll need to put up a new bookcase—nah, let's be realistic, several new bookcases—to house your extensive book collection, but I'm happy to make any changes you wish. You name it, and I'll do it. I want you to feel it's your home as much as it is mine."

Warmth floods my entire being as I gaze down at the key in my hand. Clasping it tightly, I flash Lewis a smile then announce loudly enough for everyone to hear, "Of course I'll move in with you."

A roar of approval bursts from those assembled, and applause breaks out. Lewis's eyes shine with delight.

I squeeze his hand and add, "That was your cue to kiss me. What are you waiting for?"

As the crowd erupts with laughter, Lewis beams and presses his lips to mine, sparking a chorus of whistles and cheers.

EPILOGUE
LEWIS

"Hiya, boy. How are you doing?" I crouch beside the dog bed in which our black Labrador, Bruce, is curled up.

His tail thumps enthusiastically, and he yawns before affectionately licking my hand. At one stage, Iona and I had been thinking about getting a puppy, but then Iona heard about a six-year-old Lab whose elderly owner could no longer care for him, and our hearts melted.

Bruce is perfect—a great fit for the hotel. Gentle, friendly, and well-trained, we all love him, and guests do too. He especially likes to hang out here in the snug. It's his spot.

He picks up his favourite toy—a Highland cow that squeaks—then drops it at my feet and looks up at me with those big soulful eyes that are impossible to resist.

Laughing, I scratch Bruce's chin then pick up the toy and play a game of tug-of-war with him. I adore this dog.

Guess who takes him on the most walks? Me.

Guess who fills up his dog bowl each mealtime and ensures he always has a fresh supply of water? Me.

Guess who he likes best? Iona.

It's like Molly, my childhood cocker spaniel, all over again.

But . . . I can't really blame him. Who wouldn't love Iona?

At the bar, Jamie is tapping away on his laptop.

"The snug is empty," I point out.

It's just me, Jamie, and Bruce here—there are no customers in for a drink at the moment.

"You could, if you like, help out elsewhere around the hotel?" I suggest hopefully. "Or even just go outside and get some fresh air. Maybe take Bruce for a walk?"

He doesn't even acknowledge me. His eyes remain glued to his screen, as though completely oblivious to everything around him.

Standing, I walk over to see what he's doing. Ah, once again, he's on that *Highland Legacy* game.

"I would ask if you don't have anything better to do with your life, but I know the answer."

He briefly raises one hand from the keyboard and shows me his middle finger. Okay, so at least he's aware I'm here.

"I'm being sociable," he claims, still not taking his eyes off his game. "I'm chatting with someone while we quest together."

I notice a chain of messages in the bottom-left of the screen. "Who's SassyLassie? Is she someone you know in real life or some random you've never met?"

"The second one."

"Do you even know her real name?"

"Nah, but that's part of the fun. We've gone on all these incredible adventures together, and she is *so* funny. But . . . I also know nothing about her. I mean, I'm sure she's Scottish, but otherwise she could be anyone. It's kind of exciting, really."

"Ah. You're definitely being catfished by some old granny who's into lanky lads."

"Piss off! I bet she's an absolute babe. And anyway, I may not have an odd obsession with the gym like you, but I am *not* lanky."

"Hmm . . . you kind of are."

Sighing, Jamie tears his gaze away from the screen to give me his full attention. "You know, *you're* the one who's standing about doing nothing. It's a Monday—it's quiet. The restaurant isn't open today, and although some folk may pop in for a drink, it's not going to get busy. I'm quite happy sitting here playing my game and pulling a pint for any local who drops by. Why don't *you* take Bruce for a walk?"

And so I do. The first signs of spring are starting to appear: I spot snowdrops and crocuses. What's more, the days, once short, are getting longer again. By the time I get back to the hotel, it's almost six, and yet the sun has only just set—a welcome change to what things are like in the depths of winter.

I head up to my room, where the light is on in the bathroom. I call hello, and Iona replies that she's just drying off after a post-work shower and will be out in a moment.

I go over to the window and am about to draw the curtains when I spot Emily across the way, in Iona's old room. I raise a hand in greeting, and she grins then bends out of sight, reappearing a moment later with Ru. She points me out for him, then they both wave at me, Ru especially eagerly. That boy could do this all day—he never tires of waving at his uncle from across the street. It's kind of cute, and it also reminds me of the way Iona and I would wave at each other when we were younger.

The bathroom door opens, and Iona emerges in a white dressing gown. Beaming at me, she comes over and wraps her arms around me.

Ah. It was nice growing up opposite her, but it's so much better having her here in my room with me.

It's been a little over three months since I presented Iona with a key to the hotel—five since our first date at the Glen Garve Resort—but in a way those numbers are irrelevant. It feels like Iona and I have always been soulmates, ever since we were wee.

"Oh, isn't Ru adorable?" Iona says, spotting him and waving too. "It's hard to believe he and Callie will be one next month. They're both getting so big!"

"Aye, they are. It's funny, even though it's been a couple of weeks since Ally, Emily, and Ru moved into your maw's old place, I still sometimes get a surprise when I see someone other than you in that room."

Shortly after I transferred the last of Iona's things over here, Elspeth started talking about wanting to downsize. She felt she had no need for such a big house anymore, given her two children are now happily settled in their own homes. It took a bit of time to get everything arranged, but she's in a smaller place now, while Ally, Emily, and Ru have moved across the way. It's a solution that's working really well for everyone.

Emily—perhaps growing tired of the waving game—puts Ru down and then, with a final wave to me and Iona, draws his curtains.

Iona finds my hand and squeezes it. "It's nice, isn't it, that the house has stayed in the family? Well, maybe 'family' isn't the right word, but you know what I mean. Maw, Aidan, and I may be Stewarts, and the rest of you McIntyres, but we're so close we're basically all family."

"Basically, but not quite, and that's an important distinction. Otherwise, the things you and I get up to would be *very* wrong."

Shaking her head, she gives me a playful shove. "Did you have to say that, Lewis? Seriously?"

I smirk. "Anyway, after the wedding, your family will legally be mine, and mine yours."

"Wedding? You're getting ahead of yourself there. You've not even proposed yet."

"Shit, haven't I? Are you sure?"

"Hmm . . . aye, pretty sure. Seems like the sort of thing I'd remember—unless it was a *really* lame proposal and it's slipped my mind."

"A lame proposal? Nah, that doesn't sound like me. You're right, I haven't proposed yet, but it's coming, and when it happens, it is going to blow your mind. To be clear, I'm going to spend the rest of my life with you, Iona. I don't want to get all old-fashioned on you, but you will carry my babies one day." I place my hands on her hips. "These are fine baby-carrying hips. That's the kind of thing the hero says to the heroine in a historical romance, right?"

"Er, aye. But I'm pretty sure it's not okay for a man to say that to a woman nowadays."

"Bollocks! You love it and you know it. Anyway, like I say, a proposal is coming, so you'd better get prepared. It could come when you least expect it."

"Oh aye?" Iona reaches for our curtains, draws them closed, then takes a hold of the belt of her gown. "I can do unexpected things too, you know. Any idea what's coming next?"

"Hmm . . ." Playing along, I rub my chin, making a show of having a real think. "Are you going to make us both hot choco-lates, then we'll cosy up and watch a film?"

"No."

She lets her dressing gown drop to the floor, and I shiver, taking in her naked body, admiring her from head to toe. Fuck, I will never grow tired of the sight of this woman. My cock is already reacting.

"I'm going to have sex with you, Lewis—that's what I'm going to do. Be honest with me: you didn't see it coming, did you?"

Chuckling, I shake my head. "I had no idea."

Smiling naughtily, she takes my hand and leads me to our bed.

A NOTE FROM THE AUTHORS

We hope you enjoyed *The Highland Crush*. Want more of Lewis and Iona? Subscribers to our free email newsletter can download a bonus epilogue in which Lewis pops the question.

The *True Scotsman* series continues in *The Highland Game*, Jamie and Maisie's story. Haste ye back to Bannock!

For more information about the bonus epilogue and *The Highland Game*, visit amymcgavinbooks.com.

Bonus Epilogue

Next Book

The True Scotsman Series

The HIGHLAND GAME

AMY McGAVIN

Made in the USA
Las Vegas, NV
07 December 2024

13482536R00156